CW00549124

Author

Polly Babbington

In a little white Summer House at the back of the garden, under the shade of a huge old tree, Polly Babbington creates romantic feel-good stories including The Boat House PRETTY BEACH.

Polly went to college in the Garden of England and her writing career began by creating articles for magazines and publishing books online.

Polly loves to read in the cool of lazing in a hammock under an old fruit tree on a summertime morning or cozying up in the Winter under a quilt by the fire.

She lives in delightful countryside near the sea, in a sweet little village complete with a gorgeous old cricket pitch, village green with a few lovely old pubs and writes cosy romance books about women whose life you sometimes wished was yours.

Follow Polly on Instagram, Facebook and Twitter @PollyBabbingtonWrites

Want more on Polly's world?
Subscribe to Babbington Letters at PollyBabbington.com

The Boat House Pretty Beach

Polly Babbington

Copyright

© Copyright 2020 Polly Babbington
The Boat House Pretty Beach
All rights reserved.
This book is a work of fiction. Names, characters, businesses, places, events and incidents are either the products of the author's imagination or used in a fictitious manner. Any resemblance to actual persons, living or dead, or actual events is purely coincidental.

Welcome

Welcome to the world of Pretty Beach.

A sweeping, sparkly blue inlet town surrounded by water, criss-crossed with sweet old laneways, filled with wonderful characters and overlooked by a quaint old blue and white lighthouse.

We meet the lovely Sallie Broadchurch and follow her bringing back to life an unloved old boathouse - pretty, forty and looking for a new life by the sea.

Holly and Xian are the gorgeous owners of the Pretty Beach Bakery, along with Holly's son Rory, a doctor in the city and Sallie's best friend Nina. Then there's beautiful Jessica and her bride Camilla of Pretty Beach Fish and Chips, Nel the local bus driver and the delectable David Windsor, businessman extraordinaire.

Top it all off with Ben Chalmers, dashing owner of Ben Chalmers Seaplanes, a lot of history behind him and wondering quite what's happening when a new neighbour arrives in his little town by the sea.

PROLOGUE

Sallie Broadchurch sat in the cafe downstairs from her flat, drained the last of her cappuccino and pressed the Gmail app on her phone. She scrolled through and there it was, the email from Pretty Beach Council.

Dear Ms. Broadchurch.
Thank you for your emails regarding the Boat House. I've attached the information requested and refer to my additional attachment on the status of the Boat House and properties.
I would like to extend my congratulations and officially welcome you to Pretty Beach.
Kindest Regards,
R. J. Johnson.

She finished reading it, closed the phone, said thanks to Vinnie for the coffee as he bustled around closing up and walked back to her tiny flat. Nina, her best friend, was waiting for her outside on the pavement. They climbed the stairs running up the outside, stroked Folly the neighbour's little cat as he meowed hello and unlocked the door.

Nina followed in behind her, head bent to her phone as usual, texting instructions about a case's paperwork to one of her paralegals. She looked up from the phone.

'Wow, can't believe you've got it all packed up so quickly.'

'Well, there was hardly a lot here.' Sallie pointed to the boxes stacked neatly on the left. 'So, all that there is for you to bring when you come down. I'm just taking my backpack and the suitcase tomorrow. Those are the things being shipped, and that leaves the odd few bits in the morning. Everything else came with the place.'

Her phone started pinging, she opened it up and read the messages in the WhatsApp group, informing her that the keys to the Boat House were available, clicked close and looked over at Nina. They were both now sitting on the floor surrounded by the packing boxes, a bottle of wine and two glasses sitting on the floorboards between them.

'Well, that's it then, it's all complete. I can't believe I am doing this; I've spent the last and only money I have on an old boat house in a tiny town I don't know and I have no idea what I am doing.'

Nina sighed.

'Everything is watertight on the legal side of it, Sallie. I've had every lawyer I know worth his salt ensure there isn't a single loophole in that contract. You've got yourself a piece of real-estate by the sea, in an area where the new high-speed train runs, which people are clamouring to buy. We've been through this - with your skills you can't go wrong and I'm not being funny, but the money you had would barely have got you a car would it? Being able to get that place for a song was the best thing ever.'

'I know we've been through this, but it all seems very crazy now it's real.'

'What's the worst that can happen? You come back. You now get to have a shot at making your own income, having a good go of something else and starting a very nice new life by the sea in Pretty Beach.' Nina took a sip of the wine and patted Sallie's leg.

'Let's have another look at it on Pinterest.' Nina took her MacBook Pro out of its case, closed the portal for her law firm and opened up the board they had created.

They clicked through pictures of the town which was more like a large village, just off the coast along from Newport Reef.

The old village green, the blue and white lighthouse, the memorial for the first submarine cables. They clicked through the images - beautiful old cottages, the Newport Reef Fire and Rescue Service station, the old Marina Club, the tiny museum displaying pieces from the coast guard and memorabilia from the area's efforts of the Home Guard in the war.

Sallie sighed, and Nina crossed her fingers.

'You wait, this will turn out to be the best thing you've ever done in your life.'

Chapter 1

Sallie sat looking out the window, turning the bangle over and over on her arm. The bus had slowly emptied out the further it had gone along the coast and she'd spent the last hour of the journey, since she'd changed at Rydd-on-Sea, looking out at the beautiful old houses and listening to tunes on the bus driver's radio.

She looked through the pictures of the Boat House again on her phone, as the bus slowly made its way to her new home. The Boat House looked tired and unloved, the once white walls dingy and uncared for, an unkempt driveway to the front, the sea in the background, and an old, seen-better-days roof. She could just make out the little cottage to the side and the two jetties to either side.

Signs for Pretty Beach had been getting more and more frequent. She had watched the miles count down until the big brown sign announced, 'Welcome to Pretty Beach, Twinned with St. Amer.' The bus swerved around the last of the coastal road and came to an abrupt halt at Pretty Beach bus stop.

Catching the bus was a longer route than the new train, and she'd had to change twice, but weaving its way in and out of the beaches all the way down the coast to Pretty Beach had been a lovely ride. She walked down to the door of the bus with her basket over her arm, pushing a suitcase on wheels and carrying a large backpack on her back. Just a few things for a new life by the sea.

She tapped her travel card and said thanks to the driver.

'Have a lovely stay in Pretty Beach,' the bus driver called out to her as she got off.

She stopped and turned around to say that she wasn't on holiday, but decided it was way too complicated and left it at a smile. The bus driver turned the engine off, pressed the clock on the dashboard, took out a flask of coffee and poured some into a cup.

'Not a bad stop for a coffee break, is it?' The bus driver laughed and gestured out to the sea, the lighthouse and the view as Sallie stepped off the bus and put the basket down.

'We don't get many holidaymakers up here at this time of year,' the bus driver said, taking in the slim, honey-haired woman in the white jeans, tennis shoes, a floaty sandy coloured camisole top and blazer. The bus driver was friendly and probably just making conversation on her break. You didn't get that in Freshlea.

Sallie couldn't be bothered to go through the entire story. How would it go down if she had told her, "Well no actually, I am pretty much homeless, have no money, and I'm on my way to a rat-infested building which I haven't even seen for thirty years." She thought that might be quite the conversation stopper.

'Staying up there at the lighthouse?' The bus driver pointed to the towering blue and white lighthouse all the way down the beach and up on the cliffs in the distance.

'I wish,' Sallie replied; she'd seen it on Airbnb and it was two thousand a night. 'I'm staying over by the wharf at Seashells Cottages.'

The bus driver sucked her teeth, took out her ponytail, ruffled her fingers through her hair, smoothed it to the back of her head and tied it back up. She leant forward on the counter, resting her chin on her hand and smiled, lighting up her unbelievably pretty face.

'You should've jumped off at the Lavender Bay stop then, not the lighthouse end - that's nearer to old Pete's places if you walk down the hill. Even that's a bit of a walk though, especially with that lot.' She waved her hand at Sallie's big bags. Sallie looked back into the bus at her.

'Oh, I've planned to have some afternoon tea here, have a look around, see the lighthouse and then I've got an Uber booked.'

'An Uber? Wow, you were lucky. Must be Rory up from St. Louisa's then. See, we've got two Uber drivers down here at the moment. Holly from the bakers but she doesn't do the Winter season usually, so no go there, and then there's Tony but he's in Bali at the moment. So yep, it must be Rory, I didn't know he was back yet.' She tapped her fingers on the steering wheel.

The bus driver, whose badge said her name was Janelle, said it was a lovely day for an afternoon picnic and told her about a little sheltered warm spot down by the breakers.

'Walk over there, see those two enormous trees? Through that park and then do a left along the boardwalk, there's an area there with a bench and picnic tables, completely sheltered, your very own sun-trap in the afternoon. Warms the cockles of your soul, that's for sure.'

Sallie smiled back at her gratefully. 'Thanks so much, that's just what I'm looking for.'

'It gets quite chilly though later, you'll be surprised - the afternoon winds come in and will pick up from the West and there won't be a soul around by the time the sun goes down. You'll be fine with Rory, dark blue Toyota with the Uber sign in the back window. A good looker, that's for sure.'

She looked at Sallie and lit up the electric smile again, started up the bus and put her hand up.

'I'll be seeing you then,' and she left a pause as if asking for Sallie's name.

'I'm Sallie, thanks so much for the tips.'

'Nice to meet you Sallie, welcome to the wonderful world of Pretty Beach.'

She turned on the engine, looked in the mirror, indicated right and smiled as she pulled away.

Well that wasn't a bad start - a nice bus driver who had told her about a picnic spot, you didn't get that in Freshlea and the only Uber driver in town was a good-looking man who just so happened to be a doctor.

Chapter 2

Sallie Broadchurch hauled the rucksack on her back and basket over her arm. She shielded her eyes from the sun and looked around; Janelle was right there certainly wasn't a lot going on. The car park for the beach only had a few cars in it and there were just a handful of people in the cafes and restaurants lining the road over on the right.

She walked down through the small park, dragging the suitcase behind her and made her way along the path and over towards the ocean. The wheels on the case clattered on the timber boards until she came to the small sheltered bench and table. She laid out her bits and bobs beside her and sat there sipping on her tea, and looking out at the amazing colours beyond. It was as if someone had picked every single blue in a paint palette and plopped them into the sea in front of her.

A couple of hours later, and having walked back over to the bus stop for the Uber, a dark blue Toyota came around the corner bang on time and pulled into the bus stop. The window wound down and a handsome man in a navy-blue jumper and gold rimmed Ray Bans peered out.

'Sallie? Rory, and currently the only Uber in town. You're booked to go to Seashells Cottages, right? I'm on my way to work, but covering this for my mum.' He took in the pretty woman in the white jeans and blazer and smiled.

'Thank you, I heard the walk is further than I thought, so good job I had the forethought to book this. The bus driver said it would be a long way and checked to see how I was getting there, which was nice of her.' Sallie replied as she pulled the backpack off from her shoulders.

'Ahh Nel, you've already been initiated into the Pretty Beach way then. Yes, we treat them well down here in the sticks you know, haha

- not if you're a tourist in the Summer though, then we charge you seventeen big ones for an ice cream and twenty-two for a beer.'

Laughing, he got out of the car, nipped around the back and with very strong arms and very nice brown eyes, popped the boot on the car and slung her rucksack and the little silver case on wheels in the back.

He opened the passenger door, Sallie got in, did her seatbelt up and immediately regretted the whole thing. A doctor driving an Uber? That seemed a bit odd. It was like a scene from a true crime podcast, and as they pulled away she thought she might never be seen again. It reminded her of a television drama she'd seen of a scary, unscrupulous doctor. Wild thoughts ran through Sallie's head - would he carefully inject her with a dose of some drug which would make her sleepy and it would be the last thing that she would remember?

As they drove along past the odd shops dotted here and there, it seemed to be taking ages. She began to think that not only would she be drugged, but she would, in actual fact, be murdered by Rory, stuffed into the back of the Toyota, taken to one of the old boats, rowed out to sea, never to be seen again. What was worse, was that no one would know. Or care.

They made their way down the road; the afternoon sky had faded quickly, the lighthouse glowed from above and lights started to come on here and there. They trundled along past huge old Pretty Beach homes, the Fire Station her and Nina had pinned on the Pinterest board, and the fishing boats lined up along the jetties.

As they approached Pretty Beach Wharf, they came into civilisation again, the water glistened on the left, the lighthouse now a beacon in the distance. Rory swung the car around to the left and the beach opened up in front of them, a family out for a stroll on the promenade bundled up in hats and boots and a couple of kids who clearly weren't as cold were running along in front of them.

Sitting there in the front seat of the Toyota, she thought about the life she had left and Nina, her only real friend... and the little annexe in Freshlea, it had been great, she had finally happily slotted into somewhere. If it hadn't been for the offer of a lifetime she wouldn't be here in this sleepy little town to move into a falling down old boat house.

'Yeah, not far in a car, nearly there, Seashells Cottages is accessed over on the left down that little lane - bit bumpy so I'll probably park up and walk you down there.' Rory looked over at her as she smiled at him.

'Takes ages walking around The Bends on that road, I've done that a few times with a few beers inside me that's for sure.' He chuckled and slowed the car down, pulled off the tarmac and onto a bumpy, unmade side road. Bits of gravel hit the side of the door and crunched under them.

'It's just down the end of this road, not really a pavement and you've got to be careful of the stream running along the right side, Seashell Cottages is right down the end there. I'll park up here, grab your stuff and walk you down.'

Were people really this friendly here? First of all, there was the happy bus driver and now this. In Freshlea there was no way an Uber driver would drop you off and then walk you in and help you with your luggage.

Would her neighbours be as nice at the Boat House?

Chapter 3

Sallie walked along the beach gazing up at the lighthouse in the distance, the cold sand between her toes and took in big lungfuls of the ocean air. Strange - the air felt different up here, cleaner, clearer, who knew what it was, but it was definitely different to the air she was used to.

She walked right round the headland, passing the odd daytrippers on their way up to the lighthouse. A couple of weathered old surfers zipped up in wetsuits, with surfboards tucked under their arms smiled as they ran past barefoot on the way out for a surf. A group of teenagers sat on the dunes on a blanket, rugged up in hats and jumpers, music playing from an old van behind them.

It wasn't as quiet and dead as she'd thought it would be and by the looks of the massive houses backing onto the beach, the cars in the driveways and some of the boats around, this wasn't quite the old, backwater fishing town she was expecting.

As she carried on walking along the beach, she looked up at the lighthouse to get her bearings and opened the map app on her phone. She'd worked out she could walk from the ocean beach, through the car park and sand dunes over to the other side of Pretty Beach where all the shops and restaurants were and there she would finally approach the Boat House.

She walked in and out of the sand dunes, took her coat off in the warm sun, and carried on along the road to see what was around. A line of shops all decorated in pretty pale blues, pinks, navy and whites spilled out onto the pavement. The left side lined with palms in oversized white pots and strings of fairy lights and white bunting criss-crossed above.

Sallie looked all the way along the laneway and could see Pretty Beach Boat House way in the distance down at the end. It didn't have quite the same feel as the well-kept shops and restaurants keeping up to the name of the place. From what she could make out, what was once the old Boat House, had in the past been a boat and fishing store - it now looked to be a part falling down timber building just about staying up via a corrugated roof.

She fished around in her bag for her glasses, her eyes weren't quite what they used to be since she'd turned forty, popped them on and everything crisped up. And looked a lot worse.

Weeds covered the whole front of the Boat House; it looked as if a pane from the barn door at the front was missing and someone had fly-tipped an old mattress out the front. Ivy covered the side of a gabled roof towards the rear and peeling paint adorned every single surface. Every thought she'd had that this might be an answer for her swiftly went out the window. She took off her glasses and sighed. It was better without them on.

The nearer she got the worse it became. What she had thought would be charming old clinker rowing boats, actually as she got closer, looked like a big pile of rotting junk. The little bridge that went over the stream run-off on the right looked like it needed condemning and the turret above the house looked, quite possibly, as if it was about to fall down.

She rummaged around in her basket, took out the large bunch of keys and jumped across the narrow stream of water. Knee-high weeds brushed her legs and it went through her mind that the next thing she would see would be a rat or grass snake. She looked over at the small boathouse cottage next to it, set back and to the right, it too was covered in peeling paint and overgrown with weeds.

She passed old rowing boats, huge old oil drums and piles of what looked like trestle tables, goodness knows what they were used for. The padlock on the old barn doors and the 'No Trespassing' sign were a bit of a joke really - she guessed that if anyone had wanted to, they could easily pull up one of the weathered sash windows to the side of the building and climb right in.

The padlock was rusty and eroded, covered in a white-green crust from the sea air and looked like it had been there for a very long time. Amazingly the key worked, the padlock opened, and the chain fell to the floor. She popped her other glasses on and looked through the keys, pulled out the one labelled front door, turned it and the right-hand lock clicked. She pulled open the door and peered in.

Presented with a very large, very grim looking gabled room and a lot of dust she didn't know whether to laugh or cry. It was surprisingly empty. She had thought it would be filled, like the outside, with all sorts of junk, but rather it looked like someone had been through the whole place and relieved it of anything personal, leaving everything else.

She continued to peer in and taking it all in, she slowly nodded - maybe there was a glimmer of hope. She'd had this feeling a few times before, especially when she had found the roof top annexe of the house in Freshlea to rent for a pittance. She'd got to work on that the day she'd moved in and turned it from a pig's ear into a beautiful little place with a tiny balcony overlooking the rooftops of Freshlea and a distant view of the town. This place was the same. It had oodles of potential.

As she looked in and up at the roof, it gradually dawned on her that the nuts and bolts of the building were, by the looks of it, okay. In fact, if it was structurally sound all this needed was some thought, some effort and some paint. A lot of paint, probably more than she could afford, but that was the least of her problems.

She pulled open the door a bit more, the bottom of it scraping along the faded block paving, and pushed it harder, opening it just enough for her to walk in. Stepping inside with trepidation and wondering if the floorboards would take her weight, light flooded from the other end through a bank of doors which led out onto a deck.

She looked up as she stepped forward. Wow. The whole of the back and to the right side was a vaulted ceiling, left to the natural timber and crammed full of old ships ropes, oyster baskets and glass buoys. Piled in the corner were vintage life rings, oars and old bits of timber weathered by the sea.

Huge old industrial pendant lights hung all the way down the centre of the ceiling. *My goodness,* she thought, *people pay thousands for replicas of those things.* She wasn't sure if she wanted to walk under them in case one dropped to the floor. Huge cobwebs and electrical wires caught the light between them.

She took a couple more steps forward and gingerly walked to the right. The tongue and groove shiplap roof flattened out and a tiny set of stairs came down from the ceiling with a stable door at the bottom. She pulled the door towards her, half expecting it to come off in her hand and looked up, wondering what was up there. If there was plumbing to this place and electricity she could possibly live here - with a lot of work.

She took a deep breath in and sighed. Who was she kidding - she was forty years old with two failed marriages behind her, no help and no money to do anything. That was not a great recipe for success.

This place though, goodness, this place was like a dream. She'd styled enough houses over the years working for Peninsular Styling to know the power of elbow grease, paint and a bit of savvy between the ears.

She gazed up the stairs, and then bent down to examine one of the treads - everything looked in a lot better condition than she had first assumed. If you could see past the awful paint colours, the cobwebs and the stench of what she assumed were rats or mice, the actual timber of the place seemed to be in quite good condition.

Depending on what was upstairs, she reckoned she could turn this place around.

Chapter 4

Sallie woke up in Seashells Cottages to the sound of the sea in the distance, got up, found some sachets of instant coffee and a tiny carton of milk and some biscuits and made herself a coffee. She popped on her slippers and grey pom-pom beanie, grabbed a blanket and opened up the glass doors onto the verandah and sat overlooking the sea.

The water glistened, the sun was coming up, and she could just about make out Pretty Beach Boat House in the distance. Just as she was finishing up her coffee, a very tall man walked past at the end of the garden as it tapered off to the beach.

'Hey, alright, I'm Pete.' He raised his hand in greeting. She got up from the chair and took a couple of steps down to the end.

The large, extremely tanned middle-aged man stuck out an enormous hand to her; she was a bit embarrassed in her beanie, pyjama bottoms, old t-shirt and slippers but he didn't seem to notice.

'I thought I'd pop in to tell you there's special brunches on Sundays down at the old Marina Club if you fancy it. Great for an egg and bacon buttie and a coffee.'

Sallie definitely loved a bacon buttie but went to say no. She didn't really want to go somewhere and have to talk to anyone yet and she wasn't even sure what she was doing here. Some crazy idea for a new start by the sea.

Pete Mulhoney was like a big friendly giant - she imagined he must, as well as owning the cottages, be out in the elements a lot, as his skin was heavily etched and deeply tanned. Wide, incredibly blue eyes and short, white blonde hair with a pair of sporty wraparound sunnies tucked into it on the top of his head. Even though it was cool he didn't seem to be chilly, with no shoes, board shorts and a huge roll neck jumper.

'You own this place, do you?' Sallie gestured around to the little line of tiny cottages.

'Ahh, yes I do, my Mum and Dad left them to me about five years ago. In a right state they were, but I did them up slowly and then put them on the internet for holiday rentals and now apart from in the Winter it's a full-time job keeping up with it all. Rather be out on my boat to be honest. But a job's a job isn't it? And it's better than paying someone else's rent.'

Sallie nodded. How true that was for her.

'Butties served from about eleven. I'm going out to the DIY store first and I'll be heading down about 12ish. I'll meet you out the front here if you fancy it?' He pointed down at his feet.

'By the way, you'll need shoes, not allowed in the Marina barefoot,' he pointed at her pyjamas, 'you'll be getting dressed?' Sallie laughed and replied that she wouldn't be caught dead out in an ACDC t-shirt and ten-year-old pyjama pants.

Pete waved and walked over towards what she presumed was his car and she went back into the cottage, stripped off her pyjamas and slippers, squeezed herself into the little bathroom and turned on the tap. Hot water gushed out, she'd thought it would be the opposite, that irritating low pressure water you got in the crappy hotels she always had to stay in, but miraculously, the shower head was large and the water was hot and lovely.

Well, that was a bonus - hot water and a good shower for a new start in Pretty Beach. She jumped out of the shower and opened up her little suitcase. She pulled out clean underwear, old soft jeans and a chunky jumper, pulled her hair up into a high ponytail and stuck a few clips in the back. She looked in the mirror, goodness, she seemed to have aged overnight, she might be in the back-end of nowhere but there was no way she was going out like that. Forty was catching up with her.

She took out her floral makeup bag, rummaged around for some BB cream and foundation, blobbed it all over her face and rubbed it in. A million times better. The stuff was cheap as chips but took five years off, possibly more. Quick fluff of blusher, some eyeliner and mascara. She looked back in the mirror. Wow, women had a lot of rubbish to bear in life but makeup certainly helped.

At midday Sallie did as instructed, took the little side path out past the cottages and onto the beach to meet Pete.

'Doing a work project or something, are you?' Pete asked. She looked back at him confused.

'We get a lot of writers and suchlike down here in the Winter - they take a few weeks away to get their work done, even had some dude from LA last year who was trying to finish a script for a movie.'

'Oh well no, not me,' she laughed.

'Well, you've come at the right time if you don't mind a bit of a chill in the evenings, and it's the Pretty Beach Winter Solstice Bonnie next week, don't suppose you've heard of it? Bit of a local tradition, bonfire on the beach, lots of old-fashioned hearty food and plenty of beer. You should come along.'

Sallie didn't say anything back, this was all too good to be true, nice locals and festivals on beaches.

'Gets quite a bit busier here next week - you got the last cottage as it goes - no tourists though, it's a bit of an unspoken thing between the locals, we keep 'em out for Bonnie week. You making a longer booking though, I thought to myself, what's the harm? There's a parade that goes up to the Marina Club too on the Sunday and a roast. You'll have to get a ticket for that though if there are any left - they normally keep a few back just in case anyone flies in that we forgot about. I'm sure we'll be able to squeeze you in.'

It was cold on the beach, the air was crisp, the sun bright. Sallie slipped her sunglasses on as they strolled along not saying much; she had to look up quite a bit to see Pete he was that tall and the wind was making it difficult to hear. Sallie took it all in. She had to admit, it was one fantastic beach and this was just the wharf side. There was the actual ocean beach on the other side too, if her memory and map studying was correct.

The sea fell gently onto the sand and a long line of shells and seaweed led them all the way along, she could see the sign for the Marina Club in the distance. She felt a million miles from her old life. It was only a few hours on a bus but it was almost like she was on a different planet - no city sights and sounds, no noise, no people flying around in big German cars. Shells interspersed the seaweed here and there, and she bent down and picked one up and put it in her pocket.

They strolled along in the wind, a couple of walkers passed and nodded hello to Pete, he waved back with a cheery smile and indicated they were going to the Marina Club. Arriving at the club, a big blackboard outside announced 'Pretty Beach Buttie - local eggs, lovely bacon, Holly's bakery rolls and Marnie's coffee, locals only.' Sallie wondered what constituted locals and said as much to Pete.

'That's old Brucie, miserable old bugger, he puts that to stop anyone coming in he might not like the look of. Thinks he's the Mayor.'

'I'm not a local.' Sallie raised her eyebrows in question.

'You're with me though' he said, as if that made her a local by association.

They walked into the club, she showed her identification and took the temporary membership ticket. A few people stood at the BBQ on the deck and an old guy with a huge stomach, drawstring chino shorts pulled up over the top, a big brown coat, knee high fishing socks and a fur lined baseball cap stood turning over bacon and cooking eggs.

Sallie realised she was really hungry and thought she could probably down two of the things. The buttie lived up to its reputation and afterwards she stood on the deck of the Marina Club drinking the coffee and looking out to sea and turned to see the bus driver lady who had helped her, step out onto the deck.

'Janelle isn't it?'

'It is indeed, most call me Nel though. How're you getting on?'

'Good, I've heard about these butties here and heard about the Bonnie too.'

'Oh yes, great if you'll still be here for the Bonnie - you don't want to miss it.'

As they were standing chatting, Rory, the not Uber, Uber driver strolled up to the table with a buttie.

'Hey Sallie, how are you?'

'Well, I'm loving the Pretty Beach air, thanks.'

Rory, it seemed, was as good looking in the daylight as he'd been before. Big brown eyes, that gorgeous, creamy brown skin.

Sallie sucked her stomach in a bit. *Ridiculous, what are you doing?* she thought. The local doctor, who commuted from his big job in the city, would not be interested in you or the flatness of your stomach. There was no ring on his finger, but no doubt he had a nice little wife tucked away in a beach house somewhere and three gorgeous tanned, blonde kids running around. He wasn't looking at her chest though like many men did, so that was a plus.

Chapter 5

Sallie looked into the window of the old cottage alongside the Boat House, down on the right; it looked to be in the same condition as the rest of the place. A building with three or four rooms, a tiny verandah out the front and a back-room area leading to a boat ramp. She decided to leave it as it was and headed over to have a look at the flat over the Boat House.

She wasn't sure whether or not to go up the stairs - goodness knows what she would find up there, so making sure her phone was on hand and had a signal, she slowly and gingerly went up. Each stair creaking and groaning as if in protest that someone had dared to start using them again.

She emerged into a large room with the same vaulted ceiling as downstairs, a panel of pretty French doors with peeling paint opening up into a tiny deck where an old French cafe table had fallen on its side and what looked like an old oil drum which had been used as a barbeque.

A whole bank of windows looked out over the harbour and in the corner over on the left a vintage pot belly stove sat with a chimney going up through the roof. She let out a long slow breath. My goodness it was stunning. Filthy, animal droppings everywhere, painted purple in places but pretty much surrounded on all sides by water and sky.

On either side of the large room two doors led off, she pulled one open carefully and looked in. A small corridor led to a bathroom, two small rooms and a larger bedroom with a tiny alcove to the side - somehow, someone had fitted in an old claw foot bath with a shower over the top, a pedestal sink, and a toilet with the cistern above and a rusty chain hanging limp to its side.

She looked down into the pan of the toilet and the bath. Layers of dirt and grime stared back, stained with brown and orange, but there was hope. Hours, days, possibly weeks of work, but hope. An old, stained mattress lay directly on the floor and piles and piles of old rotting fryer oil containers were stacked up inside one of the cupboards.

At the window, a filthy, old, dark green seventies blanket was draped on a couple of nails. There was not a single personal item or sign of an actual individual anywhere though. It was like someone had removed anything of the past and left the rest to rot.

The other door led to the turreted room and another room off to the side housed an old stove, and a wall of timber cupboards with yellow plastic handles and what looked like a butcher's top worktop that someone had painted with plastic paint across the top.

A double butler's sink sat underneath the window and two old copper taps ran up the back of the wall and over the sink. She stepped nearer to the sink and looked inside; the bottom of it was black with grime and congealed gunk. Sheesh this needed more than a good clean, that was for sure, the years of neglect and a previous life of filth needed to be wiped out with paint.

Ivy crept in through one of the windows and where a window on the other side had come open, mould had formed on the wall. The carcass of a dead rat lay on its side near the bottom of the stove and an old piece of blue net curtain nailed up to the window flapped in the wind.

This wasn't out of Homes and Gardens. Obviously, the place had been rented at some point to what looked like druggies. Old red plastic milk crates sat in a circle around the pot belly stove and the window at the end, looking back out over the laneway and to the shops down the road had been painted out with white emulsion paint.

Her phone pinged with a text from Nina.

How are you getting on?

Not too bad. Could be worse I guess.

Send me some pics. xxx

She walked back down the stairs, taking photos for Nina. Went over the main floor and to the French doors at the back, fumbled around with the keys and found one to open one of the sets of doors. It opened out to a deck whose legs straddled the beach. Right down at the end water lapped up against the bottom, a pergola above held row upon row of old fishing nets, crabbing pots and old canvas sails piled up on the left.

She closed the doors behind her and walked down the side of the downstairs deck, which sloped away as it met the shore where masses of reeds and weeds engulfed it, but she could just see her way through and to the neighbouring property. It was another old house with a huge sign saying *Kayak hire, bait and fishing gear available.*

She pushed through the weeds at the front and looked over the road. A gelato shop with a pale pink and striped white awning sat to the front, a pink cruiser bike with flowers growing in the basket, plus a florist and a bakery. *Looks a bit better on that side of the road than over here,* she thought to herself.

To the other side, another house with what looked to be a renovated building at the back and a big sign read Ben Chalmers Seaplanes. Wow, the place had seaplanes too. It was like something from a movie.

She'd seen enough, she wasn't sure if she was up to it; it was vastly overwhelming. She walked to the front, turned to the right and sat herself down on a decrepit looking old bench, took her small flask from her bag and poured herself a milky coffee.

She took a sip of her coffee and made a decision. She was going to give a new life by the sea, a new start and the Boat House at Pretty Beach a good go.

Chapter 6

Sallie walked past Pretty Beach Fire Station, along the path and over to the tiny museum housing the council offices and a small community hall out the back. She smoothed her hair down, pushed open the door and headed into the dark hallway and approached a long counter, where three women sat at their booths. One was chatting to an old man waving around a council bill and informing the whole place that he wasn't ever going to go paperless and why did they keep sending him a paper letter to ask him to.

Sallie stood behind the sticker on the floor saying, 'wait here' and looked at the touch screen and wondered whether or not to add her details and get a ticket - the place was deserted, surely she didn't need a number? She was wrong, according to the sign on the counter she did need a number. She punched her name, mobile number and details in and a second later a text alerted her that she was in line to speak to a council representative and would be instructed when a member of the team was free.

She remained there, looking at the two women, who were chatting about last night's episode of the baking show and discussing who had been eliminated. Five minutes went past and she had wondered if the system had actually notified either of them that she was there. Neither of them had looked over, she wasn't even sure if they'd seen her. Just as she was about to say something the screen flashed above her head and instructed her to step forward and up to Counter Two.

'Hello, I'm Julie Fanan, how can I help you?' The woman beamed at her.

'Hi, I have a meeting with Mr Johnson. I emailed him last week to talk about the listed building regulations and he said I might as well pop along and have a chat.'

The blonde-haired woman, with bright pink lipstick from the eighties and electric blue eyeliner on her waterline, smiled back at her.

'You didn't need to get in the system for that! Hold on I'll go out and get him.'

Sallie had to laugh to herself; there was no reception desk, no concierge to tell you what to do and no one even looking up to see who was in the place. She'd had no other option than to put herself in the system. Julie came back in the door on the right, strolled back over towards the counter, ruffled her hair to puff it out a little bit more and smiled.

'On his way, just making himself a cup of tea - are you wanting one too, if so I'll go up and make you one?'

So, this really was the Pretty Beach way then, even the people in the council offices were friendly. Slow, yes, but offering to make you a cup of tea. In Freshlea they were behind a perspex counter and looked like they were possibly holding a gun underneath for protection.

'Actually, yes that would be lovely, thank you Julie.'

Julie came back a few minutes later with Mr Johnson and a cup of tea, and a text informed Sallie that her query with the council had now been dealt with. He took her over to a small sofa and coffee table in an alcove off to the side.

'Right Sallie, I have all the details you need here in this folder and I've also emailed you a zipped-up file of every single thing you need to know about what you can, and can't, do in Pretty Beach in terms of the building.'

Sallie secretly heaved a huge sigh of relief at Mr Johnson who had held out his hand and told her to call him Roy. With the emailing back and forth she'd had visions that Roy would be some evil little jobsworth. She'd envisaged that she would end up making a voodoo doll of him and spend her evenings sticking pins in it. In fact, he was a happy-go-lucky chap with a massive round face, a bright pink shirt and missing a finger on his left hand.

'Basically, you can't do anything that changes anything too much and you have to keep everything in the colours of Pretty Beach. If you're not planning on building anything or pulling anything down, you should be ok. That's right, isn't it, from what you said in the emails?'

'Yes, and no, I won't be building anything. The only thing I have to worry about really is one part of the corrugated roof is quite rusty and will need to be repaired at some point and the bridge over the stream.'

'The regulations need to be consulted for that when you get to it, but on everything else you should be good, and I for one will be happy to see that old place brought back to life.'

'And then there's the floating house - I haven't been able to work out which one it is.' She pointed to the note on the file.

'Also in the email, in a separate folder. Now that's a bit trickier because it comes under 'waterways' and actually, there's a whole other world of red tape around those things - some of them go back to the war and were built as temporary homes for the returning soldiers, so it's more complicated.'

'Yes, I saw that. Well, I think Roy, I will cross that bridge when I come to it.'

'If I was going to give you any advice on the matter, that would be a very good idea.'

Chapter 7

Sallie took her phone out of the backpack, plugged the charger into the wall and clicked the lead into the phone. She looked around the little room at Seashells Cottages - such a lot of potential if someone with an eye for it got hold of it. Tongue and groove clad throughout, with a beautiful bath, handmade kitchen and little verandah area to the front.

Unfortunately, Pete had painted it a dreadful garish blue and furnished it with bits and bobs from the local charity shop by the looks of it. While Sallie could do that with her eyes shut and pull it all together, this effort looked to be exactly what it was - a load of used furniture thrown together in a rush.

Not that she was complaining; it was very clean, warm and more importantly it wasn't too expensive. As her battery charged up again her phone beeped with a text. Her friend Nina flashed up in the little green box on her phone.

Hey Sal, you won't believe this, someone's moved into the annexe - a bald bloke in his fifties who stands on the balcony in the morning belting out Elton John songs in the worst voice I've ever heard at the top of his lungs!!!

Hilarious! You'll have to complain to Jude.

I know, can't believe it, maybe I'll be moving out to Pretty Beach too - tbh I'm getting sick of the noise here. Bet it's quiet there?

It is but it's not quite the sleepy little place we thought. Lots of fancy boutiques, all the lovely old cottages but also done up houses, seaplanes, some nice restaurants...

Only an hour on the train now Sals, I might have to look on the internet and have a little sea-change myself.

You can buy an old falling-down house if you like.

You'll work it out. I'll speak to you Wednesday, I'm in court all day tomorrow and then straight out to clients in the evening, I'll be back late.

Tx, spk soon.

Chapter 8

Sallie opened the fridge, took out one of the bottles of wine she'd put in there the day before, and poured a long tall glass. She needed a drink after the realities of the hard work and sheer vastness of what would need to be done to the Boat House.

Other people bought grand estates, perhaps a chateau in the south of France they renovated and did up as part of a TV show. In romance books, down-on-their-luck women got new jobs in sweet little cafes with handmade cakes and fruit trees out the front. Lovely, long-lost plump aunties in gingham aprons would take them under their wing and men swept them off their feet. Not her, no, she had an old Boat House in a town where she didn't know a soul.

She walked into the bathroom, poured some shower gel into the bath, lifted the mixer tap and ran the bath. A glass of wine in the bath solved a lot of things. She sat on the toilet looking at her phone as the tub filled up and the wind outside howled - the evening had quickly drawn in, the ocean had picked up and didn't sound quite as friendly as it had earlier.

Scrolling through lovely lives on Instagram it crossed her mind that this was one of those situations she found herself in in life where she wished she had someone by her side. Not that she was looking for a man per se, but sometimes just being able to talk to someone else about what the heck you were going to do helped. What was that saying about a problem halved?

She let the water run until it reached the top; a full bath was a luxury for her and as she wasn't paying for the water here, she was going to make the most of it. The complimentary shower gel had done surprisingly well at providing a huge tub of bubbles. She stripped off her jeans and jumper and climbed in.

The warm, bubbly warmth seeped into her bones and instantly soothed everything - the last few months, the journey getting to Pretty Beach and the huge mountain of work that was the Boat House and the decision on whether she would stay and hope it worked out... or risk another failure in her life.

She knew something though, she was sick of feeling like she was swimming through mud - always trying to catch her tail, always trying to keep her head above water. Maybe up here she could finally get away from that.

She would make a list. This conundrum of whether to stay or go wasn't exactly rocket science. She'd have to work out what she would need to spend to make it liveable and if she had enough to cover doing that, then she would stay.

The actual renovation wasn't so much the problem - she had done it before with her second husband. The problem was more the money. They'd bought 'renovator's delights' and spent years doing them up and living in gardens in a tent. Then they would sell, buy another one and rinse and repeat the whole formula. Sallie had spent the best part of her thirties in old overalls, shovelling around in dirt, living in tents and going to the toilet in the elements.

The last one they'd finished and when they were finally on their way to some stability, her husband had decided he rather liked the look of the neighbour more than he did her. The property market had dipped, they'd just about broken even on it all, he'd refused to move out and she'd found herself in dingy rented accommodation in Freshlea looking for a job.

The best thing about that experience, though she hadn't thought about it at the time, was that she had come out of it with a skill and that was how she'd ended up with the casual job in property styling. It had taught her to look at the bones of a place, the shape of a room, what you could do with what you already had and how to do things and keep on budget and that was exactly what she was going to do now.

She took out her notebook and pen, leant over the side of the bath onto the little side table and wrote a list of things she would need to do. It was quite simple, first things first. If she wanted to live in the Boat House she would need to sort the garden, find something to sleep on, make sure it was safe and work out a way to make some money.

Chapter 9

Four days later and Sallie was standing in the middle of the Boat House, she'd been in every day and had started to clean things up. A long, slow, tiring and tedious job whereby at the end of the day it seemed as if no progress had happened at all.

The first day she'd managed to squeeze the old mattress, stinking of old wee and covered in stains, out of the large hallway window. She'd gagged, dragged it over the floorboards, opened the windows up, looked about to see if there was anyone nearby and slowly pushed the whole thing out and it had landed down the side of the house with a huge crash. She'd heaved it over and tucked it behind the side so it couldn't be seen from the front and decided she would deal with it later.

She went around the whole place pulling down the old blankets and net curtains nailed up to the windows, chucked out the plastic milk crates, emptied the cupboards in the kitchen, ripped down creeping greenery growing through the window and wedged it shut to stop more entering. In rubber gloves and using a dustpan she'd scooped a dead rat carcass into a plastic bag and lobbed it out the window.

Her head was stuck in the old oven, seeing if there were any signs that the thing worked, when she heard a car pull up out the front, footsteps on the gravelly path under the weeds and a knocking on the barn door downstairs.

Someone called out. She removed herself from the oven, wiped her hands on her old jeans and thought she must look a fright. Scraping her hair back to neaten her bun she carefully walked down the stairs, crossed the Boat House floor, walked over to the doors and opened them up to see a tall, blonde-haired man dressed in shorts, working boots, an astonishingly white polo shirt and a cheery smile.

'Hello, I thought I saw someone in here. I looked over a few times thinking that there was movement in the old Boat House.'

'Ha, err yes there is, it's me... I'm Sallie.'

'Ben.' He stuck his hand out and Sallie looked at her filthy hand and apologetically took his firm grip.

'Ben Chalmers, as in Ben Chalmers Seaplanes.' He stuck his thumb up and pointed to the signwriting all over the adjacent corrugated roof building. He was the owner of the property next door.

'It was the turret window being open that made me realise there was someone in here; I've been here nearly ten years and never really seen a soul.' He looked at her kindly and then looked further inside at the interior of the Boat Shed.

'Never judge a book by its cover though eh, pretty good in there, isn't it?'

Her eyes widened, 'I don't know about that Ben, but it's got good bones I think. Come in and have a look if you like.' She pulled open the door and he stepped inside.

'This has more than good bones - look at the ceiling and the view out the back, a property developer would be all over this. And those vintage industrial lights are worth a couple of thousand each. I'll whip them off for you if you like, pop them on eBay and you'll be better off in no time.'

'Thanks, but if I can get those to work they'll be staying.'

He sucked air in and shook his head, looking up at them.

'Would be great if they are working wouldn't it? If they're like the ones in my place next door they were made to last for years, not like that old rubbish from China nowadays. The problem is the globes, unless you get the fittings changed those things will cost you a fortune to run...'

He paused for breath and she answered his question that yes, they worked. Amazingly everything worked. A plumber had been in and said the hot water tank had a few more years in it if she was lucky, the electrician had put in a new box and replaced some wires and everything had gone a lot more smoothly than she had hoped.

'Anyway, good to see someone in here. I came up here about ten years ago now, bought an old house down at the beach in Seafolly, rented that one out now and I live out the back here too.'

'Ahh thank you Ben.' Ben with the honey-coloured skin, curly blonde hair and the strongest legs she'd ever seen. He walked around, looking at the faded timber, the view out to sea and the vaulted ceilings.

'Hmm, needs some work...' Then walking down to the end of the building and out at the deck behind.

'Wow, this is gold!'

'I know.' She laughed. He mumbled something quietly that she didn't quite hear.

'Sorry?'

'Oh nothing, my wife - she would have loved this, she loved old buildings. She passed away about ten years ago. Breast cancer - took her very quickly. One minute she was here, a year later, gone.'

'I'm so sorry to hear that.'

'Yeah, well, it is what it is, I'm finally getting used to her not being here.' He looked up at the vaulted ceiling.

'That's some carpentry up there, isn't it?'

They both stood there in silence looking up at the roof and all the old junk in the eaves. Standing next to him, she could smell a mixture of clean laundry and some kind of fresh lemon aftershave. Not a bad combination, that was for sure.

'What are you going to do with the place then? All I know about it is it was rented out years ago through the council and the awful tenants sat around all day smoking pot.'

She looked up at the blue-green eyes on the lovely skin and thought *I could definitely get used to living next door to you.* He looked out the front to the water.

'What about those moorings down the side there? What are you going to use those for?'

'I've no idea, they're included and a floating house too, but goodness knows where that is.'

'There's a few of those old floating houses out there, it must be one of those. Look, I'm always after moorings, they're like gold dust in Pretty Beach - if you can let me use one of those moorings every now and then for my planes, I'll lend you a couple of my eighteen-year-old apprentices for a few weeks to help sort this place out - not much going on in the Winter up here and they need some good old-fashioned hard work.'

'That's so kind of you! There are two spare moorings there and I can't see that I will be using either of them anytime soon, not having a boat and all that.'

'Don't you believe it, everyone in Pretty Beach ends up with a boat.' Ben smiled at her.

'It's a fabulous place to live. When my wife got sick, it went around in seconds, even though she was very private about it all and didn't want anyone to know or to see her looking like she did. But, I tell you what, you won't find any better people. The people in Pretty Beach, they will help you out. Did all sorts for me when she passed away - left me dinners on the doorstep, even a case of beer one night.' He looked away as if talking about his wife had brought back another time.

He stood there as if contemplating how nice the people of Pretty Beach had been to him and then snapped out of the memories.

'If you want those young fellas to give you a hand just shout - we've not got a lot on at the moment and by the looks of this you're going to need more than your elbow grease to get it sorted out.'

'That Ben would be marvellous, I don't even know where to start, so generous of you.'

'It's the Pretty Beach way,' Ben replied. 'Some of the folks are a bit odd, and it all feels weird at first, but you'll get used to it.'

He walked back towards the door, she said goodbye, turned around, walked across the huge floor and up the creaky old stairs back to the oven.

And you, Ben Chalmers Seaplanes, I could get used to you too, she thought.

Chapter 10

Three hours later, Sallie pulled her phone out of her pocket and looked at the time. The morning had flown past, it was a tad before two, no wonder she was feeling hungry. And exhausted too - since she'd left Ben downstairs instructing his youngsters to pull all the junk out of the roof and vacuum it, she'd swept every single floorboard in the little flat with a broom, mopped it, emptied bucket after bucket of thick grimy water down the sink and wondered if it was making any difference at all.

It felt almost pointless to even try to clean it all up, but as each layer of filth left, the place began to look the tiniest bit better. Just as she was pouring another bucket of brown water down the sink in the kitchen, she heard Ben call up the stairs. She stuck her head around the corner and looked down.

'Yeah, popped over to see how these blokes were doing and told them to go and get some lunch, they've done a good job. Amazing what a few hours and a bit of muscle can do.'

'That's music to my ears. I didn't realise the time, I'm starving too - I'll have to pop down to the shops and get something to eat.' Sallie stood at the top of the stairs looking down at him.

'I've got some pies over in the fridge; if you like pies and a beer I can sort you out with one of those.'

Sallie thought to herself that actually she was in no doubt at all that she would like Ben to sort her out, but kept that to herself. She was forty and did not have a good track record with relationships, and romance was the last thing on her mind.

'Where's the sun? I'll get the pies and we can sit over there in the warm.' He winked and went back to his yard.

She watched as he came sauntering back along the pebbles and hopped over the little low fence between the two properties. Carrying a small blue lunch bag in his right hand and beer in the left, there was no doubt that he was quite easy on the eye.

'Sorry, I didn't check to see if you liked beer or not? But I brought over these extras anyway, thought you could do with a few in your fridge. I've got hundreds of the things left over from a function we did last week.'

'Actually, I do love beer, but there is one small problem - I am not the owner of a fridge.' She laughed and he pulled two beers out of the case, popped the lids and handed her a brown bag with a beef pie in it.

'Now that's something else I can also sort you out with - I've got a fridge, a microwave, an outdoor seating set with a matching table and a bed in my garage from a house I flipped down in Gypsy Bay and haven't gotten around to selling them on yet. No one has even sat on the bed let alone slept in it.'

She took a bite of the pie. 'Oh, that's kind of you, but I'm on a bit of a budget, so I will have to wait on that.'

'No, it would do me a favour, it's been blocking the garage for months and I need to get my finger out and do something about it.' He sipped his beer.

'That would really help me out.' She put the pie down on the paper and took a sip of the beer.

'So, you'd like the lot then would you? Well, I'm your man...'

They both leant back against the old Boat House the sun beating down, he held out his bottle to hers and clinked.

'Here's to being sorted in Pretty Beach.' She said.

He took another couple of beers out and offered her another one.

'Thanks Ben, you really are too kind.' She looked up at him and the eyes.

'Nothing about being kind Sallie, it's the Pretty Beach way.'

Chapter 11

Pretty Beach Bonnie Festival planning had been in full swing, posters were on every lamppost, flags and bunting adorned the streets, and a huge bonfire had slowly been built day-by-day down on the main beach. Sallie had passed it every day and watched it get bigger and bigger on her way to the Boat House.

The morning of the big day dawned bright and cold - she had been for a long walk on the beach rugged up in an old flannel shirt, grey beanie, a huge pair of sunglasses and a chunky scarf wrapped twice around her neck. It was chilly and clear, she loved these days, the only way it could possibly get any better was if it snowed. Sallie Broadchurch loved snow.

It was so early and so cold that she'd made a take-away cup of coffee and headed out not bothering to even wash her face. She walked for an hour and on the way back looked over towards the old Boat House as she came around the corner in front of the bakers. It didn't look any better from the outside, the only visible difference was a vague path of trampled down weeds on the way in and the window in the very top of the turret was now permanently open. It looked sad, dark and unloved compared to all the beautifully adorned shops in pale hues and the vast beach houses all decorated and getting ready for the festival.

She walked into the bakers, a line of about three people queueing up for fresh bread ahead of her - clearly a popular place or maybe just the only place. She ordered a large iced bun, a loaf of bread, and took a bottle of milk out from the fridge and placed it on the counter.

'Hey, I'm Holly.' The woman smiled at her and Sallie did a double take that the owner of the bakery was quite so friendly.

'Mother of Rory, Uber driver - he told me all about you.' She extended her hand across the counter.

'Ahh nice to meet you.'

'Did you hear about what happened last night?'

'No, what do you mean? I was up and out early and haven't seen anyone.'

'The thing last night down at the Marina Club. Someone robbed the place, tied up old Brucie, stole all the cash and all the stock. It's all over the news.'

Holly was beside herself with it. Clearly not much went on in Pretty Beach. Sallie almost laughed to herself - old Bruce, the guy with the long socks and huge stomach getting tied up, it was like someone had made it up, in fact you couldn't have made it up, it was so bizarre.

'Are you sure?' Sallie frowned at Holly.

'Sure!' Holly replied, 'Nothing ever happens in these parts, the nearest we get to any crime is when some of the rich kids from the City bring up some dope in the Summer and sit around smoking it on the beach. He's in hospital now too, nasty little sods whoever they were. He was so stressed they reckon he might have had a heart attack.'

Wow, this was horrible, a real crime in sleepy Pretty Beach. Sallie went over it in her head, she had popped in the Marina Club on her way home that night too. Typical, the week she arrives in a backwater town to start a new life and would be living alone in an abandoned house someone is assaulted and robbed.

'Sounds like something from a television show,' Sallie replied.

'Yeah, hope it won't put you off being over there in the Boat House.' Sallie looked back at her with a frown wondering how Holly knew she was there.

'Sallie, nothing goes on in Pretty Beach without old Holly knowing, I've seen you over there.' She did a funny little chuckle and tapped the side of her nose.

'I'm the baker, the Uber driver and the local bush telegraph.' She laughed at her own joke.

Holly, lovely and funny, with the same deep brown eyes as her son Rory and not a line on her face, a super-shiny straight black bob, blue shirt and jeans with a baker's apron over the top, flicked her hand and pointed over the road to the Boat House.

'It's a great spot, I've been waiting for the day someone would take it on. Let me know if you want any help.'

'Thanks, I'll keep that in mind.'

Sallie walked to the front of the shop, pulled open the door, the little bell tinkled as she left and she wondered what other characters she would meet in this funny little town.

Bread under her arm, she crossed over the road, jumped over the stream and walked along the beach back to Seashells Cottages and past the old Marina Club to see if there were any signs of what had been going on.

Glorious, warm sun glinted off the sea, the sky deep and full and the sand cool between her toes, she ripped a piece of French bread off and stopped in the sand, hand over her eyes squinting down to see the Marina Club.

Gosh, Holly was right, there were three police cars lined up at the driveway of the club - two police women looking bored guarded the entrance and what looked like red tape was tied around the whole building.

Chapter 12

Sallie walked back along the beach following the line from the tide of seashells, no wonder it was called Seashells Cottages - thousands of them lined the shore. She opened the door of the cottage, went into the kitchen, made herself a bacon sandwich and a cup of coffee and went outside onto the verandah to think about the Boat House. Thank goodness for Roy Johnson and Ben; they had been extremely encouraging and like everyone else had seemed more than happy to help.

She sliced the sandwich further and thought about what she was going to do with the place. Ben Chalmers was right, it was gold, but she had no money for seaplanes, boats or in fact any kind of work at all and the only experience she had was in cafe jobs or property styling. Even that was not a skill. It sounded fancy and some of the girls she'd worked with had a qualification in interior design - but in reality, it consisted of lugging around furniture, adding a load of lamps on any free surface, scattering a few throws around and tidying all the clutter up. Throw in a few large vases of flowers, place big bowls of lemons everywhere and people let rid of themselves of ridiculous amounts of money.

Maybe that was an idea - maybe she could do something with styling, use it as a base for a styling business. The trouble was Pretty Beach was tightly held and according to Pete, there was one house a year for sale and that would either get passed on to a local or someone from the City would throw a load of money at it just to make it their holiday home.

She finished up her sandwich, tidied up the kitchen, went into the bedroom, picked up yesterday's jeans and her oldest, faded work t-shirt. Then quickly slung together a cheese sandwich for lunch, made up a bottle of cordial and slipped one of the bottles of wine into her basket. At the last minute she grabbed her laptop just in case the thieves came anywhere near Seashells Cottages too, locked the door behind her and headed down the little cobbled path to the laneway.

Adjusting her hat, remembering to spray her face with sunscreen and turning the corner she bumped straight into bus driver Nel, who she hardly recognized without the regulation bus driver's hat and uniform. Behind her sunglasses Sallie looked her up and down. Nel was stunning, real soft blonde, almost baby-like hair tied up in a ponytail with a pretty scarf, a fantastic figure that had been hidden by the bus uniform, beautiful luminous skin and deep brown eyes with lashes which looked like they weren't even real.

Nel waved her hand in recognition and smiled.

'What are you up to, off to the Boat House?' Sallie stared back at her - Janelle hadn't paused for breath and was still going. 'Are you coming along to the Bonnie Festival? How about finding yourself a Pretty Beach man?'

'I think I'm a bit too old for a new man.' Sallie answered.

'Haha, old, no one's too old in Pretty Beach Sal, not many of us to go round you know! See you, then.' She looked at the basket with the bottle of wine poking out the top.

'Wine for one is it, at the Boat Shed, or will there be someone joining you - someone like Ben?' She chuckled again to herself, and before Sallie could think of what to reply or attempt to answer, she held her hand up in a small wave and walked on.

***

Sallie carried on along the lane, gazing up at the houses wondering about the conversation. Would she actually be interested in starting anything with someone in her new town? No. The last thing she wanted to do up here was get involved with any of the locals. On the other hand, Rory, very handsome doctor and Ben unbelievably good looking seaplane owner... neither of them were the sort of men one would ordinarily kick out of bed.

Shaking her head and blinking she pulled herself up, what was she thinking? There was no way either of them would look at her in the first place. Getting on a bit Sallie with the too big boobs and wrinkles around the eyes.

No, she decided, whether a seaplane owner or doctor, she was not fraternizing with anyone. This was her last chance to get on with her life, get a real job, forget about the two failed marriages and the lousy perv she'd worked for for the last few years and actually put some roots down and start planning for the future. And a romance, dalliance or even harmless flirtation was not part of that.

She quickened her pace, walked west along the lane, turned left as it branched down towards the sea and around the inlet and through the main street of Pretty Beach. Lots of pastel coloured gift shops selling all kinds of trinkets sat beside each other along the lane, a tiny bookshop with an old cruiser bike outside, a beautiful florist with White Cottage Flowers across the door, diving trips centre, a fish and chip shop decked out in navy blue and white, an old-fashioned grocer, a boat tours reception, three cafes and right at the very end a pastel pink and blue oyster bar.

As she stood back and looked around, she realised that everything was painted in the same ice-cream colours. She remembered Roy saying something about a Pretty Beach by-law and she realised now she hadn't seen anything painted in any other colour since she'd arrived. She'd ask Ben about it if she bumped into him later.

Arriving at the Boat House she crossed over the stream, was just about to get out her keys when she noticed a newspaper had been left in the decrepit old post box. She pulled it out of the box and flicked it open. The Pretty Beach Daily, screamed:

Crime in Pretty Beach!

Old Brucie tied up and left for dead by gangland members from the city.

She sighed, folded it back up and popped it in her basket. Gangland members in this place? Not quite the sleepy little feel she'd been hoping for.

She trampled through the grass and weeds to the barn door, unlocked the padlock and dragged the door open. As she opened it up she was amazed at how different it looked. Ben's youngsters had made an immense improvement. She'd been so busy in the accommodation upstairs, and exhausted when she'd left that she hadn't had a proper chance to see it in the daylight.

Anything and everything old and dirty had been pulled out and stacked up on the outside of the house where it couldn't be seen. They'd vacuumed the whole place with industrial vacuums and lightly jet washed it afterwards to wash the place down. She'd been a bit nervous about the jet wash on the timber, but Ben had said they'd done the same in the place next door and it had come up great. She had taken his word for it and held her breath. He had been right.

It was still damp though, so she walked all the way to the end and opened the doors at the back to the deck overlooking the water. Light flooded in and cool crisp air swept into the Boat House. Yep, that should do it. She took a double take at the view; she hadn't truly appreciated it since she'd been upstairs cleaning and tidying. It undoubtedly was fantastic, indeed breath-taking. The sea, the air, the sky... just the magnitude of nature.

She stood there for a few moments, the sun beating down on her face, then crossed the floor of the house, opened the door to the stairs and carefully stepped up. Every tread creaked and groaned and she was sure that the next time would be the time she put her foot through the things.

Her job for the day was to do something about the state of the kitchen - it was way past a little bit of bleach and a scrub, and the only thing that would get rid of the filth and stench was paint. Bleach on the old double butler sink and some paste on the copper taps would get them shining, but the actual cupboards, well they needed a few layers of paint to get them looking good.

With a podcast playing on her phone and putting on a pair of rubber gloves she started to roughly wipe out the kitchen cupboards; whoever had made them had obviously done most of the other carpentry in the place too. Her gloved hands worked over the beautiful tongue and groove panels to the front and dovetail joints... the drawers ran like a dream.

She stood back and surveyed her work. The only thing keeping it from looking like a high-end bespoke kitchen on Pinterest were the revolting handles someone had put on and the lurid green woodchip wallpaper hastily glued to the wall behind the gap for the fridge.

Yes, this kitchen would scrub up really well. It reminded her of the first place she'd renovated with her second husband. That place had been in a worse state than this, with melamine cupboards and a dirty brown splashback. They'd sprayed the whole lot with laminate paint, blasted the old tiles in a light grey and by the time they'd finished the whole thing had looked as good as new.

Examining the worktop more closely, she could see it was definitely butcher's block underneath, the top had been painted with what looked like plastic paint, probably to try and make it wipeable. There were two ways of getting that off; try and dissolve it or sand the whole thing back. She would do the latter.

She pulled disposable overalls out of her basket, climbed into them, dragged over the industrial tin of paint and dipped in her paintbrush. Standing on the worktop, head to toe in the cheap overalls, her head inside the cupboards she slowly and painfully started painting the whole thing.

A few hours in, bored of podcasts she jumped down off the counter, walked down the stairs and found the old radio in the cupboard on the ground floor of the Boat House. They didn't make them like this nowadays. Plugging it in, a deliciously old-fashioned sound came out and she realised it was tuned to Pretty Beach radio. The music ended and a voice came over sounding suspiciously like Pete at Seashells Cottages.

'What a beautiful day it is today down here in Pretty Beach and only a day to go before the Bonnie Festival.'

Sallie worked for a couple more hours without taking a break, chuckling away to herself at Pete on the radio and hoping to get all of the upper cupboards painted with undercoat by lunchtime.

The clock was ticking now, she had limited time left at Seashells Cottages, she had no more in the budget to pay Pete and overall, the sooner she could move into the Boat House the better.

Just as she climbed down off the worktop and examining her work a text came in, Nina's name flashed up on her phone.

How u getting on? OMG I read on Facebook that Pretty Beach made the Crimestoppers Facebook Page and someone got tied-up and mugged?

Yeah, the Marina Club apparently, I don't know much more than that, I was in there that evening but way before it happened!

Had to laugh Sallie, nothing up there for years, and u move there and there's a crime - meant to be from that Robo Brothers lot.

I know, typical right? So much for a relaxed, casual Pretty Beach lifestyle.

What's yr progress like?

Yeah good, I've got the whole place cleaned out and now started on the upstairs.

Fab. It'll be in Country Homes magazine next.

Hardly, I don't think so!!!

Sallie, you've sent me the pics and remember I've seen what u did to those houses u flipped and I've seen u work yr magic on the annexe. I reckon it will look amazing and don't forget the view. BTW my sister has some furniture going - a couple of white sofas, a desk and an old trunk. From that fancy French furniture place she loves but now she's going boho chic, I told her u might be interested.

Aww thanks - but no money.

It's free. She was going to take it to the tip! I asked her and she said she'd get it shipped if u want it?

That's so kind. Can you send me some pics?

If it was from the French homewares store that Sallie used to frequent often, and couldn't even afford to buy a bar of soap from, let alone a sofa, then she thought there was a good chance she would love it.

What are u going to sleep on though, the floor???

Sallie laughed to herself; she'd done it before. When she'd first moved into the little annexe by Nina her bed hadn't arrived and she had spent two nights on pillows in the bath. It had been more comfortable than she'd expected.

She would be getting the bed from Ben so that was good enough for her. She did cringe a bit about the mattress but he'd said it was unused and that was the last of her worries. Her text pinged again.

So what's going on at the weekend?

Believe it or not I'm going to a festival, the Pretty Beach Bonnie Festival no less, which is a bonfire on the beach and a big lunch on Sunday. The guy I rented the cottage from invited me, apparently all the locals go.

Look at u being invited by a guy to a lunch, don't get that in Freshlea too often.

Yeah Pete's not exactly dating material Nina.

You never know Sal, anyway going into court now. Boring - another murder.

Chapter 13

Sallie opened the wardrobe at Seashells Cottages. What did you wear to a festival that involved a huge bonfire, lots of drinks where everyone got very drunk and did stupid things?

She wondered if the locals would be dressed up, as in dresses - it was cold and she didn't want to be clambering around by a bonfire in a skirt. She decided on black skinny jeans, a black silky shirt, a stack of sparkly bracelets, curled her hair and put it up on top and held it there with a tiny little diamante clip which sparkled and caught the light.

There was life in her yet. She loved the power of simple dressing; the whole lot including the sparkly hair clip had come from H & M, not that you could tell. The shirt gleamed and the jeans were that cut that took five pounds off, pulling in the tummy at the front and keeping the rear end from sliding down the legs. In her ears simple, faux diamond drops sparkled - she'd read that putting pearls or diamonds in your ears brought attention to your face and in a good way. She had no idea if it worked or not but had given it a go.

Pulling on black boots with a chunky heel and grabbing her huge wool coat off the hanger, she doused herself in perfume, popped a narrow brown belt over the top of the coat to cinch in her waist and looked in the mirror. Forty - yes, fat - not yet, and with a whole lot of life experience behind her.

She wondered why she was even bothering to go to this. She wasn't particularly interested in new friends, had been bitten too many times with men and wanted the quiet life as much as possible. However, everyone here had been so friendly to her and it seemed as if this Bonnie night was a big deal, so she thought she'd make the effort.

Go along for a couple of drinks, show her face, stand around the fire and enjoy it all. Then, she'd walk back along the beach, have a nice warm shower, make herself a cup of hot chocolate, put on her pyjamas, get into bed and scroll ideas for the Boat House on her phone.

Chapter 14

Sallie Broadchurch stood at the side of the fire, she'd made the right call on the dress, smart casual. Most of the other women were dressed similarly, in nice but warm clothes, except for Nel who was in a beautiful floaty boho dress. *I'd be wearing a dress like that if I was her age again and looked like that,* Sallie thought. She really was particularly stunning tonight for sure.

Once the fire was lit everybody took a spot next to it and they all started to sing a song similar to the national anthem, but all about Pretty Beach. How sweet, the place even had its own song. At the end they all stood up, stamped their feet three times and turned around. She must ask Pete what that was all about.

Soft golden light flickered from the bonfire and caught the faces of everyone around, she took in lungfuls of the clean, cold night air and looked up at the stars.

Holly, Uber driver and baker stood on the other side and she saw Ben Chalmers a few along from her with a beer in his hand, a beanie pulled down over his hair. Rory was standing next to Pete, who was still in shorts and all of what she guessed was his family were standing beside him, including a young woman holding a baby and a toddler holding her hand.

Sallie rubbed her hands together, she hadn't brought gloves and pulled up the collar on her coat. She looked up at the sky, if only it would snow, that would make this scene even better. She loved snow - she could smell it when it was on the way. She held her hands up to the fire as slowly people started to drift away. Staring into the fire Rory came by on his way in.

'Are you coming in, getting a bit cold now out here isn't it?'

She nodded, followed him up the beach and they walked all the way along. She stepped off the beach, stamped her feet to get rid of the sand and he walked over to the tap, turned it on and cold water gushed all over the floor.

'Brrrrr, are you crazy?'

'Ha, not too bad once you get used to it.'

She didn't believe that for a second and started to rub her feet in the grass wiping off the sand.

'You'll have sand in your socks and your boots if you do that.'

'I'd rather that than run freezing cold water over my feet in this weather!' Sallie exclaimed.

'Maybe you have a point... the water is like ice.'

She brushed her feet until most of the sand was off, flicked some more off with her socks and put the boots back on. She could feel that flush to her cheeks from being outside in the cold and was looking forward to getting inside in the warm and a drink inside her.

Chapter 15

Sallie undid the belt on her coat, held open the door with her elbow and followed Rory into the pub. The place was rammed with people, she pulled her bag round to the front, took out her phone, opened her credit card slot and went as if to move forward to the bar. Rory touched her arm.

'No, no, I'll get these. What would you like?'

'Sauvignon Blanc would be great please.' She looked around, saw Pete talking to Ben and who she thought must be one of his sons and his grandchild and Holly stroking the back of the child's hair. She took a couple of steps over towards them.

'Hey Pete, haven't seen you for a couple of days, how are you?'

'I'm good thanks mate, it's sad about old Brucie though isn't it? Sorry that happened in your first bit in town, we don't get that much up here just so's you know...we are wanting you to stay.' He joked. 'What have you been up to then? I heard you've been going into Pretty Beach's best kept old building - you didn't tell me about that.' He threw his head back and laughed but there was a bit of an edge to his voice. Sallie took a step back and looked him straight in the eye.

'Ahh well, I do like to have secrets, but I'm learning that it's quite hard to have them here in Pretty Beach.'

'That's for sure.' He paused for a bit, looked around and then back at her. 'All good with me Sallie, you'll get to know what this place is like.' His deep tan skin crinkled and something about the way he spoke to her made her feel uneasy. She didn't want to get on the wrong side of this very tall, very suntanned man, who knew everything about her new home.

Just as she was about to reply, Rory came back with the drinks and took a position next to Pete. She took her wine, and managed to take a huge sip without anyone noticing, when Pete gestured to his right.

'Anyway, Sallie, my son Jake, his daughter Ava.' He ruffled the little blonde curls and looked as proud as punch.

'Nice to meet you Jake,' she said and held out her hand. He took her hand firmly at which point Nel appeared and she saw Jake take in the fantastic figure in the lovely dress. Nel's hair was pulled up into a pretty high ponytail and huge dangly black earrings contrasted against her gorgeous hair and luminous young skin.

'What a beautiful dress, Nel.' Sallie touched the fabric on the sleeve.

'Thanks, this old thing - had it years!' She winked at Sallie and pulled her gently to the side away from the three men, gulped down another mouthful of her orange coloured alcopop, opened her handbag to the side and showed Sallie a little nondescript bottle with a retractable spout at the top.

'Sssshh don't tell anyone, I top up my drink with this budget Russian vodka from the off-licence. Saves me a fortune - bus drivers in Pretty Beach don't earn much you know.'

'Tell me a bit more about yourself then Nel.'

Janelle screwed up her face, puckered her lips and dropped her head to the right as if she was deciding on world peace. Her ponytail flipped over. She was quite funny, Sallie liked her from what she had seen so far - raw, honest, real and friendly without any of the fake stuff you get in the City and all the airs and graces.

She told Sallie all about how she had been born, gone to school and lived in Pretty Beach all her life. Quite liked her job as a bus driver and that she wasn't interested in much other than Pretty Beach and quite content on what it had to offer. What a way to be in life, Sallie thought - totally content.

'What about a man then, anyone in your life?' Sallie asked.

'Oh well, now, there's been a few.' She gestured around at the place and at Rory and Ben.

'Had a thing with Ben, did you?'

'Ahh Ben Chalmers, bit out of my league, Sallie. Tried that years ago when I was a bit too young and he'd just lost his wife. Bloody gorgeous thing, she was. So sad, they hadn't been here long then either.'

'I did hear about that, yes.' Sallie looked over at Ben who was standing there chatting to Rory.

'He's a multi-millionaire, but he likes to think he's the same as the rest of us, not sure why. If I had all that dough behind me I'd be shouting it from the rooftops and driving around in a convertible flashing my diamonds. Bet he didn't tell you that bit yet, did he?' Sallie didn't get a word in to reply, Janelle was on a roll.

'Pretends to be a run-of-the-mill Pretty Beach boy like the rest of us, but his parents own half of the South and run race horses all over the world. Millions just for one little pony. Apparently they sell them all over the place. Yeah, you look him up on the internet Sallie, I'm telling you - he's loaded. Anyway, bless him, he wasn't interested in anyone for years and certainly not someone like me.'

'What do you mean?' Replied Sallie, 'someone like you, you're absolutely stunning, so pretty, have you seen your eyes and skin?'

'Thank you for that, doll, but I know my place in life and someone like Ben Chalmers is not, you know, in the business of being with someone like me, and I can tell you this thing for sure - he was in no way interested in a quickie behind the toilets.'

Nel threw her head back and laughed, took another big sip of the orange drink and Sallie's eyes widened much further than she thought they ever could. Nel was a hoot and now she thought about it she couldn't quite see lovely Ben Chalmers behind the toilets with her.

Nel poured another lug of vodka in her glass, closed her bag and left Sallie to the little group. The club was getting busier and busier, she'd mistakenly thought that the busiest bit would be the bonfire, but the bar was now four deep and more and more people bustled in through the door.

Sallie stood there looking around, and realised she had no one. Her only real friend was Nina who now lived three to four hours away, and a distant cousin in Australia. There was no one for her to call when she was in trouble, no one to give her a helping hand when she needed it, no one to just call her up and ask what are you up to and are you okay? She put the wine glass down on the table, took her phone out of her bag and wandered in the direction of the bar to get another drink.

Maybe Pretty Beach was the place to change all that, where she would stay, find some friends and maybe even be accepted into the local community and be part of it all.

***

Ben Chalmers was at the bar. Goodness, she hadn't seen that one coming, a multi-millionaire. It all made sense now though, the square jaw, the good diction, the nice clothes and broad shoulders. Ben Chalmers didn't come with an old white van and tracksuit bottoms, he came smelling of expensive scent, good hair and seaplanes.

As she approached him at the bar she smiled to herself recalling the story from Janelle and the back of the toilets... it was obvious now Nel wasn't his type - she was silly, flirty, young and impossibly pretty. Ben turned just as she was about to steer away from him and get herself a drink at the other end of the bar.

'How are you? What are you smiling to yourself about? I've been away for a few days in the country at my family's place.' He rolled his eyes indicating it had been painful.

'Yes, your lads told me.'

'What can I get you to drink?'

'You can't get me anything to drink Ben, I owe you a million drinks already. What can I get you?'

'Well that's very kind,' he replied. She loved it when men were gracious enough to take a drink from a woman without making a big fuss and turning it into an issue. He peered over the bar and analysed the beer pumps.

'I'll have a LO pale ale please.'

She ordered herself another glass of wine and the ale for him, and the barman placed the drinks in front of them. Ben with the honey skin and lovely eyes raised his glass.

'Cheers to you, my new friend, Boat House Sallie.' He chuckled.

As he raised his arm, she noticed his watch. It wasn't one of those look-at-me watches that made her cringe, the ones with the big face and even bigger logo where she'd think to herself *yes, yes, I know, I get it, you've got money*. It was more understated than that, but she recognised the brand because Nina, top barrister for top law firm, had treated herself to one for her fortieth birthday. It had cost Nina more than a car. Sallie had been staggered at the price and quickly calculated she would have been able to put a deposit down on a flat with the timepiece strapped to her friend's arm.

As Ben placed his drink back on the bar she looked closely at it when he wasn't looking. It was set with tiny diamonds alongside the numbers. Yep, Nel was clearly right. If he had a watch like that on his arm he wasn't scrabbling around for money and buying his boat shoes in H & M, that was for sure.

They stood at the bar for a while chatting. It really was pleasant to talk to him, he just seemed so friendly and relaxed. And he really was quite easy on the eye too, she remembered that from the lunch they'd shared leaning up against the shed wall.

They'd had a few more drinks when suddenly the music turned off, a petite woman with blonde hair and a pouty upper lip who Ben told her owned White Cottage Flowers took to a tiny stage and began a drawn-out presentation with all sorts of awards for the locals.

On and on it went, and they stood there at the bar ordering more drinks and listening to it all. Culminating in awards for best butcher (she'd only seen one), best school teacher (a pretty dark-haired girl, named Miss Hicks who Sallie thought looked about twelve) and best boat, at which point Ben had laughed and said under his breath. 'We all know that will be Pete.'

Indeed it was, and Pete walked up to the stage, turned around to everyone and waved and jogged up the steps to take the award. He thanked the Pretty Beach Community profusely, rattled on about his love for his boat for a bit and told everyone how grateful he was to live in such a close-knit town where no one had any secrets.

Sallie had smiled to herself - well, Suntanned Pete, you don't know mine.

***

Sallie took another sip of her drink and had suddenly had enough. The Bonnie had been fun and Ben was still looking bright eyed and bushy tailed, but after lots of glasses of wine and then a Margarita, Sallie was feeling decidedly warm and definitely on the tired side.

She leant forward, chin on her hand towards Ben, who stood with his elbow propped on the bar smiling and listening. Some distant voice somewhere in the back of her head was telling her both to shut up and not to have any more to drink. She ignored the voice and insisted on finishing her Margarita.

As she drained the last of her drink, she'd slumped on the bar giggling, and was finding herself quite humorous. Ben thought this highly amusing as she rambled on further, mostly about how lovely Pretty Beach was, how she should have made the move years ago and bizarrely the power of a man with a good aftershave.

Looking around as the club slowly started to empty out, she suddenly felt extremely tired. It seemed so relaxed with Ben - she'd thought he might be a bit boring, a bit stilted or perhaps that the conversation would be slow, but it was the opposite. She felt as if she had known him forever. She kept looking at him as she sat there on the bar stool thinking he was quite perfect.

'Shall we go and sit over there?' She heard herself slur a tiny bit as she indicated to a free sofa, feeling the need to sit back and rest her head.

Ben laughed and shook his head. 'No, I don't think so Sallie, I think it's time we hit the road. I'll walk you back to the cottage.'

Sallie didn't take much persuading, hopped off the stool, and pulled her coat from the coat hook.

'Good idea. Yes, I'm tired.' She said as she fumbled getting her arm into the sleeve and laughed to herself, 'Haha I'm a little tipsy, how funny Ben, I was only going to stay for one drink.'

Ben helped her into her coat and replied, 'Always the way when you think you'll only have one - you've definitely had more than that...'

He chuckled and they started to walk out to the other side of the club to the door. Sallie bumping into a few people on the way. 'Ooops sorry.' She heard herself hiccup.

Continuing to squeeze her way out of the club laughing and giggling, it was taking so long that Ben eventually grabbed her hand and led her decisively out of the back door of the club.

He yanked the door open and the cool evening air hit Sallie squarely between the eyes. She stumbled over the funny little half step; somehow her brain remembered it, but her legs weren't quick enough and she lurched forward. Just before hitting the ground, she grabbed onto a palm planted in a huge white pot. As she held onto a branch and steadied herself, she then wobbled, toppled ever so slightly backwards, couldn't get her balance and plonked down in the pot, a leaf in her head and feet hanging over the edge. Her knees slammed into the corner of the pot, she swore and then started to laugh.

'Sallie and the palm tree, ha!' She chuckled and tried to pull herself back up.

'I think we'd better be getting you a coffee when you get home, Sallie.' Ben said, jumping down the step.

'I don't even like coffee.' She replied and started laughing as if it was the funniest thing she had ever said.

'Hmm,' he replied, 'Funny that, I could've sworn I saw you with a cappuccino the other day.'

With that he popped one arm around her waist and one on her elbow and heaved her out of the plant pot. His neck got ever so close to her, she took a big breath in.

'Mmmmmm, you smell lush.' She heard herself say it and knew she was being totally uncool and giggled at the thought of being uncool with the pilot, with the good legs, nice shirts and seaplanes.

'What's so funny?' He said as he steered her along the pavement down the little lane.

'Oh, just me really, well, me and you. I mean look at you, all fabulous and seaplane-y. And then look at me, just met you really and I'm a bit… tipsy, totally uncool and you're just, just gorgeous and lick-able.'

He replied laughing, 'I'm happy you think I'm gorgeous, but I have to say, no one has ever told me I'm lick-able before. However, at my age, I'll take that as a compliment.'

'Hah hah hah,' she heard herself slurring 'At your age, I mean you look bloody good for your age in my opinion, I mean look at me.' She pointed to her face.

'Thanks, now come on let's get you back to the cottage and I'll make you a coffee.'

She looked at him, so fresh and clean looking, everything around her twinkly and sort of blurred… she felt more relaxed than she had in ages as he held onto her waist and they slowly made their way to the cottage. Ben took the keys from her, opened the door, grabbed her hand before she fell over the step and steered her in.

She plonked down on the tiny table, took her boots off while he put the kettle on and made them both a coffee.

'White?' He asked.

'Yup.' She replied with a hiccup.

The warm coffee, walk home and fresh air sobered her up quickly and she felt a hundred times better.

'I'll be off home then, you'll be OK?' Ben said as he picked up the coffee cups and put them in the sink.

'I'm fine, thanks for walking me home.' She said as she walked him to the door and just as he went to step out he turned around. She looked up at him and he bent down and his lips brushed her cheek and then he kissed her gently.

Her heart pounded in her chest and seemed as if it skipped a beat as she felt his lips against hers. Time stood still and she breathed in his delicious smell as she stood there in the doorway with him, the cold air from the ocean whistling around their feet, his hands gently resting on her waist.

Chapter 16

Sallie woke up, turned over, head screaming, touched her swollen, bulging eyes, tried to lift her head off the pillow and felt like someone was banging on the inside of her head with a mallet. Everything around her seemed super loud; seagulls screeched around outside, even the sea was crashing in and out making her head feel worse. She rolled over, tried to plump up the pillow quietly, and thought that she would try to get back to sleep.

She laid there for a few minutes with the pounding head and dry mouth, even her limbs hurt. There was no way she was going back to sleep, everything ached, her head was thumping and as she moved the cover to get out of bed even her hands felt bruised.

She couldn't remember how much she'd had to drink, but it was bad. Her head pumped as she sat up in bed, swung her legs to the floor, walked over to the kitchen, poured herself a glass of water and sunk it down in one. She felt it go all the way down through her body and leant against the counter with her head resting on the kitchen cupboard.

The last thing she could remember was standing at the bar with Ben, lovely Ben Chalmers with the lovely forearms, and the lovely watch, and remembered him saying, as she stood swaying that maybe it was time to go home.

She vaguely remembered him saying something about keeping Pete on side and telling her that he was harmless enough. Sallie had remembered replying back that he was very orange and very small town, and Ben had suppressed a laugh.

It was all coming back to her now. She lifted her head away from the coolness of the laminate cupboard, scooped her hair off her face and re-tied the hairband. She put her glass underneath the tap, turned it on again and drank another glass of water and was hit by a wave of nausea and hoped the water would stay down.

Sun caught the light on the glass doors as another beautiful Pretty Beach day was in full swing. She opened them up, watching the sea pounding against the beach, took big gulps of ocean air, grabbed two paracetamols from her bag and washed them down with another glass of water. She needed to make a cup of tea, that would help clear her head. She put two teabags into the pot, poured in the boiling water and stood leaning against the tiny little kitchen while she waited for it to brew.

Remembering more, she laughed pulling a gaudy, yellow and white striped mug out of the cupboard. Goodness, she'd called the man who about ran the place orange and small town.

Muttering to herself, she picked up the teapot, the mug, some milk, hooked open the door with her foot, went outside to the veranda and sat looking out to sea. Thinking about what else had happened the night before she remembered the strong arm of Ben Chalmers at her waist and walking unsteadily along the lane. Yes, that was right, she'd fallen into the plant pot and had laughed as if she was hilarious. He'd grabbed her, set her straight and she had clung on to his arm the rest of the way.

A wave of embarrassment flooded through her. *Oh no*, she thought, what had happened with him? She didn't even remember putting her pyjamas on, or for that matter having a wash, let alone taking her makeup off. Whatever. She was grateful that he'd got her home safely.

She took a sip of her tea - actually she didn't care. Who cared if she'd got tipsy and been a bit silly, wasn't that what this Bonnie festival was meant to be all about? No, she wouldn't worry herself about last night.

It slowly came back to her; slurring all sorts of things to Ben as they were walking along the lane, rubbing his arm she'd told him that he smelt nice and that he was good enough to lick. He'd laughed, his hand around her waist stopping her from falling over as they'd walked along.

Sallie cringed recalling she'd found it all highly amusing and had laughed and laughed so much that she'd slipped and nearly toppled both of them into the verge lining the side of the road.

She winced to herself. She would not be able to even look in Ben Chalmers' direction now. He would have been surrounded his whole life with all sorts of highly-educated, well turned-out women that he hadn't had to virtually carry home and put to bed in a crappy little holiday cottage wittering on about the power of a good aftershave.

Pretty Beach newcomer Sallie, who didn't even finish high school and had only just met him, had drunk way too much, told him he smelt wonderful, proceeded to witter on and on about the dangers of too much sun exposure and informed him he was so nice she would quite like to lick him and then had kissed him on the doorstep.

Well that was absolutely great. Way to go about handling yourself around your new extremely easy on the eye neighbour, Sallie.

Chapter 17

Sallie got out of the shower and was getting herself dressed when she came to a decision. She would not dwell on the fool of herself she had made the night before with Ben Chalmers. She would only spend time worrying about what she needed to get done so that she could move into the Boat House.

Mentally she went over it all - she'd have nowhere to sit and it would be quite cold until the Spring but she would have something to sleep on, something to cook on, a fridge, running water and a very nice view of the beach.

Nina started calling her on Facetime. She pressed accept and Nina popped up from her house in Freshlea with her hair done and makeup on.

'Whoa, I guess the Pretty Beach Festival was a good one then by the looks of you.' Nina smiled and laughed.

'Oh dear Nina, I did have a few drinks for sure, and told the seaplane guy that he smelt nice and that I would like to lick him.'

'Nothing changed there then - at least you didn't fall over, which we both know you've done before.' Nina was laughing and smiling into the screen.

'Actually, yes that's a bonus, I was quite well behaved on that front.' She didn't mention the falling into the flower pot and told her all about the night - the story of Rory on the beach, of Ben in the bar, and getting a bit tipsy.

'Anyway, enough of all that. I've decided what I'm going to do. There's nowhere that does really good, well styled accommodation here - it's either places like Seashells Cottages or the big mansions overlooking the cliffs that sleep like twelve. There's nothing that seems to say to me casual, seaside, shoes-off style and that vintage coastal thing. I'm going to start slowly doing the cottage down the side up, and then I'll list it online, it would give me a bit of income.

Then in the evenings I can do a course. It's not really what I want to do, I'm sick of hospitality but I do have a skill in it I guess.'

'Great idea! Stop putting yourself down, you'll have it looking amazing and half of the internet eating out of your hand on day one.' Nina smiled into the phone.

'Hope so.'

'I wish I was up there with you, in the sunshine overlooking the water. I have a case to prep for next week, it's cloudy and cold here, and my mum is coming over later to talk about her divorce.'

'When you put it like that, actually it does sound better here.' Sallie laughed.

She clicked end on Facetime and decided that Nina was right; she was very good at hospitality, she'd done all sorts from running a cafe to cleaning a hotel. Renting the boathouse cottage out would be like styling the houses she had done over and over again - it was all about a whole lot of hard work and a huge load of marketing.

And the old cottage beside the Boat House was a marketing dream - overlooking a beautiful panorama on the beach, complete with an authentic vintage setting, beautiful established trees and the odd seaplane flying past just to really set the scene.

All she would need to do would be to throw some hard labour at it and work out how to make it look a whole lot fancier than it really was, on a very low budget.

Chapter 18

Sallie took off her sunglasses as she walked into the shop, took a can of soft drink out of the fridge, paid for it at the front and walked back towards the door. She walked back along the beach to try to banish the lingering pounding in her head - it was certainly true, something was in the air in Pretty Beach that made you feel better.

She walked along the laneway - even the shops were looking quiet after the Bonnie. The homewares stores were closed for the day, the beautiful florist White Cottage Flowers had piled all their stock inside and a couple of the cafes had their blinds down and closed signs up.

Sallie approached the Boat House, its old tin roof glinting in the sunshine and the little boathouse cottage at the side now visible after she'd hacked away at some overgrown bushes. Just as she stepped over the stream, one of Ben's seaplanes came in to land from the left. She sighed to herself and thought *could be a whole lot worse places to end up.*

As she trudged up the apartment stairs and walked over to the kitchen she was delighted with the efforts of the day before - the painting had come up really well, it was amazing the difference a coat of paint made. She didn't know why she was surprised, she'd done it so many times in previous renovations and every time it had come up a treat.

Looking around the apartment, every room was brighter, cleaner and fresher even though she'd touched nothing else in the place yet. There was still a lot to do, she wasn't out of the woods yet, in fact it would be a good few weeks before she would be even halfway happy with it, but it was really getting there.

The floor was now stripped back to the floorboards and while not perfect, they had come up well and were now clean. The walls were still a dirty, cream colour but she had wiped them down with a soapy solution and they were now ready for a good coat of paint. The window at the front, while still covered in paint, had been scrubbed and repaired and now opened.

She took a mug of tea and a packet of chocolate digestives over towards a patch of sun on the floor by the old paned windows and sat down, warming her whole body in the sun and made a list of things she needed to do to move in. The main thing was the fridge which was coming the next day along with a microwave - she would make do with that for now. She might be able to get the old stove working at some point, but it had seen better days and needed an industrial level clean to even look at it, a tetanus injection to actually use it.

She looked over at the two pot belly stoves, one at either end of the room and wondered if she could get them to work. She had no idea about what kind of wood she would need to burn or how to even work out if it was safe, but it could be an option. Even if she could get the one in the bedroom or kitchen working she would be at least able to keep one room warm. It was only six weeks until the cold part of Winter ended, and then it would be warm enough to not need it.

Just as she was getting her painting clothes on her phone pinged on WhatsApp, she took her phone out of her pocket and saw 11 pictures had arrived from Nina with the castoffs from her sister. She knew Nina's sister was absolutely loaded, obsessed with home decor and changed her 'look' every season, but she didn't think she would be happy to just give her, for free, her pristine cast-offs from the French boutique.

She scrolled through the pictures. There were two huge white linen sofas which looked like they had ten or more enormous feather filled cushions running along the back, two wingback chairs in a co-ordinating fabric but slightly different shade of white and a large, wide, buttoned footstool. The pictures went on, it was like going shopping on her phone for free - a large wicker tray, a huge basket full of throws and blankets, a smaller two seater love seat sofa which looked as if it might be velvet and a low bleached ash chunky coffee table.

Nina had written a note underneath it.

Are u interested in any of this? She's getting rid of it but said she'd be happy to get it shipped to u to save her the hassle of taking it to the dump.

The dump! Sallie thought the world was crazy, this stuff didn't even look like it had been sat on.

Interested? I'd love it. You sure she couldn't sell it?

Pah. She would never stoop so low as to sell stuff second-hand.

Wow how the other half live eh?

Tell me about it.

Sallie closed the phone and thought, *well that's that problem sorted out*, walked over to one of the pot belly stoves and bent down to have a closer look. It was small and squat and someone had painted it white years ago... she thanked her lucky stars they hadn't painted it techno green. The white paint had rubbed off in a few places here and there giving it a nice old patina. Layers upon layers of compacted ash sat on the bottom and would need to be cleaned out, but it seemed functional by the looks of it - no holes and the door closed properly.

She closed the door up, it would be the flue that would be the problem - she tried to crane her head behind but couldn't see much more than the fact that it was old - she would need to get someone in to look at that before she did anything.

She moved back towards the sun spot and added flue to her long list of things to do - glazier to fix the broken window panes on the barn doors and the windows of the boathouse, paint the inside of the main rooms and make some blinds and or curtains. Find a locksmith to fit a new deadlock on the door at the bottom of the stairs, the French doors at the back and fix a keypad to the main barn doors.

Find out the cost of firewood, sort out some kind of house insurance, (goodness knows how much that would cost) and get the plumber back to sort out plumbing for a washing machine.

Thinking it all through, she leant back on the old timber tongue and groove wall, they were soft and almost moulded to her back and she could have sworn they moved in sync with movement of the sea outside.

Chapter 19

Sallie had spent the day with her list of jobs and was about to open her emails and check whether or not she had received the deposit back from the estate agents in Freshlea when she heard someone knocking on the door. She contemplated not bothering to go down and open it, she wasn't interested in the slightest in talking to anyone.

She crawled along the floor to the painted in window at the front and peered through trying to make out who it was without them seeing her. It looked like it was Holly from the bakery over the road with what looked like bags full of bread. She'd have to go down and see - Holly had been really friendly to her so far, and her lovely son Rory too. She walked over the floorboards and down the creaky stairs, pulled the lock up from the inside of the barn door and pushed the door open.

'Delivery of Bonnie Buns for you!' Holly was holding up a white paper bag filled with buns. 'Pretty Beach tradition and I thought you might not know about it so I brought you over a bag before they all go.' Holly smiled.

'How kind of you, thanks so much.'

'So, it's official then, you're in and you're staying?'

'Well I guess I'll have to.' Sallie laughed.

Holly was tiny, much smaller than she looked when serving behind the bakery counter, her hair was dark and gleaming and she looked lovely, wearing straight leg navy-blue jeans, ballet flats and a navy-blue blazer with a silk t-shirt underneath.

'Where are you off to then? You look beautiful.'

'I've just a few of these to deliver and then I'll be going to pick up my mum and then over to Rory for a meal.' Holly shifted to her left foot and peered in behind Sallie. 'Looks like you've really been busy then. I loved this place when we first moved here, a lovely old build-

74

ing it was - lots of people stopped here and then came over to me for their bread. It was a bit different in those days and I was the only Vietnamese I think any of them had ever seen. Took them a while to get used to me and for me to get my English going, but everyone was so good to me then.' She smiled fondly at the memories.

'It's lovely here. Pete thinks he runs the place and old Brucie too, but the place is wonderful, you'll love it here. Pretty Beach needs a few actual pretty locals like you as well. About time we had a fresh face or two about the place.' Holly looked further inside and at the garden.

'By the way, I was thinking you might like to borrow some of my gardening stuff. I keep a whipper snipper and one of those small electric mowers out the back of the bakery just to keep that strip along the lane nice and neat, I can't stand it when it's long. I used to come over here every now and then but, you know, I am getting on a bit now. It'll be slow going and you'll have to be careful with it, but it doesn't take long if you go over it first with the whipper snipper then keep going over it with the mower - it should come up well.'

'Oh, that would be fantastic, I'd really like to have a go. I've hacked at some of the bushes with some old shears I found but that's all. I can't afford to get a gardener in, and there are a lot of bugs and insects with all this undergrowth. I can't imagine what it's like in the heat of the Summer.'

'I can tell you, you'll be eaten alive if it's this long.'

'Yep, thought so.' Sallie sighed back.

'Just pop around the back of the laneway. If I'm not there, put your hand over the gate, slide the bolt across and then the mower and the whipper snipper are in the shed. Key to the shed is under the loose patio stone on the right.'

'Great, thanks Holly.' Sallie smiled back at her. 'I'll have to add that job to all the others on my list.'

'Looks like you've done a grand job so far. Enjoy your Bonnie Buns and I will see you around. Pop in and say hello.' With that she turned, waved and walked away.

Not such a nosey parker after all, thought Sallie, *maybe I should wind my neck in a bit.*

Chapter 20

After a decent meal and a warm bath, Sallie woke up the next day feeling a lot better than she'd done the day before. She had another full day ahead and a telephone meeting with the insurance company to extend the house insurance to include letting the boathouse as a holiday rental.

Just as she was putting her breakfast dishes away and was about to jump in the shower there was a knock at the door. What did Pete want? She hadn't seen him since the Bonnie presentation and she was quite happy to keep it that way.

She walked up to the door and looked through the peephole to see Rory, handsome doctor Rory, standing there, dressed in what looked like working clothes and holding a whipper snipper.

'Hey Sallie, local gardener calling, not just part-time Uber driver and highly-qualified doctor.' He laughed - clearly, he was as good humoured as his mother.

'I'm going over to do Mum's garden at her house and she said you had added the garden to a long list of jobs to do. I'm due back in the hospital soon but I am trying to get as much fresh air and exercise as possible and can give the grass at yours a first go over with the strimmer if you like?'

'Ah, you guys, really that's so nice of you.'

'You don't know what we're really like, wait until you get to know us properly.' He winked as he replied, winked the lovely chocolate brown eyes with the long eyelashes and creamy brown skin.

Sallie suddenly remembered not only was she in her pyjama bottom and a flimsy old t-shirt, her hair was piled up on top of her head in a giant messy bun but also, that she was braless. She crossed her arms over her chest self-consciously and replied.

'I didn't see any garden bins though, I'll just have to pile it all up and then order some from the council.'

'I think if I remember there are some bins right down the end of the property near the old fence and gate, near Ben's place, I was down there a few months ago and noticed them. They are the old council bins though, you might have to get those changed over. Bill drives the refuse truck and no doubt he's all over it that you've moved in so shouldn't be a problem. I'll pull them up to the front and then leave them outside and see what happens. If they fit on the truck you should be good.'

Sallie smiled at him and thought how he seemed to genuinely have that air about him where he wanted to help people, which was always handy when one was a doctor.

'There used to be a whole gravel driveway and car parking section there in the old days, we used to skid around it on our bikes, all overgrown now, I wonder what will come up when you get that sorted out?'

'Who knows? I am finding all sorts of things!'

'And when Ben Chalmers first moved into the seaplane building, there was a gate in the fence all the way down the back, and I think there was a shed there too - all completely overgrown now, with trees and weeds.'

'Yes, Ben told me something about that,' replied Sallie. 'He seems nice too, is he?' Sallie looked at him quizzically.

'I'll have to let you work that out for yourself Sallie. He had a hard time a few years ago, that is for sure. Terrible with his wife, she was trekking down to St. Louisa's all the time for the treatment too. He has a few secrets though does old Ben, I'm sure you'll work those out living next door to him.'

'The place seems full of secrets from what I'm gathering.' Sallie laughed and raised her eyes upwards.

'Ahh, you've seen nothing yet of the deep and dark secrets of Pretty Beach,' Rory chuckled, picked up the strimmer and strode off to his Audi.

Chapter 21

Sallie was in the bathroom of the apartment with her head under the claw foot bathtub, rubber gloves on and pulling out grime and layers and layers of tangled cobwebs when her phone pinged.

Sallie, Ben here, furniture is on the way over. BC

Cheers, thanks Ben, I'm here all day, it would be great if they can bring it right in.

Nice Ben with the lovely blonde hair and fabulous eyes. She cringed in embarrassment thinking about the lick-able comment and her behaviour when he'd walked her home, put the phone back in her pocket and carried on scrubbing under the bath.

An hour later, she heard a van pull up outside. Lochie and Ollie, the two lads who had been helping her out, called out from the driveway, she slid herself from under the bath, went down the stairs, opened the doors and walked down to the van.

'Hey Sallie, we've a bed, a fridge and outdoor table and chairs for you in the back.' Ollie said, smiling and pointed into the back of the van.

'Thanks, the fridge goes in the gap in the kitchen, bed in the back room looking over the water with the pot belly stove in the corner, and I guess put the outdoor stuff anywhere out here. I'm going to pop over and get some lunch, have you boys had anything yet?'

'Yeah, we have but we never say no to some of Holly's bakery stuff.' They laughed together.

'Rightio, lunch coming up.'

The boys opened the doors at the back and started to get to work while Sallie strolled over to the bakers in her oldest painting clothes, thinking that the good thing about being unknown, was that you didn't give a hoot what you looked like.

The little bell tinkled above her as she pushed open the door of the bakers and waited in line. There was always a line at Holly's - for such a small place it was quite amazing. Sallie stood back and observed making a mental note to analyse why she was so successful.

She got to the front of the queue, ordered three meat pies, three sausage rolls, three cans of coke and a few rounds of egg and salad sandwiches.

'That's a lot of food for one small woman.' Holly joked.

'It's not all for me, just the sausage roll. It's for Ben's lads, they're helping me out for a few weeks.'

'Well Ollie won't be eating a sausage roll, he's vegetarian, so I'll change that for a cheese one and Lochie likes lemonade not Coke.'

'Wow, do you know everyone and everything around here Holly?'

She tinkled a little laugh out, 'Ahhh it's good business Sallie - I make it my business to be known and to know everything, remember everyone's names, their kids, and what they order, it's why they come back to me.' She nodded a few times as if agreeing to herself and bustled around getting the order together.

Sallie took the bag full of goodies from her - well there was one part of the answer about why the bakers did so well already there for her... know your customers and treat them well.

The sky was coming in and getting darker as she walked back over the road, it looked like there might be a storm rolling over Pretty Beach. She walked back into the Boat House, it sounded as if the lads were upstairs in the bedroom, goodness knows how they had gotten the bed up the tiny little stairs. She walked up the stairs, popped the bag of food down and walked into the bedroom.

'Yeah, there is no way that bed out there is coming up those stairs.' Ollie said as she walked in.

She hadn't even seen the bed and walked over to the window they were pointing at and looked down at the bed outside on the drive, propped up against the wall. Looking back at her was a beautiful old-fashioned iron bed. She couldn't believe it, she'd thought it would be a modern thing and had been quietly praying it wasn't black leather or worse button-back retro grey. What she was looking at, though, was a bed that was right up her alley.

'Everything dismantles apart from that bit, so we are going to put it on ropes and hoist it through the window.' Ollie seemed to know what he was doing. *Thank goodness I sorted out that insurance,* she thought.

'Well, there's food out here, so why don't you have a break and eat that before the pies get cold and then we'll get that bed in?' Sallie asked Ollie.

She walked back outside into the main room, picked up the bag and took it into the kitchen, and stopped dead in her tracks, Ollie nearly bumping straight into her as she nearly squealed.

'Oh. My. God! He didn't tell me it was a SMEG vintage style fridge.' She turned to the boys.

'Yeah, bit weird, some stylist bought it for that Gypsy Bay house - she was a bit nuts. Ben was funny when this turned up, we thought he was going to lose it, he wasn't at all happy about it. Went for an absolute bomb though, so obviously she knew what she was talking about. Probably would have preferred a nice brushed stainless steel one, to you know, spruce the place up a bit, wouldn't you?' Ollie asked and looked around at the old floorboards and cupboards.

'Are you kidding me? I'm so happy I could die, I've had my eye on one of these fridges for like fifteen years!' They both looked at her as if she was completely mad. Ollie walked over and opened it up and showed her that it had never even been used. She was almost jumping with excitement.

'I'm going to have to give Ben some money for this!'

'You're joking, Ben Chalmers has money coming out of his ears! Everything he touches turns to gold. He has properties galore, the seaplane and the helicopter business and he just won a tender for the government. He won't be needing any money for a fridge he doesn't want.' Ollie laughed and started opening the bag of pies.

Lochie, who didn't say much at all - in fact she hadn't really heard him speak - nodded in earnest and added, 'My mum said he's dripping in it.'

Sallie didn't reply. So maybe that was what Rory was talking about and it seemed Nel was right; Ben Chalmers Seaplanes had more than a few planes and an old workshop down at the wharf.

Chapter 22

Sallie had spent days and days painting - the whole of the apartment was now different shades of white. Most of the walls were painted in simple, white trade paint. The others in various shades of white from the fancy heritage paint company whose prices made her wince. She'd stalked their tins of paint on the 'reduced' table and ended up with the tongue and groove clad walls in strong white, the architraves around the doors in a soft white, the twenty-centimetre-high skirting boards in antique white and the actual doors themselves she'd stripped back to timber, loved the patina of the wood and left them to their natural pale state.

She'd stood back when it was finished, head cocked to the side and couldn't quite believe it - the result was absolutely stunning, all the different shades of white bouncing the seaside light around and she'd done the whole place with hardly any budget.

It was slowly coming together, she now had a fridge, a slow cooker and a microwave, outside furniture and a bed.

There were still a lot of problems. The mould on the wall in the sitting room was still there though it was drying out very slowly, there was a small piece of ceiling that had fallen away in the bathroom, and the light fitting in the bathroom flickered every now and then. She could put up with that.

The next thing she needed to sort out were the window fixings, there was no way she was going to live without anything at the windows - as a woman on her own she'd rather not invite anyone to look in.

She finally found the solution to the window dressings one day when she was putting the mower back in the shed at Holly's - piled up on a bench seat were loads of old flour sacks with faint grey writing on them and numbers stamped in a faded blue. They were incredibly dusty and covered in cobwebs, but she knew that they would look fabulous up at her windows. She had no sewing machine but could just tack them together at the top, run a rod through them and attach ties to roll them up.

Her mind had whirred - not only would they look absolutely beautiful, but you couldn't buy antique fabric easily and if Holly wouldn't mind her having them the whole of the window dressings throughout the place and the boathouse cottage would be free.

She'd gone into the shop later on that day, bought a bun and a sausage roll and asked Holly who'd said to take them. She'd thought it hilarious that Sallie was even considering putting them up at her windows.

***

The day before her last day at Seashells Cottages Sallie was ready enough to move in - she had hot running water, a kitchen with fridge, a bed and two old Bentwood chairs she'd found one morning with a note saying 'free' on them as she walked back from the beach.

It had become very quiet at Pretty Beach since the Bonnie Festival and she hadn't really seen anyone at all. It was strange how deserted it seemed. Rory had gone back to his stint at St Louisa's and wouldn't be back until the end of month, Ben Chalmers was at his parents' horse farm helping out as his dad had just had a knee replacement and she hadn't seen much of Suntanned Pete since the Bonnie night. She'd mentioned it to Holly at the bakers.

'Make the most of it lovely - only a few more weeks of peace and we'll start ramping up and by the time Summer comes you'll be sick of the sight of people and tourists everywhere.'

Sallie couldn't quite believe how this place could turn into a thriving town with day trippers and reams of people spending money but Holly assured her that not only did it happen but it was nuts.

'You need to get that boathouse cottage finished - if you put that up for rent now you'll have it rented out for the whole season. Pete has the same clients back year after year now. Half the time they book directly, the same week every year, generations of the same family coming down too. And between you and me I think he made a pig's nose out of it.' Sallie laughed so hard in agreement.

'It's a pig's ear Holly and yep I know exactly what you mean - not exactly got the touch has he?'

'So, you're staying are you?' Holly winked at her. 'I'll tell Rory that then,' and she chortled away to herself, picked up a load of French sticks and started loading them into the baskets behind her.

Sallie smiled to herself - you can tell Doctor Rory whatever you like.

Chapter 23

Sallie walked the long way round the bay back from the Boat House, pushed open the door of Seashell Cottages and the heat hit her. The central heating was pumping lovely warm air around the place.

She looked at the tiny little cottage, one more day and she would be leaving. It wouldn't take long to get packed, she'd not brought much with her and the rest was yet to arrive. She couldn't wait to get out now, it was all very well being in a holiday cottage but it got old pretty quickly without the real home comforts. She was ready to get back to a routine, her yoga and gardening.

She missed growing things. Back in Freshlea she'd loved to potter about on the tiny balcony in the evenings, potting up seedlings and growing all sorts of things - lavender, herbs, salads. It was truly amazing what she'd grown on the tiny balcony. Nina had taken to popping over when she was cooking dinner, helping herself to a few bits and exclaiming that fresh herbs had changed her life.

Yes, she certainly was missing the home comforts in her life and now she had more than a crappy falling down balcony with pots on it - she had her own land and now that the Boat House grounds had been cleared she could see that there was lots of potential for a beautiful garden. There were even a few apple trees, a plum which unbelievably had survived all the years of neglect, two olive trees and a magnolia tucked away down on the left.

She missed cooking and baking too; she'd started making everything from scratch when she'd found herself in the crappy little bedsit after her second marriage had ended as a way to save money. She'd taken a book out of the library on basic cooking, joined a budget cooking Facebook group and thought she would have a go. The next thing she knew she was overrun with all sorts of things - a freezer full of breads, curries and casseroles and enough sourdough to supply the whole of Freshlea.

It had become a little side income too, after she'd run out of room in the freezer and had taken some of the loaves into the cafe downstairs, they'd snapped them up and the next day ordered ten more - she'd made quite a profit on the ingredients and added all sorts to her menu, including pies, slices, soups and stews.

Maybe she would just start a similar gig up here. She sat thinking about it all, her mind wondering what else she could do with the property to provide her with an income. That was the whole beauty of the place - it offered her the opportunity to not just settle down, but more importantly the chance to thrive, not just survive.

Chapter 24

Sallie had moved into the Boat House without any mishap and a few weeks later, Nina drove down to Pretty Beach with the last of Sallie's stuff from the annexe.

After a day unloading the car, more cleaning and painting, Nina and Sallie showered, dressed and walked over to the fish and chip shop to enjoy a meal and a bottle of wine. They walked out of the Boat House, the sun dropping low over the ocean, a breeze coming over the hill and the air just starting to warm up, a hint of Spring about the place.

Walking into the restaurant they sat down at the table in the window and looked around. It was gorgeous, just down the road from Holly's bakery and, surprisingly, Sallie hadn't really spoken much to the owner Jessica at all.

Jessica was a similar age to Sallie and from what she could tell there didn't seem to be a man around. Sallie loved seeing a successful woman running a business. Nina was one of them - barrister extraordinaire who ran a fabulous business, owned a gorgeous old house in Freshlea, had a portfolio of properties and not only that a fantastic social life. No man though. She'd never found a man who could keep her interest or entertain her brain for long enough.

They finished the dinner and sat in the window of the shop watching the world go by and ordered another bottle of wine - it was going to be one of those nights.

Jessica had finished serving and had pretty much shut up the take-away shop when she came over to Sallie and introduced herself. She smiled at them both, holding her hand out to Sallie.

'Well now, I know who you are, but we haven't officially met. I'm Jessica and I know that you are the elusive owner of the Boat House and every single person in Pretty Beach talking about you!'

Sallie quipped back at her, 'Yes I've heard.'

'You'll be ok, it will only take you five years to get yourself in with the locals.'

The wine had gone to Sallie's head a little bit, Nina was doing her usual trick of drinking like a fish but showing no sign of it and the evening was looking like it had quite a way to go.

On a whim Sallie asked, 'Want to join us Jessica? Or do you need us to pay and get out of here?'

Jessica flipped the watch on her wrist and checked the time.

'You know what, I normally have to get back for the babysitter, but the children are at their Dad's tonight for a change, so I might just take you up on that.'

She started to take off her apron, walked back over to the back of the shop to get a wine glass, locked the front door, turned the lights down low and pulled up a chair from another table.

Jessica was a bit of a chatter and the wine and the food had made Nina and Sallie the perfect listeners.

She'd come to Pretty Beach as a teenager with her parents and couldn't stand the place, couldn't wait to leave and as soon as she'd finished school she'd headed off, moved into a flat share and started doing a make-up course. Those were the days she had laughed. Turned out she had been in the right place at the right time and had ended up doing makeup for some of the biggest names.

She soon had a thriving business and fifteen other makeup artists working for her in a small agency. And then she'd met her husband Martin, had two babies and they'd decided to sell up their flat and bought a large house overlooking the ocean in Pretty Beach.

They'd also bought the fish and chip shop, rented out the flat above it and once they had settled in she had decided that actually she didn't like men at all, chucked Martin out and took up with an older woman.

'And that didn't go down well with the Pretty Beach locals. No one could look me in the eye... throwing out my husband and going out with not only a woman but one fifteen years older than me.' She threw her head back and groaned.

She'd kept the fish and chip shop, Martin had moved out to a house down at Gypsy Bay, quickly taken up with a string of women and never helped with the kids or the business so on the side at the weekends she did wedding makeup and hair.

They finished up the wine listening to Jessica's stories and Sallie announced that they should carry on their drinks and go to the Marina Club.

'I reckon we need some fun,' she said.

They gathered up their bags and walked across the beach to the Marina Club - it was packed, a live band playing, blaring Abba tunes from the stage and Suntanned Pete was leaning up at the bar with a pint.

'Here she is, the Boat House owner herself,' he ribbed her good naturedly.

Sallie decided to be nice to Pete - really she needed to keep him on-side around Pretty Beach, she didn't know when she might need someone like him.

'Hi Pete, ahh yeah, just call me a property tycoon with that place. This is my friend Nina, she's up here from the city for the weekend.'

'Nice to meet you Nina.'

Nina shook Pete's large hand and the wine talking she told him he was very bronzed. Sallie left them chatting about her job as a barrister and how it all worked, while she went off to get the drinks. They finished the first drink, got in another round and standing next to Pete she'd turned to chat to Ollie and Lochie.

Ben Chalmers had arrived and Jessica was telling him about her plan to hopefully expand the fish and chip shop brand down to Newport Reef, when on the other side of the bar old Bruce came in wearing a neck brace, limping with a walking stick and his ankle in a protective boot.

The music stopped, everyone turned around to look at him, he held his hand up and did a little regal wave around the place. He made his way through the bar, stopping to chat to various locals, relaying the tale of his ordeal until he ended up approaching Sallie.

He didn't say anything to anyone, lifted his walking stick off the ground and pointed it in Sallie's direction, roaring at her at the same time.

'Hope you didn't bring those blokes down with you girl - funny how the robbery happened just after you got here!'

Sallie felt the blood rush to her face, the mix of the wine, the stresses of the past few weeks, him shouting in her face and the rudeness of the comment flushed her with anger.

'How dare you call me 'girl' and point at me, you miserable old bastard!' The whole place had gone silent.

He was a bit taken aback that she had answered at all. Going in for the kill and burying herself further, she continued, the wine doing the talking.

'Who do you think you are in your ridiculous knee-high socks anyway?'

Too stupefied to move his mouth - he wasn't used to anyone talking back to him, and especially not a female, he lifted his stick again, wrangled it towards her and went to say something else but he wasn't quick enough as she raised her voice.

'Oh, and don't even get me started on your stupid signs about the place and don't you dare point at me with that stick again!'

There were gasps everywhere, a few sniggers and a stillness. No one moved, everyone now mesmerised by Sallie, the newest resident of Pretty Beach and Bruce, the oldest, having a stand-off in the Marina Club.

She went to say more, she would wipe the floor with this miserable old man's head. Nina looked at Ben and sliced her finger across her neck. She could see Sallie was on a roll, she'd been here before, someone needed to shut Sallie up, and quickly. It would not end well.

Ben Chalmers clocked the look on Nina's face, took Sallie by the elbow and went to lead her away from Bruce. He leant down into her ear and whispered, 'Leave it, Sallie, he's just a silly old fool who thrives on the drama, he loves a huge row. He'll be enjoying this.'

She yanked her arm away, but he steered her deftly out of the club, through the reception doors to the steps and outside onto the beach. Sallie was still furious at what Bruce had implied and Ben asked her if she wanted some water, but she replied that no, she was just going to sit down and get some fresh air, stalk back in and tell Bruce a bit more about what she thought of him.

'That's really not a good idea. Come on, let's get you home.'

'I can't go home, I need to keep a check on Nina. She always drinks loads and can't handle her alcohol.'

He'd smiled at that, 'I've already checked, and Ollie and Lochie are going to drop her off on their way home. Nina will be just fine.'

He took her hand and they walked along the laneway, stopping at the late-night Spar and getting a coffee from the machine. She'd sobered up with the coffee, the night air and the reality of walking along with Ben.

'Grrrr, I was so angry, how rude can someone be?' She said and looked up at Ben as they walked along sipping their coffees.

'Not known for his charm that one, I'm afraid,' Ben replied.

'Well, I may be new to Pretty Beach, but I'm not having that. He pointed that stick right in my face!'

'You made that quite clear.' Ben laughed and she started to giggle.

They finished the coffee silently - approaching the Boat House they stopped and she mentioned how pretty the lighthouse looked at night up on the cliff. The air felt thick between them as if both of them were wondering what to do next. She could feel the heat of him right beside her and could smell that same heady, fresh linen smell from the night after the Bonnie.

At that point, he'd reached down and put his hand around her waist as a strong feeling surged through her. She'd put her arm up and felt the soft hair at the back of his neck and fell into the warm folds of his jacket as he bent down and kissed her gently, pulling her closer to him. She leant into his strong body, intoxicated by the feel of him, the way he held her to him and kissed her softly.

Chapter 25

Sallie was sitting in the kitchen on one of the Bentwood chairs she'd found on the side of the road when Nina came into the kitchen. Nina made herself a cup of tea, sat down next to Sallie, who carried on looking out the window, down the beach and over towards the Marina Club.

'What was I thinking? I told one of the locals he was an old bastard!' They both burst out laughing.

'Have to say it was quite funny though. The face of the old idiot was absolutely priceless and you know most of the locals were thinking the same.' Nina was laughing into her tea.

'I'm really sorry I just left you. I did check though before Ben took me home.'

'No worries, I quite enjoyed talking to Pete. He's not anywhere near as bad as you said and it was hardly out of the way for Lochie and Ollie to drop me off.' Nina shrugged.

'I can't believe I said all that!'

'No-one will probably even remember; the place was rocking and there was a lot of alcohol flying around.'

'You're joking, it went silent when I said that.' Sallie said as she remembered.

'True.' Nina nodded in agreement.

'What am I even thinking of trying to make it here? It's a ruddy backwater with a load of crazy old locals.'

'It'll be fine, you just might have to do a bit of creeping to make it up to old Brucie, but he had it coming I reckon. You and alcohol Sallie, you do like to put the world to rights... remember when you told that guy who lived next door to stop acting like a jumped up little twat with a naff man bun and too short trousers and no socks?' They both laughed again at that.

'His face was a picture too - never saw him in those cropped chinos again either.'

They sat there talking about the night, how lovely Jessica was, how Suntanned Pete probably wasn't all that bad and all the nights they'd been out in the past where they'd ended up doing silly things.

Sallie sat there in her pyjamas with the cup of tea and thought some more about what had happened the night before. The part of the evening that no one else knew. The bit that she was hugging to herself and keeping quiet about. She considered telling Nina how something had happened inside her she had never felt before, but thought better of it.

She decided that another kiss with, what appeared to be, the multi-millionaire who just so happened to live next door was just a bit of fun. There was no way it would be anything more than that to him.

She would not say a thing to anyone; the last thing she needed on this new adventure in Pretty Beach was a romance. She had such a bad track record with the two failed marriages and other losers who'd messed her about over the years, she didn't want to start anything just to see how long it would be until it went wrong.

So she decided to keep it quiet about the kiss outside her house, where bathed in beautiful silvery moonlight, she'd giggled and told him how nice he smelled and how she really would quite like to lick him again if at all possible.

What was she thinking, kissing the extremely good looking, very rich man who lived next door? She'd thought. The very rich man who had taken her hand after the kiss, smiled, looked into her eyes, told her that he liked her very much and asked her out for a drink.

Chapter 26

It was calm and peaceful in the Boat House since Nina had gone home. Most of the deliveries had happened and there were no workmen around. Sallie Broadchurch relished the peace, and the meditative sounds of the ocean and nature all around her... it was so different to living in the City. She opened up the doors and sat looking out as a seaplane went past and Luke's fishing boat bobbed by. She'd just poured herself another coffee when a text arrived from Ben.

Hey Sallie, just checking you are alive after the other night ;) Hope you are ok? BC

Fine thanks.

She hoped he didn't mention the kiss. He didn't. Then she wished he had mentioned the kiss and was very much hoping he would follow-up on the date. He did.

Good to hear, let me know if you want to go for that drink, I'll be back in Pretty Beach tomorrow, just up at Seafolly Bay today.

She sat there for ages deliberating her reply. And finally, unable to come up with anything that sounded witty or as if she was not that bothered without sounding rude she simply sent back.

OK. Great. Love to.

* * *

Ben Chalmers checked his phone and kept re-checking it. No mention of the kiss then. He wondered if there would be a follow-up text, but nothing. She clearly wasn't interested, but it had seemed like she was the other night.

Even though he'd very much wanted it to go further, thankfully he'd stopped it before anything happened either of them would regret. He had to remember he had to live and work next door to this woman... this very pretty, tiny woman who had something about her he couldn't put his finger on.

It was strange; women hadn't even crossed his mind since Tana had died, and now all of a sudden, all he could do was think about Sallie Broadchurch. Loads of women had come on to him too, most of the women in Pretty Beach for sure. His parents had tried to fix him up with several but he hadn't even listened long enough to find out who they were. Sweet Nel had tried several times in fact, and had even offered a one night stand just to 'cheer him up.'

But as soon as he'd seen Sallie standing in front of him a few months ago, shading her eyes from the sun in skinny jeans, an over-sized, faded old t-shirt, no make-up and hair knotted up on the top of her head, something had changed. She was different to all the other try-hards that had chased him in the last few years, especially the ones his mother had tried to set him up with - little rich bitches with no idea about actual life.

Sallie had seemed almost indifferent to him, and he supposed that was what made her attractive. It was nothing to do with her huge blue eyes, lovely skin and the fact that she looked good even in a pair of old jeans and a mucky old t-shirt covered in paint.

She seemed not to give a stuff about anyone else or what they thought and she was sort of vibrant but not showy and talking about herself all the time - he hated that. There were no flies on her either. She'd ripped into the renovation of the Boat House better than many he knew, written up a business plan, finalised a profit and loss sheet and worked harder than he had for a long time. She was strong and straight to the point, which was exactly why she'd told old Bruce what she thought of him the other night and had hit the nail right on the head.

Maybe it was time he could finally move on from Tana. It had been ten long years. He still missed her every single day and thought about her all the time, but it had recently eased off. In the first few years everything had seemed empty, his house, his business, even his head without her around, but it had been a very long time grieving and it had all finally got a bit better.

He'd never thought he would even look twice at another woman again. Sure he'd gone with the odd one over the years and Pippa, a family friend, had been in and out of his life, but this Sallie Broadchurch had come along and that day he had first met her, standing in the decrepit old building, a dead rat carcass lying on the floor in front of them and cobwebs in her hair, he'd looked over at her and felt something that he hadn't for a very long time.

Chapter 27

Sallie had predicted that not having been in the Boat House for that long, kissing her neighbour, having verbally abused a senior citizen and the creaks and sounds of the old place, that she would not sleep very well and toss and turn all night. Before she'd gone to bed, she'd had visions of that awful slot during the hour between three and four in the morning, when she would lie awake going over all the crappy things in her life and wishing that it had gone better. She would lay there under the duvet and wish that rather than being alone in a scruffy old house, she had a handsome husband beside her... three lovely little boys would be tucked up sweetly in another room in matching beds and pyjamas and her main worry would be what new dress to buy for her holidays and when she would next get her nails done. It was a much nicer scenario to think about than where precisely her next meal and indeed pay cheque was coming from.

In fact, she'd slept like a log. The next morning, she lay there looking out the door to the beach. The secret to the good night's sleep must have been warmth... after filling up the pot belly stove with wood, a long soak in the bath and putting on her warmest flannel pyjamas, she'd made herself a hot water bottle and sat in bed with a book on her Kindle, a Baileys at her side. When she'd found herself hardly able to keep her eyes open, she'd turned the light off early and had slept surprisingly well.

The wind rustled around howling outside, the fire was down to a low glow and pulling the blind right back from the window she felt icy air blow in and big, grey and purple clouds coming in over the sea. Outside, huge waves rolled in and crashed on the beach - the dark skies had changed the usual blues and greens to greys.

Sallie pulled on some tracksuit bottoms, shivered going over to the kitchen, made herself a bacon sandwich and a cup of tea and went outside to eat it on the deck. She drew in her breath as cold air hit her cheeks and whipped her hair around her face. There were no boats around on the water today, no seaplanes for sure and not a soul in sight. She'd noticed that no one at all went out when Pretty Beach was cold and wasn't quite so pretty.

Today she was getting the old boathouse cottage next door ready for rental - she'd taken the advice of Holly and had a really good deep dive into Pretty Beach accommodation and what it was being let out for. There was nothing much on the water like the Boat House, the old boathouse cottage and its grounds, and none of the other holiday rentals were beautifully decorated - most of the places were the usual open-plan interior decorated in a beachy theme of seashells and starfishes.

Her vision was completely different to that dated beachy look, and she knew she could make the little house right on the water into a rustic and charming holiday home with a vintage coastal feel - and she could sell the dream pretty easily, without a whole lot of outlay.

She needed to start clearing the place out, order a bed, a small fridge and a few essentials. With a bit of work she could get it done, photographed and online in the next month or so. And then she would sit back and wait for the bookings to come in. *Pah,* she thought to herself, if only it would be as easy as that. It was elating though, the thought that she might be able to have a secure income of her own without having to rely on anyone else.

She got up, had another cup of tea and then put a huge jacket over skinny jeans, tied up Timberland boots, popped a slouchy beanie on and wound a large cable knit scarf around her neck. The wind nearly whipped the door out of her hand as she'd walked out, it was actually colder than it looked with a howling wind. She needed to pop up the laneway to the shop to get milk and some bits and bobs to make a curry.

She pulled her coat tighter around her, headed off back past the Marina and around the other side of Pretty Beach, past Seashells

Cottages and down towards Seafolly Bay to the supermarket. She walked along the coastal path amazed at the difference the weather made - the sea and sky a mass of dark greys and angry purples.

Just as she'd gone past the Marina Club and rounded the corner at the door of the supermarket coming out with a bag of shopping was Suntanned Pete, still in shorts and flip flops but today rugged up in a big sheepskin coat, a hat and a scarf. For someone she had rubbed up the wrong way he was smiling - maybe he was a harmless old sod after all. She walked over to him and his dog who was tied to the railing outside. The dog wagged his tail, she bobbed down to stroke him and say hello.

She was just waiting for him to tell her she was bang out of order with the comment to Bruce when he completely avoided mentioning the evening's goings on, and said nothing about old Bruce at all.

'I bumped into Rory and he said you were clearing the yard. Years of overgrown weeds there, what a chore! Anyway, it reminded me, I have an industrial drum of weed killer leftover from when I did up the cottages. I found it when I cleared out the shed recently. Not organic obviously, but nothing else did the job. Costs an arm and a leg - yours if you want it for nothing.'

To say that Sallie was taken aback was an understatement. This must be old Suntanned Pete's way of being nice. She could definitely do with it; she'd seen weed killer online and the amount she needed would be in the hundreds, if not more.

She wasn't going to say no to this offer. Pete was scrolling through his phone looking for a picture of the weed killer. He took a glasses case out of his pocket, opened it, perched a pair of glasses on the end of his nose and looked through.

'Yeah, here we are - blimmin' litres of the stuff.'

'Thanks, that's really nice of you Pete.' Sallie smiled at him.

'No worries, if there's one thing about me, I like to be generous to everyone around here, you can be sure of that. Speaking of that - Holly said you're going to rent out the Boat House then?'

'No, just the old cottage down the side. I thought it might as well be put to some good use.'

There was no way she was going to tell Pete that she was basically going to take his business model of cottages on the beach, turn it on its head with much better styled places, an elite clientele and artisan experiences to boot.

He screwed up his nose and looked at her over the top of his glasses.

'Well, I can help you out with that too then, pass over my enquiries if you like. I'm nearly fully booked already.'

'That will come in so handy, excellent,' she doubted whether the clients who looked at Pete's places would be interested in the old boathouse cottage but she was grateful for any word of mouth recommendations, that was for sure. She went to turn around, stroked the dog.

'I'll be seeing you - I need to get a few bits for a curry and then get myself back along the beach and in the warm.' She went to open the supermarket door.

'By the way, there's a meat raffle over at the Marina Club in the week, that's if you'll get past old Brucie.' He winked and started chuckling. 'Must say, in all the time I've lived here, which is my whole life, I've never seen anyone take on Bruce and win.'

'Ahh well,' she looked right back at Pete in the eye, 'I don't let anyone walk all over me Pete.'

Chapter 28

Sallie had just shut the door behind the old beach house after spending the day cleaning all the junk out, clearing out cobwebs and working out what she needed to get together to make the place look good. She was picking up the vacuum when she looked over the fence and saw Ben walking along his jetty on the way to the workshop. Her heart flipped over.

'Busy day?' He called out.

'I haven't had a rest since I've been here.' She laughed.

'Fancy that drink we spoke about the other night?' He didn't mention the kiss.

Would she fancy a drink with the handsome man she'd kissed who lived next door? Hmmm, debatable. She remembered the kiss - even though she'd been married twice, things had stirred in her she'd never felt before. What even were they?

They'd seen each other a few times since over the fence in passing, but neither of them had mentioned it and she remembered she had vowed to herself to keep Ben Chalmers very much at a distance.

'I'd love to go for a drink,' she said and then trying to act nonchalant carried on, 'By the way, I bumped into Pete a few days ago and he offered a load of weed killer for all of this - that was kind of him.' She gestured around at the weeds lining the side of the drive.

'Trying to find out what's going on if I know him. Nosey old thing - too much time on his hands, that's the problem. That's good though, that will get rid of the weeds.'

'Yep, so it's all coming together - the electricity and internet booster should be up and in there by tomorrow afternoon and then all I need to do is style it properly.'

'I employed this stylist on my last renovation... three thousand on a fridge.' He shook his head in disbelief.

'Yes, I heard you were cranky about that fridge, but now I've got it thanks to you and I love that fridge more than your stylist did I think.' She laughed.

'Surely a fridge is a fridge?'

'Not if you love decorating,' she chuckled.

He looked at her as if she was speaking German, 'Okay, see you out the front later?'

'Deal.'

***

Ben Chalmers got out of the shower, dried himself off and thought about the drink.

She probably hadn't even realised that he'd been trying to manoeuvre bumping into her since he'd got back, but every time he'd seen her and was going to ask her for the drink, he'd lost his nerve.

Or that he had stopped himself from texting her a good few times. He didn't want to seem desperate after the kiss, even though he was, couldn't stop thinking about it and definitely wanted the date.

***

Sallie raced up the creaky stairs of the Boat House; what the hell was she doing saying yes to Ben and the casual drink? He might be thinking it was just that and she was wondering all sorts of other things. Like a date. Other things, like the kiss and how much she loved the look of him. How when she looked at him it was like she could drink him in.

She stripped off the old working clothes and raced to the shower. Hopped in, washed her hair, scrubbed her nails and soaped every single bit of her body to remove every last piece of dirt, cobweb and dust.

Getting out of the shower she dried herself quickly, pulled on clean, ironed jeans and a navy blue oversized linen shirt, roughly dried her hair, stuck it back at the nape of her neck in a low bun and pulled a few bits out at the front. Spritzed herself in two layers of perfume, did her make-up and was quite pleased with the difference from the grimy, mucky woman that had arrived half an hour before to the one who looked back at her in the mirror.

***

Strolling over to one of the bars down the laneway Ben showed Sallie to a seat out the front catching the last rays of the day's sunshine and ordered a beer and a glass of wine. They chatted for ages about what was going on in Pretty Beach, about the time he'd had back at his parents and she told him about some of the states of the houses she'd renovated back in Freshlea. She had surprised, even herself, with how quickly she had skimmed over the part with the two husbands, the two divorces and the sadness of the lost babies. Who wanted to hear all of that?

'Well then Sallie, unfortunately it's been really lovely and a welcome break, but I'm going to have to head off, will you be walking back home?' It had been a lovely few hours and probably would have lasted a lot longer, but Ben had a video conference with his lawyers.

'I might actually go the long way round. By the way, I wanted to, well, errr, mention the thing the other night. You know, apologize. Where that came from I'm not sure, sorry about that.'

Ben Chalmers looked at her, sitting there enveloped by the huge chair, clutching her glass of wine to her chest.

'Right, I'll take that on-board, Sallie.' He got up to leave the table, leant over and kissed her on the cheek to say goodbye. Just as he went to go he turned back.

'I actually quite liked it myself.'

Chapter 29

Sallie sat there in the huge chair, people-watching and trying to digest quite what Ben had just said. She'd gone hell for leather telling him how she regretted the kiss and how sorry she was that it had happened and he had said he'd liked it! What the heck did that mean? Should she be kicking herself? No, she had done the right thing, even though she really liked him, this was remaining as a friendship.

On the walk home Sallie heard her name being called. Jessica from the fish and chip shop was tidying away the chairs at the front. She looked tired and with less than the immaculate makeup normally in place. Sallie crossed the lane strolling over to say hello.

'Hi, look I hope you don't think I'm being cheeky, and say no right away, but you said the other night that you ran a cafe back in Freshlea, that's right isn't it? I was wondering if you'd be interested in helping out here for a while, what with the wedding plans and everything I'm flat out at the moment?'

'Yeah I've worked in loads.' Sallie didn't need much time to think about it; a casual, local, job was exactly what she wanted, especially for only a few nights a week so that she would still be able to concentrate on the property.

'You know what, I might just take you up on the offer.' Sallie smiled at her. Jessica heaved a massive sigh and continued stacking the outside chairs one on top of each other.

'That's great then, I can do most of it myself, but need help for the busy bits.'

'No worries, I would love to help out.' Sallie replied.

'Okay. How about starting this Friday?'

'Great, works for me, see you then.' She carried on walking along the road, turned the corner and bumped straight into Holly from the bakers carrying a vast armful of flowers and fruit.

'Hey Sallie, how are you?' Holly was squinting at her over the flowers.

'All good. Sorry I haven't been over, I've been working flat out on the boathouse - I looked into your idea for holiday accommodation a bit further and I reckon it's got more legs than the cafe idea to start off with.'

'I knew it! Would you like to come over tomorrow? I'm doing a special Indian dinner for Rory, he loves a good curry. And my mum will be there - we can chat all about it. I've been in business a long time. There's much to learn.'

Sallie really liked Holly, they'd clicked as soon as they'd met and she loved a grafter, she was really pleased to be invited to dinner too as she'd missed the suppers she had shared with Nina.

'I love Indian food Holly, I'll take you up on that. I'll make my famous dahl and bhajis... and I'll bring the wine.'

Chapter 30

Sallie finished up cleaning and headed back to the Boat House, she needed a quick shower and to make herself look presentable before she arrived at the fish and chip shop.

Crossing over the laneway and seeing the shop was still shut, she walked round the back which was a similar set up to Holly's bakery - a small courtyard with a patch of grass and a fence all the way round.

Jessica came out to let her in - she was very attractive, and it seemed a little bit odd that she was with the much older woman, but each to their own. Sallie had bumped into them down at the beach a few days earlier and met Camilla, a tall, older woman with large hands, badly highlighted hair and big feet.

'Hi, how are you?' Jessica said as she let Sallie into the back of the shop.

'I'm good, bit tired, but it's all coming together.'

'Ready for the craziness that is serving people their Friday night fish and chips?'

'I think I'll be able to handle it - you want to be in a cafe in Freshlea with all the hipsters, that is nuts!'

'Okay, let me take you out the back and show you the set up and then I'll get you an apron and then it will pretty much be go, go, go. All I need though is for you to help out so nothing too taxing on the brain.'

Sallie looked properly around, it was the fanciest fish and chip shop she had ever seen. The whole thing was liveried with navy-blue and white, and the fish and chip sign had a little crown over it. It was plain and simple and the menu didn't sway very far away from just fish and chips, no other extras like you found in a lot of places. The logo read simply:

Fish and Chips
The Way It Used to Be

Everything was white inside - the food boxes, the wrapping paper, the cups, even the fridges - everything else was navy-blue. It worked - simple colours in a striking combination. The details were meticulously planned, with paned windows to the front, the restaurant completely sectioned off from the noise of the take-away and a small separate serving bar.

Small, round tables were covered in navy-blue oilcloth tablecloths with a white lantern and candle. From the ceiling canopies of white fabric gave the place a soft almost ethereal feel. Little fairy lights were strung in between the fabric and there was not a faux fishing net or plastic orange lobster to be seen. At each of the tables sat navy-blue painted Bentwood chairs and the menu was chalked up on an enormous old barn door.

There were four starters, four mains and four desserts and one plate of the day - a fixed price deal consisting of a starter, a main and a glass of wine. Clever, efficient, cost friendly and not a fancy label bottle of kombucha in the vicinity. Sallie decided this was exactly the process she was going to follow if she ever got a Pretty Beach cafe up and running.

Jessica's older daughter, who was the spitting image of her, was sitting at one of the tables sorting out the knives and forks and other bits and bobs.

'I'm Caitlin.' She said to Sallie and smiled - she was just like her mum, only younger.

'So that's it really. You said you've worked in a cafe before so it might be better for you to work in the restaurant side, Laura runs it pretty well but she can sometimes get stressed if it's manic.'

'Everything is on the iPads, and as you can see,' Jessica pointed to the blackboard, 'there are only a few options and just a few selections of wine and beer to keep it all really simple and straightforward. At the end of the day this is fish and chips. All you have to do is key the order into the iPad, add on if they have drinks - then the order goes straight through to the kitchen and you get a notification when it's ready. We are fully booked from about six so it will be busy.' Jessica flicked her hands as if it was all easy and continued, 'Have you worked with iPad ordering before?'

'Yep, all good.'

Jessica sighed with relief and handed Sallie a butcher's apron in navy-blue, an iPad and a navy-blue t-shirt with the shop logo on it.

'All the money goes through here too - most people pay with a card or their phones nowadays, all you have to do is get them to tap there,' and she pointed to the top of the tablet.

'And then if it's cash just come and get me and I'll put it through, but I doubt very much we will get that tonight unless it's one of the old timers. If you wouldn't mind putting that on that would be great.' She pointed to the polo shirt.

'Sounds like you know what you're doing.'

'Yep, I've been doing it a long time and then before that the makeup gig. All you have to do is make your costs super low, work really hard, give it a few years and make sure you diversify your income streams.' She smoothed back her hair, tucked her polo shirt tightly into her jeans and put an apron on over the top.

'When I moved back here this place was a failing fish and chip shop relying too heavily on take-away. Now we deliver fish to the local restaurants, added the restaurant side which is really just the same food with a few extras and I still do the makeup at the weekends which means we have three or so income streams.'

Sallie took it all in, yes it made sense. She needed to get the boathouse cottage going and then she would need to diversify too with a cafe, and maybe other ideas that could work on the property.

'You also have to think about being new to the place and work at being nice to the locals.' Jessica laughed.

'Maybe not having it out with Bruce wasn't a wise move - though I have to say, it was entertaining. Even though I'd lived here before it took some time for the locals to get used to me and then when I chucked out Martin and moved in Camilla, it was like I'd grown six heads. Now that took a while, I even noticed a drop in takings when all that happened.'

'You need to keep people on side and you need to watch them like a hawk especially ones like Pete, he will stab you in the back as quickly as he can. Never liked it when I started this place, he doesn't like anyone else in Pretty Beach being more successful than him. I got a brick through the window when I started going out with Camilla. No proof of it and I don't know why, but I always think it was him somehow. Old-school as they come and not willing to see anyone else's point of view.' Jessica picked up the knives and forks. 'Anyway, enough of me, what are you going to do over there, have you decided on a cafe?'

'Actually, no, I'm going to start with a holiday rental of the boathouse down by the water.'

Jessica did a long low whistle.

'So, you'll be going into competition with Seashells Cottages, rightio - then you really need to keep Pete on-side.' At that moment the first of the take-away customers walked in and Jessica scooted off.

Sallie finished putting the lanterns on the tables, turning on all the little faux candles and switching on the fairy lights. She hadn't remembered just how lovely it was in here. The soothing music was instantly relaxing and the food smelled amazing. No wonder it was the right environment to get drunk the other night.

The first customers came in, Sallie showed them to their table and handed them the small timber clipboards with the menu, pointed to the door and opened their wine.

Sallie was naturally friendly with the customers, you could tell she had worked in hospitality before, taking the orders and asking the customers if they were ok but not being too over the top. The whole evening was going swimmingly.

Jessica watched from the bar of the take-away area and smiled to herself witnessing Sallie scooting around thinking of things before she needed to and generally keeping on top of things way better than Laura did. *She is going to do fine at the Boat House* she thought. *Watch out Pete.*

Just as the evening was ending and the last of the restaurant people had left, the door opened and the bell tinkled above. A man walked in in blue shorts and a grey hoodie.

'Sorry, just about to close.' Sallie said as she looked up.

'I'm David, Jessica's brother, you must be Sallie?' The man in the blue shorts said. Another time when one of the locals knew who she was and she had no idea who they were, she had to admit she was getting used to it now.

'Yes I am, nice to meet you,' she smiled and finished up with spraying and wiping the tables, as Jessica's daughter came out.

'Hi Uncle David, how are you?'

'Hi lovely, how's the studying going?'

'Yeah, on top of it, bit stressy, but I'm okay.'

Sallie carried on clearing up around them and chatting, David looked over.

'By the way Sallie, well done with your baptism of fire in Pretty Beach. I witnessed the whole thing the other night with old Brucie boy, made me laugh, and Jessica too. It was then and there that she said she'd ask you to work here for a while if you had the time to help out and also then that we knew you were a keeper in Pretty Beach.'

Sallie smiled up at him and started to clear the lanterns off the table.

'I have to ask the details on the Boat House - what are you planning to do with the place?'

'Get in line! It's the million-dollar question in Pretty Beach at the moment, you'll have to ask your sister,' she laughed back.

'There's a bit of a rumour going round that you're going to turn it into a biker's cafe, you know, considering that you brought the City gangland mafia in with you.' She laughed back at him.

'What do you do then David?' She asked.

'Ahh, a boring job in insurance in the city, commute there and back, horrible trek, I get sick of it.'

Jessica's daughter's eyes widened while she sorted knives and forks for the next day.

'It's hardly just boring old insurance Uncle David!'

'Yep, that's what I said,' he replied with a corresponding look on his face to suggest to Caitlin to hush up.

'And the holiday business Uncle David, don't forget that.'

'That's a side thing.' At that point, Jessica walked in and joined in the conversation.

'Actually Sallie, you might want to have a chat with David, it didn't even cross my mind. He has quite the thriving sideline with a holiday apartment business. A little bit different, going for the golfing crowd but really high occupancy.'

'That was a definite learning curve. Insurance was a lot easier in the start.' David shook his head.

'Oh don't tell her that!' Jessica tapped him on the arm.

Sallie had ascertained a lot about him in the few minutes she had spoken to him. Firstly, that the good looking genes clearly ran in the family and secondly, that he was another of the Pretty Beach locals who was confident in his own skin. Little bit cockier this one though. Liked himself quite a bit by the looks of it, which wasn't surprising, he was not at all offensive to the eyes.

She also noted the car keys with the Mercedes badge, the loafers with the shorts and the very clipped cut of his hair. *Bet he looks a bit different, all dressed up to go to the City,* she thought. Caitlin came back with his package of fish and chips.

'Well Sallie I'll be seeing you, nice errm... necklace.' He definitely looked at her chest.

'You'll have to pop over for a drink, there's loads of little tricks with short-term letting and I know a few locals who can help with it all if you want to go away or you need anyone to manage it for you... I've got a whole team of cleaners, someone who brings in all the supplies etc and there are agents who can do all the chatting back and forth and all of that side of it. It takes ages, you won't believe some of the questions people ask - they want a hand-hold on how to book a holiday house!' David said.

She nodded and smiled back. What a joke, her getting a manager, she would be lucky if she could make ends meet, she certainly didn't have the need or the budget for a manager and she would be doing all the cleaning herself.

He smiled, gathered his things, waved goodbye, clicked the button for his Mercedes and drove off.

Chapter 31

The aroma of spices, garlic and onions hit Sallie's nose as she packed the dahl and bhajis into a white china dish. Her dahl recipe was like an old friend; it went with her everywhere and had become quite the local dish in Freshlea, with the cafe below selling out and ordering more and more every week.

She'd tweaked the store cupboard ingredients over the years until she could make it with her eyes closed. It was comfort food of the Gods and had seen her through freezing nights in the annexe, long days property styling and many an evening with Nina discussing all that was wrong in the world. She put a lid on the dahl, wrapped up the bhajis and headed out for the walk up to Holly's.

Sallie checked the position on the map on her phone - she was never much good with directions, but Holly had said the walk was a ten-and-a-half minute walk from Pretty Beach over towards Gypsy Bay, that it was number forty-five Ocean Road and that it was a white house. What she hadn't said was that it was an incredibly large white house with a triple garage at the bottom, a black Porshce 4 x 4 on the drive and views over the whole of Pretty Beach. What had Sallie been expecting? She didn't know, something a bit more regular, humble in fact, like an old cottage or something a bit more normal. This was more like an estate.

She checked the address again, looked up at the big, black electric gates and pushed the button on the intercom. Holly answered, and the huge gates started to slowly slide to the left. She walked in, the whole thing in view now. It seemed that selling bread in Pretty Beach was lucrative.

'Holly, this is amazing, I wasn't expecting this!'

'What were you expecting, the silly baker, with an old run-down house?'

'Ahh no, I wasn't saying that but... this is unreal.' She looked out over the back at the views.

At that point a tiny, bird framed woman, dark hair piled up on the top of her head, a tablet in her left hand and playing what looked like some kind of game came in, didn't look up and shuffled over to the counter.

Holly shouted at her.

'Mum, this is Sallie from the Boat House, the one I was telling you about. Sallie my mum Xian.'

'Slower.' Xian replied.

Holly tutted and said quietly to Sallie, 'She knows exactly what I'm saying, she's just being awkward.' She repeated it and Xian stuck out her hand to meet Sallie.

Xian's face was etched in soft lines with velvety lips and she wore a pretty gold necklace with a diamond encrusted elephant pendant.

Sallie gave Holly the dahl and bhajis and they sat up at the over-sized, engraved table, laughing and chatting while Holly pottered around cooking the curry and rice. A bottle of wine slipped down quite nicely and Xian enjoyed a few of her, what they termed, 'special drinks.'

By the end of another bottle they'd put the world to rights, talked about some of the gossip in Pretty Beach and they had told Sallie how they had arrived from Vietnam with nothing and had to sleep on the floor for a long time. They'd slowly saved enough money to buy the Pretty Beach bakery, both worked sixteen hours, every day, every week for years until they'd slowly expanded. They had bought more and more properties, renting them out and paying off the mortgages from the rental income. Sallie didn't ask too many more questions, she'd heard about the stories of the people who had arrived in those days and it wasn't nice.

Holly went out to get another bottle of wine and some more of Xian's special drink when Xian said something to her quietly.

'Ach, no she won't want to be doing that.' She replied crossly.

'My mum would like to know if you are interested in a bit of an old custom - matchmaking... she thinks she's an expert at it!' Holly sighed and shook her head.

Sallie had absolutely no interest in matchmaking and this woman had only just met her, but she didn't want to offend either of them. The old lady was hilarious and interesting. She had a good aura about her and Sallie liked how they had both made her feel really welcome - she needed a couple of good friends and maybe it was these two.

'I can't see it will do me any harm...' Sallie laughed.

'Well, you never know, sometimes it's worked, it's quite uncanny. We set Rory up on a date and he ended up nearly married to the girl, and then there was Jessica when she threw out that lazy husband of hers, that was good too.'

Xian started to chat to herself and continued tapping the iPad while Sallie and Holly cleared up, loaded the dishwasher and sat back down with the coffee. Xian leant over and took hold of Sallie's hand looking at her earnestly.

'I think there are two options for you in Pretty Beach. I would include Rory, but he's a bit of a flight risk.' It was amazing how much Xian's English had improved all of a sudden.

'There's David Windsor - very nice, but having a few issues from the past. There's one of Pete's sons, definitely an option but baggage from family life and then of course, the one you have probably already spied... Ben, the very handsome Ben Chalmers.'

At this point, Sallie wanted the conversation to stop right there. She didn't want to be rude to Holly or her Mum, but Xian had uncannily hit the nail on the head right away and she wanted to steer the subject away from him.

'Ladies, I think I will be quite happy on my own in my new life up here.' Sallie chuckled and pulled her hand away from Xian.

Holly and Xian gave each other a knowing look, the conversation wrapped up and Sallie looked at the time on her phone and started getting ready to head home. She got her coat, said thank you for the dinner, they showed her to the door and she walked home in the moonlight.

When she got back from the dinner she ran the bath, got her book out from her bag, took out fresh pyjamas and made a mug of cocoa. She stepped into the bath and thought about the last few days - the shift at the shop, the late afternoon drink with Ben and how she had wanted to just stay and chat with him Her mind had wondered to what it would have been like if he had ended up at her place at which point she had pulled herself up - it wasn't even something to daydream about, it was just friends.

He'd said that he'd quite liked the kiss though. She smiled to herself, making sure to remember that.

And how funny that Xian, Holly's Mum had honed straight in on it... maybe her matchmaking skills were quite good after all.

Chapter 32

The next day Sallie was up early and ready to go, on a mission to get the boathouse cottage ready and on the internet. She walked over towards it and didn't know how she hadn't seen it before - the place was built for a cosy little holiday home. It had been constructed to the right of the old Boat House and sat down by the water near, but not too near, to Ben Chalmers Seaplanes. A small white pebble driveway led down to the doors from the laneway and on the other side an old, steeped timber boat launch tapered gently down to the sea.

Fruit trees to the left sectioned it off from the main Boat Shed making it unseen from the apartment and huge terracotta pots, currently filled with overgrown weeds, rustled in the ocean breeze. She'd cleared all the undergrowth from outside to reveal a small block paved patio, on the right-hand side, and a magnolia tree sat in a flower bed under the shade of a large willow.

She walked down to the front to look past the tiny jetty to where the seaplanes landed and out over the spectacular view. As the sun filtered down through the trees it fell onto the huge old antique windows lining the left side of the house. Sallie had never seen anything like them and after examining them closely, Googling and trying to find something similar on Pinterest she'd finally ascertained that they may have come from a church.

Inside and out, tongue and groove cladding butted up to the windows under a faded old corrugated tin roof. Old vintage pendant lights hung in the corners, a small line of timber cupboards and what looked like an old tool/workbench functioned as a small kitchen area and an old pot belly stove sat tucked into the corner.

The three clinker rowing boats she'd seen when she'd first arrived stood lined up and to the right, an old table and chairs with peeling paint and a matching bench sat in a sunspot under a tiny bullnose porch and a small deck with just enough room to sit and step down onto the beach led out the back from double French doors.

She walked over to the right and ran her hand over the timber of a small log store built into the fence and peered into the middle of the cleared grass area where she'd found a beautiful vintage beehive. Time and the elements had stripped it back to the natural timber but she thought it would look fabulous painted up and restored.

She would start with the basics, get it stripped of the junk, whitewash the inside and out, then begin the hunt for a bath and old tapware and source the smallest least intrusive dishwasher, fridge and cooker she could find.

Chapter 33

Sallie had set up all the things she needed to rent out the boathouse - accounts with various online holiday lettings companies, synced all the booking systems to her phone, and had an exclusive clause put in the insurance to cover holiday letting.

She'd done the numbers and quickly came to the conclusion that rather than the pile-them-high-and-sell-them-cheap model, she was going to go for the elite Pretty Beach holiday-maker. This customer was discerning, wanted a quality environment in stunning surroundings with all the luxury frills you'd normally get from a hotel, only more rustic and friendly. The environment fitted that whole ethos - secluded in its own grounds, with its own access to the beach and private jetty out onto the water.

She'd poured over Pinterest for inspiration to build on the bones of the amazing old building sitting in its own piece of paradise, and made it her mission to create a city dweller's dream idea of what it was like to live by the sea - a rustic boathouse shimmering in the sunshine as the water lapped in, lovely fresh food, fancy sun umbrellas, jugs of lemonade, piles of books and newspapers, a pot belly stove, a barbecue pit on the beach. There would be picnic baskets and blankets, cruiser bikes to ride around the little town, striped beach towels, old oars, lots of bunting and a flagpole down by the sea.

She was sure she could make a go of it and tap into the elusive market that abhorred the tacky plastic shells cliche. These clients wanted soft grey linen, a claw foot bathtub looking out to sea, perfectly white sheets, huge fluffy bath towels, a garden with fruit trees backing onto the beach, fairy lights that magically came on at night and high-end toiletries in the bathroom.

They wanted bare feet and tans, lovely puffy sofas to relax back into after a day in the sunshine, bare floorboards, old windows, beautiful antique doors, pillows everywhere to relax on... an old hammock swinging in the seaside breeze.

In the cupboards of this dream abode would be artisan bread, locally home-made jams and honey, superior coffee, milk in old-fashioned milk bottles and a morning delivery of fresh croissants. Beautiful sourdough bread, eggs from nearby chickens and orange juice freshly squeezed would be delivered in cold vats.

It was all a very do-able dream to create and she worked like a Trojan to get it going and sat down after the first week of work and opened up the spreadsheet to work out the numbers. With all the costs she would be cutting it fine, but with only utility bills to pay, and the relatively low costs of the start-up and her frugal lifestyle she recognised that it could, potentially, be making money from the word go.

If bookings didn't come in, then she planned to find some more shifts somewhere or get the bus out to Newport Reef and try and find some casual work until she had enough money racked up again to start setting up the cafe side of her new small empire - Boat House Enterprises.

She was just about to get onto her laptop to try and find some further info on social media marketing when her Facetime started ringing. It was Nina, dressed in her barrister robes... never did anyone look so different, one minute in a skimpy white string bikini, the next donning a black gown and a silly old-fashioned wig.

'Hey, how are you, how are you getting on with it all?' Nina asked.

'Yep I'm good, I've got everything set up just about, all I need now is all the expensive stuff, to make it look good, get the photos done and it'll be ready.'

'That's why I'm calling, remember my friend Josh? He does interior shoots for magazines. He can't get up to Pretty Beach at the moment but he said if you take loads with your phone, he'll tell you what details to get etc. and all the right angles and he'll process them and then run them through his filters.'

'Oh wow, that's great, to be honest though Nina, I've completely run out of budget now.'

'Well, I've just offered to talk to one of my lawyer friends who is an expert in divorce - his sister is wanting to leave her jerk of a husband and he said that a barter system suits him, so I will do a call with his sister and he will do the photos.'

'But it's for me, where do I come in in all this?'

'Let's just say that you styled my house a few years ago for free and saving me thousands of dollars was the payback.'

'You're really kind, thanks, anyway I have to go, loads to do.'

'Me too, I'm back in court soon.' She waved and clicked end on the app.

Sallie got up from the sofa and went down the stairs and was just walking over to the boat house when she saw Lochie and Ollie over at the seaplane dock, washing down a plane.

They looked over and waved and she walked over the driveway and stood looking over the fence for a chat. They were great young lads, well brought up, polite and living the Pretty Beach dream and looking the part too - tanned, blonde, year-round shorts wearing and trendy sunglasses perched on top of their heads.

They'd seen her with cobwebs in her hair, paint on her face and even in her pyjamas early in the morning looking like death warmed up. She bet they thought she was ancient, but they were sweet and seemed genuinely interested in the old place. Like Rory, they had told her they used to play in the grounds when they were little and had fond memories of screeching around the Boat House on their bikes and were sad that it had gotten so run down.

She stood there chatting for ages, and they mentioned the crime at the Marina Club. It had now been confirmed that the CCTV camera had not been broken but had been turned off the night of the burglary which was suspicious.

'You were up there that night weren't you Sallie, wasn't it one of the first nights you were here?'

'Ha, yeah, are you thinking it was me who tied-up and robbed an old man?'

'I don't think so,' said Ollie with a smile.

'Yeah, just that you would have walked along the road back to old Pete's holiday cottages and they are saying that whoever it was got out along that way because there was nothing at the front after 9.30pm. The library next door's new system is so advanced that it reached over into the Club's drive and apparently no one left that place after 9.30pm by the front and there's only one other way out and that's down that lane that runs behind Seashells Cottages.'

'You seem to know a lot Ollie.' Sallie leant against the fence thinking back to that night at the club.

'Not really, I don't know anything at all, just saying.' He smiled and winked.

Lochie, who said about six words every week, responded.

'His Dad's the local cop, that's how he knows it all.'

Just then Ben Chalmers came out of the workshop and very much not in workshop clothes. Decked out in navy blue pressed chinos, tan boat shoes and a crisp white shirt with navy blue epaulettes on the shoulders with four gold stripes.

She had to clutch the side of the fence. Was she imagining that a flutter just happened in her stomach? Along with a Captain's hat tucked under his arm, a brown leather briefcase in his hand and Ray Ban sunglasses on top of his head, he waved and said hello.

As he approached the glorious vision in front of her got better - he smelt of fabulous aftershave, of just stepping out of the shower, of everything that she loved.

She was standing there in a pair of too-tight, paint-covered cargo pants, her hair piled on top of her head in a messy knot, a very old paint splattered shirt tied at the waist, no makeup and as he got nearer, she suddenly realised with horror she hadn't cleaned her teeth. Thank goodness she had put a bra on.

OMG. Ben Chalmers was absolutely beautiful. And dressed in a pilot's uniform. The vision stood in front of her and started to speak.

'Hey, I thought that sounded like you, how are you?'

'Yeah,' said Ollie, 'just telling her about the burglary and the new CCTV development.'

'Sounds a bit suspect, doesn't it?'

'I've no idea, but I was in the Marina Club that night - it was one of my first nights here.' Sallie said and couldn't stop staring at him. There was a real-life, walking, talking, very easy on the eye pilot in front of her.

'You'll be getting a visit from the Pretty Beach men in blue then!'

He walked past her and she jumped back quickly to make sure he couldn't smell her - she definitely didn't smell fresh and delightful like him. She felt like a bag of old slugs and probably looked like one too.

'Well,' he said, indicating the plane down the end of the jetty, 'it's definitely getting nearer to the season, just going into the City to pick up my first lot of rich, posh people going up to Fisherman's Point for a fancy lunch.' He started to cross over the jetty and propped open the door to one of the seaplanes.

'Like he's not rich and posh...' said Ollie jokingly.

Ben Chalmers put his briefcase down, put his sunglasses on and adjusted the hat so it sat perfectly on his head, looked over his shoulder and casually addressed Sallie.

'By the way, talking of lunch, want to join me next Saturday for lunch on the boat?'

Sallie stood there in the too tight pants and the unclean teeth. If she were a cartoon her eyes would have love hearts in them and her tongue would be droopy, hanging out of her mouth and full of longing. She stumbled on her words and coughed a bit.

'Love to Ben, yes, love to.'

Ollie started to hum very quietly, 'Love is in the air, every time you look around,' as Ben Chalmers of Ben Chalmers Seaplanes started up the engine, gave it a few revs and trundled off into the sea.

Chapter 34

Sallie walked down the end of the road, the sun toasting her skin - she could feel the nicer weather in the air. Today was her favourite kind of day... warm, dry and the sky a deep, cloudless blue. She crossed over the road at the end of the main part of Pretty Beach to walk in the sun and out of the shade. It wouldn't be long before Pretty Beach would be roasting hot and if she believed the locals, the place would be teaming with people.

She flipped over her watch to check the time, she had timed her walk to the ferry stop perfectly, and looked down as the ferry chugged around the headland, sunshine glistening off the water as it weaved its way in.

A teenager, ear pods in, wearing the tiniest denim shorts and an oversized grey jumper and boots leant up against the bench. The Pretty Beach uniform - short ripped denim shorts, very tanned legs and boots.

What a place to grow up. It made her sad all of a sudden about the babies and the stillbirth. A sadness she accepted would never go away but never got used to when it popped into her mind when she least expected it, like now. She had accepted, but it didn't make it feel any better - the only thing she knew was it would always be there with her like a deep sadness she couldn't quite get to grips with, couldn't quite believe was true.

She followed the teenager, said hello to the dockhand who she knew was a friend of Nel's, headed to the right behind the girl in the short shorts and up the stairs. The teenager turned left at the top of the stairs to meet her friends at the back, Sallie glanced to the right - the whole of the front was free. She took her seat, placed her basket next to her on the seat and took a sip of her coffee.

Thirty-three minutes of uninterrupted bliss. She sat back on the seat, her bones aching from all the physical work of the Boat House, and her brain was tired of thinking about it all. Her phone pinged in WhatsApp, it was David - they'd arranged to meet at eleven so she had plenty of time to get there and still have time to walk along to the shopping centre and go into the discount stores for a few supplies and then walk along the harbour path to the Yacht Club.

Looking forward to coffee. Just checking all is good for 11am at the Royal Yacht Club?

Sallie nodded her head in agreement, she was definitely still good for coffee with a very nice man like him. What was she thinking, she'd seen from his wedding ring that he was married? He was a hottie though.

She leant against the window and thought to herself that she couldn't have predicted this - invited by Ben Chalmers for lunch and here she was today having coffee with another man. Back in Freshlea she'd had a series of loser dates and a boss who perved on her chest all day and now she found herself in the company of two men who not only seemed genuinely nice but successful and happy in their own lives too.

Yes, a beautiful day for it. See you there at eleven.

Deciding against any kind of emoji, she hit send and left it at that. He replied back with a thumbs-up. Thirty mins later and the ferry had made its way around the headland where the breath-taking, glistening view full of blues was mesmerising.

The ferry stopped, she climbed carefully down the stairs, tapped her travel card next to the crew member and said thanks.

'See you, enjoy your shopping, don't go spending too much,' he said and laughed as she adjusted her bag on her shoulder.

No chance of that, she thought as she stepped onto the wharf, tucked her black shirt into her jeans, took a tiny little bottle of perfume out of her basket, sprayed it behind her ears, popped on her sunglasses and headed to the shops.

Walking along she thought about David - yes, he was in a completely different boat to her in terms of finances, but he had knowledge and expertise in holiday rentals and he had said he'd learnt a lot along the way and made a lot of mistakes. If a meeting with him could stop her from making any costly errors at the start, she would gladly pay for a coffee and a slice of banana bread to learn about it.

She finished her shopping and arrived at the Yacht Club. She should have realised when she had seen the word 'royal' that it was a members-only yacht club and a quite fancy one at that. Thank goodness she'd decided to wear dark jeans, a silky shirt, blazer, pretty little ballet flats and had washed and dried her hair and put some makeup on.

She walked into the reception, gave them her name and her ID and walked into the club past the old-school navy-blue and gold upholstery. Well-to-do retired men in pink starched polo shirts with the collar standing up and white-haired women with set hair seemed to be milling about all over the place. David was sitting over on the left with a laptop open and as he spotted her approaching, closed it, turned towards her and strolled over.

'You look lovely, Sallie.'

She didn't reply, but thought to herself that he looked more than stunning himself, he was absolutely gorgeous. His skin was so good she thought he might have some of his sister's makeup on. He took her double-buttoned blazer off her and placed it on the back of a chair.

'I've never seen so many tanned people with coiffed white hair,' she joked.

'I know. Most of them haven't worked a day in their life and rely on trust funds from all over the place. Not like the rest of us who have to work for their living.'

She had no doubt that David had not worked in places like she had, or that he had ever put his hand down a toilet to pull out the most disgusting stuff as she had in the hospitality jobs she'd had the misfortune to do over the years. Or had to put up with what was basically sexual harassment just because she was a woman in a low-paid job. She left that topic for another day - not the easiest of conversations to have with someone who'd offered to have a coffee with you to give you some advice.

'What will I get you?' He was very gracious, charming and kind.

'Just a coffee please.' He went over to order the coffee, strolled back to the table with it and sat down opposite her.

'So, learning about holiday rentals. Well goodness there's a lot to talk about, where to start?'

They talked for ages. He told her how he had started off with a small block of flats in Gypsy Beach and naively thought he had a license to make money. However, it had taken a long time for him to realise that to make money you had to get repeat bookings.

His whole advice had been to drill down to that - repeat customers not only recommended you, they led your marketing. They suggested you, shared your profile online and they took snaps of themselves carefree on holiday, sharing it all over social media to show anyone who cared that they were having the best time.

She hadn't even thought about that - the power of social media word-of-mouth marketing, not just adverts and throwing money at things.

So, even if nothing else, the coffee with him had been worth it. It had also been worth sitting there having an intelligent conversation with a handsome man. A handsome man in a very nice place. She was a long way from the twice-divorced woman with no money of a few months ago when she was wondering how she would ever be able to turn her life around.

They sat there chatting and she hadn't realised the time and suddenly felt hungry. While he was telling her about the little tricks for smoothly run changeovers, she slipped out her phone to look at the time and saw that it was after twelve. They'd been talking for well over an hour and a half - no wonder she was hungry.

He saw her look at her phone, 'Sorry do you have to get somewhere else?'

'No, not at all, just a bit hungry.' She was actually ravenous.

'I was just thinking the same, listen I've got a very boring conference call at two-thirty but nothing more before that if you want to get a bite to eat here?'

Sallie didn't really want to pay the club prices but she now felt indebted to him - he was clearly interested in helping and had given her some great tips. He took some menus off the next table, she scanned one up and down, the prices weren't that bad actually, she was surprised.

'What will I get you?' He gestured to the menu.

'Oh no, you paid for coffee.' She went to take her phone out to pay.

He shushed her away, 'No I'll get it. Firstly, I get it subsidised for all the business insurance I give them and secondly, you're a godsend for my sister. She's had a string of useless people working in there and that loser ex-husband of hers offers no help, pays nothing and goes with any woman in any town from here to the City - so I want to say thank you for that.'

'Ah well, I would be delighted to accept your kind offer of lunch.' She laughed.

'Will I be getting you a nice glass of something with whatever it is you're having? Only the one for me though, or I'll be dialling into Singapore a bit the worse for wear.'

She thought to herself that he could never be the worse for wear even if he'd had sixty drinks, thrown up and woken up the next morning feeling like death, but she kept that quiet too.

'I'll have the calamari, that would be lovely, thank you.'

'And how about a side of chips to share?' She nodded in agreement.

'Thank goodness, a woman who says yes to side orders and is not doing that boring thing about the calories.' He rolled his eyes.

'Oh I hear you - the friend who asks you out for dinner, then orders a piece of celery and a knife and fork and you sit there with steak and chips.'

'I have been that man, sitting opposite that woman.' They both chuckled.

He walked off to the bar to order and left Sallie sitting there daydreaming about the business and the plans... and all the things that could go wrong, plus the money she could lose. He came back down with a little stick saying number twenty-three, they chatted some more, the food arrived and she felt bold enough to ask a bit more about him.

'So, I have to ask David, partner? I heard Caitlin mention a Rianna?'

'Oh that, no,' he looked down, a bit sad, she thought he might even have blushed a bit, he coughed.

'Yes, Rianna, the girls still see her. Divorced about eighteen months but separated a while, and long before that she was messing around apparently. Got home early one day from work with a bunch of flowers and a bottle of champagne, super happy about my promotion to find my wife in bed with the guy who came over to clean our carpets. She's been with him ever since. They've got a baby and another one on the way already. The worst thing of all is that I walked away from it with nothing and he's living in my sodding house.'

David continued to tell her about Rianna, how the first time he'd seen her he had felt overcome, he'd loved it when she walked into a room, he'd loved everything about her and he had loved the idea of a family and growing old with her. He'd realised though once she'd tossed him aside that she had never really felt the same way.

As Sallie sat there listening to him talk about his ex-wife, it slowly dawned on her that there was now someone in her life that gave her that same feeling when he walked into the room.

Chapter 35

Sallie had been waiting for lunch on the boat to arrive with a mixture of excitement and trepidation. Now though, that feeling had changed. She was wishing she'd said no after she'd done some online snooping on Ben Chalmers. Sitting there one evening, with a nice glass of wine and bowl of ramen noodles in bed, she'd opened her laptop and started to Google.

Right, okay, now the penny dropped. It was now obvious why he was so charming and witty and handsome and confident. She didn't know why she hadn't seen it in the first place - he was dripping in that self-assurance you get from old money. Old established money that gave you a root system, a network of not only old school and establishment, but also of security and opportunity. Often referred to by the less-impressed as elitist.

Ben was part of the Chalmers family - she'd even heard of them, one of the oldest and most established families in the country, with a vast property portfolio including estates all over the place. They were also the majority holders in some of the country's biggest media companies. The 'farm' he had referred to was not quite the little country farm with a few chickens she had envisioned in her head, but rather a race horse breeding empire, known and respected worldwide.

She'd clicked and delved further and further - Ben was one of four brothers and the only one who didn't work directly for the family business, and their money spread far and wide with fingers in many pies. He'd also had a sister who had died tragically in an accident.

There were some old newspaper mentions of his wife Tana and a few pictures. A few pictures confirming that not only was Sallie punching way above her weight with Ben Chalmers, but that she was also, quite simply, out of her depth.

Tana Louindarni was a descendant of one of the oldest and richest Italian families. She'd grown up in the best part of London, gone to one of the leading schools and then finished her studies in no other than Rome. According to the obituary in the City Morning Times she not only spoke four languages, she'd worked as an advisor to the Prime Minister and was a passionate and outspoken feminist.

Sallie had stared at the laptop, nursing the glass of wine and thinking about the vast difference between this beautiful woman Tana Louindarni and herself. She'd not finished school, her mum had left her when she was three years old, she spoke one language with an accent and had grown up in a town she would rather forget.

She would very much like to be a passionate feminist, but when you were working dead-end jobs in hospitality, you had to put up with men looking down your top and making rude suggestions. She swirled the wine around the glass thinking - you may be able to be a passionate and outspoken feminist in political circles, but when your bosses were misogynist men who thought feminism meant you stomped around in Doc Martens and grew a moustache you had to keep your mouth shut to keep your job.

On top of all that, Tana Louindarni was extremely good looking in an aristocratic noble way - long, perfectly curled glossy brown hair, huge dark eyes, a small pert nose, tall and slim almost athletic build with gorgeous, luminous skin. There was a hint of some help from a surgeon around the plump cheeks and unbelievably perfect nose but Sallie thought she would have done the same in her boat.

Sallie glanced right to the old mirror she'd found down in the garden, painted white and propped on top of the vintage drawers. There was no way she was aristocratic or noble. Nor slim nor indeed athletic. Short and petite with light tan skin, mousey brown hair she dyed with a box dye to hide the greys and pull it up to 'honey,' big blue eyes framed now by a smattering of wrinkles showing the long hours she'd worked over the last ten years. Boobs too big for her frame that had to be kept locked down in a super-sized, super-ugly bra and a little mole above the left side of her lip which certainly had never seen any botox but definitely needed it.

The picture of Ben's wife made her feel extremely lacklustre compared to the likes of someone like Tana Louindarni. Even their names were no comparison.

Sallie Broadchurch, or Tana Louindarni? She shut the laptop and sighed and decided that she would definitely be bowing out of the lunch. She wasn't good enough for the likes of Ben Chalmers - she was more suited to old Suntanned Pete.

***

A few days later Sallie had explained the whole thing to Holly and told her all about the invitation to lunch, the subsequent Googling and the now feeling of doom that she'd agreed to go at all.

'Goodness Sallie, I've never seen a woman with that man since his wife died, the odd one a few times in a fancy car but nothing else. I can tell you, many have tried but he was just not interested.'

'Even more ridiculous then to think that he would be interested in me. I just think he's being neighbourly and anyway, I've decided I'm not going to go down that route, I am keeping everyone here around me at arm's length.'

'No, no, noooo, you're not doing that, you're going to lunch - a multi-millionaire who hasn't been seen within a metre of a woman in five years has asked you on his boat for lunch and you are not saying no!' Holly was almost jumping up and down in excitement and scrambling in her bag for her phone. Sallie shook her head and looked down at her work beaten hands and short nails.

'It will all go wrong, I'll end up upset and embarrassed - it could even end up hurting my business in some way. No, I've decided, I'm not doing it. And look at the state of me - my hair needs cutting and I can't afford the hairdressers. Look at my nails, and what on earth will I wear on a boat with a millionaire? I don't even want to think about my legs and the hairiness situation...' she trailed off.

'Don't worry, I will do a plan, I am a pro at this and very good at making the best of what God hasn't given you.' Sallie frowned back at her. Holly pointed at her face and circled a finger at her skin, cheeks and hair.

'Lots of nice botox in here and my hair is dyed every five weeks,' she lowered her voice to a whisper, 'I've had my eyes lifted and tummy frozen.' Sallie widened her eyes in amazement.

'Oh what? I can't believe it, you don't look like it at all, it must have cost a fortune!'

'I know, I told you I am an expert at it - the experts make it happen, but make sure no one else realises. I will come over next week with people and supplies.' Holly tapped the side of her nose.

'People, you have people?'

'Yes Sallie, I have people for all of these things and they all owe me lots of the favours. Don't you worry, we'll get you looking worthy of the millionaire next door.'

Chapter 36

Sallie had finished helping out at the fish and chip shop; it had been manically busy, her legs ached and she smelt of frying oil and washing up. She enjoyed being there with Jessica and the time flew by, plus there were much worse places to make some extra money, but at forty, it was definitely a lot to take on after a day working on the boathouse cottage.

It was still quite early, the rush had been right through from about five and then slowly petered off at the end of the night. They'd cleaned up, she'd mopped the floor, hung up her apron and was heading home along the laneway ready for bed.

It was strange how quickly she'd settled in Pretty Beach and there wasn't a whole lot she missed about her old life - yes the friendship with Nina, she definitely missed that. She missed that she knew a lot more people there and it was easy to get around, but she felt grounded here in Pretty Beach already. Maybe it was because she had for the first time ever, a home that she could really call her own and if she played her cards right would actually stay in for the future.

Something had changed in her in the last few weeks - she was working harder than she probably ever had, but it felt easier somehow. If you included the work she was doing in the evenings on the website, the marketing and all the other stuff that was finally coming together, she was working 14 hour days and on top of that the fish and chip shop, but overall she felt like something had shifted. Was she happier? Was it because she knew that what she was doing was for herself and that she had no one else to answer to? Not a boss, a husband, a bank manager or anyone else at all. The only thing she had to answer to was the Boat House and what it offered her and her future.

She stepped onto the beach, Ben Chalmers was right about the change in temperature and that the season had started to change, she still had her beanie on and big puffy coat but the wind wasn't as cold, the ocean was calm and looking clear.

The beach was beautiful at night - it was so different, so silent, full of contrasting twinkling lights and different sounds to the daytime. She looked up from the sand and saw her place down at the end and sighed to herself. It looked beautiful in the moonlight, it was really starting to come together.

Unlocking the door to the apartment, the stairs creaked and groaned as she went up. The lamps were already on and the whole place was bathed in a golden light, the blinds at the back on the French doors were still up and the lights from the boats, the water and the moon glistened outside.

Silently walking over to the pot belly stove, she opened it up and threw on another couple of logs. It was lovely and warm and just the place to sit and wind down after the craziness of the shop. Carrying two rounds of toast, smeared liberally with butter and jam over to the sofa and looking out at the sea, she thought to herself that yes, she was indeed happier in this new life in Pretty Beach.

Chapter 37

It was getting nearer to the lunch with Ben, and despite much deliberation Sallie had decided to go. The date for the 'help' as Holly referred to it from her 'people' was all set up and Sallie was sitting out the back of the bakers with her looking at pictures of outfits and hair.

It was just as they were talking about a few slices of caramel highlights going through her hair and Sallie was thinking the only slices of caramel she knew were in a chocolate bar when Rory walked through the swinging doors from the courtyard, past the ovens and over to the table where they were sitting with a coffee.

'Hello ladies.' He walked over to Holly and kissed his mum on the cheek.

'Ahh,' she said 'I didn't know you were coming back today, I thought it was the beginning of next week.'

'Yep, had a whole list cancelled because of the train strike so I thought I'd get back up here early, didn't bother to text you and got a taxi from Newport Reef.'

'A taxi, that must have cost a bomb!' Holly sucked in her teeth and tutted.

'Mum, I'm a doctor, I have no wife or dependants. You have ten bakeries, a Porsche on the drive and you still insist on doing Uber driving, there is no shortage of money here and I can afford a taxi.'

'Ahh you never know what's round the corner Rory.'

He rolled his eyes at her, and pointed to the tablet with Pinterest open on it.

'You're both looking extremely engrossed, anything interesting?'

Before Sallie could stop her, she heard Holly proceed to inform him that she was needing help for a date - help with her hair, her face and her clothing. Not that it was really a secret, but Sallie didn't want it broadcast to Pretty Beach that she was going on a date and actually she didn't want Rory to know either.

'What exactly are you going to help her with, she's fine as she is! Don't tell me you're going to go and shove some filler in her too Mum - you know what I think about that.'

Sallie said nothing and Holly slowly shook her head.

'Well, I guess if you are really unhappy with yourself there's a place for it. But I've seen people go through all sorts of horrors in my job and the last thing you need to worry about is whether or not your forehead has a line on it.' He laughed and crinkled the eyes. The deep brown eyes, next to the gorgeous creamy, brown skin.

He was certainly nice, Sallie thought, actually quite dashing in a normal way - not the way when a man is too over familiar and smarmy or says things like 'I like you as you are' when you and he both know that all he wants is to find his way into bed. Rory didn't seem like that at all. Not trying too hard was charming.

'I guess it's each to their own, I'm certainly not adverse to some help' said Sallie and couldn't stop looking at his eyes. 'I really could do with some of your Mum's grooming and I'm grateful to have a new friend like her who has offered to help. At my stage of life, I'm like give it to me, I'll have the whole lot done, surgery, give it all to me, give me the works. Put me under and don't let me out until I look like a new woman.' She joked and they all laughed as the little bell in the shop tinkled and Holly, Rory and Sallie looked up and over towards the counter.

There pushing her way through the door, short skirt, tight skinny jumper and beautiful face leading the way was sweet Nel with her lovely blonde hair freshly washed and her adorable smile on the pretty face.

'Not much between those ears,' said Rory, 'at least she's got a coat on today.'

'Hello, how are you all? Hi Sallie, have you all heard the latest? They reckon that the thing at the Marina Club was an inside job!' Nel told them animatedly.

Sallie sat back in her chair. That was interesting, she had been there that night and after Ollie had mentioned it to her she'd done some serious thinking and had suddenly realised that there were a couple of things that didn't add up.

First of all she'd thought she must have been mistaken, but the more she remembered and thought about it, the more she thought that she had seen Pete walking down the lane when he had said that he had come back along the beach.

The second thing was there was an old shed down the back of the cottage and when she'd first arrived, she'd noticed a load of rope pulled out from behind it and left in a messy pile out the front. There wasn't anything unusual about that in itself, other than the fact that it had caught her eye as special marine rope. Reading the report on the Facebook page the police had said it was a specific marine rope that had been used.

She'd gone back the next day after reading that and all the rope had disappeared - the whole shed had been cleared out, all its contents gone and the area around it smelled like it had been washed down with bleach. There was no way she was telling anyone any of that though, so she'd kept quiet.

Chapter 38

Sallie bit the bottom of her lip. It hadn't even got to the date on the boat yet and Ben had asked her if she fancied going for a walk. A walk with Ben Chalmers, also known by Nina as Seaplane Ben, to a special little beach with a waterfall... now that sounded nice. She spritzed herself with perfume, a dab of pink lipstick and hoped for the best. Didn't they say something about putting on your best face by arming yourself with lipstick? Ha, who knew about that, but there was no doubt it was worth a go.

She stepped out of the Boat House doors, clicked the dead bolt over and crunched across the pebbles. Ben Chalmers stood on the jetty looking at his phone and as he saw her approaching, closed the phone, put it in the pocket of his navy-blue jeans and walked back down the jetty towards her.

'Morning, how are you? What a fabulous day for it.' He kissed her on the cheek and she inhaled that smell, the mix of whatever it was that made her heart dance.

The sun was shining and brilliant white clouds bobbed across the Pretty Beach skyline. She looked up at the lighthouse beyond; it was almost like someone had dipped the whole scene in pastel blues - the lighthouse, the sky, the clouds and the sea all blended into a wonderful hue.

'Hi. I'm great, lots going on and I definitely need some fresh air and a walk to clear my head.'

'Fancy grabbing a coffee and some cinnamon buns before we go?'

'What an offer. I would not be saying no to that.' She smiled and laughed as they walked along.

'Have you tried the LO cinnamon buns yet? I suppose you've already been anointed with a gift from Holly?'

'Actually, I haven't, hmmm, perhaps I've not been here long enough to get a Locals Only bun.' She chuckled.

'I don't know about that, looks to me as if Holly's taken you under her wing. Let's hope they've baked them today. They're only made on specific days and no one is allowed to know either the secret recipe or the day they'll appear. It's a highly regarded Pretty Beach secret...'

'The more I'm learning about Pretty Beach and the strange customs, the more I'm loving it here,' laughed Sallie back to him. 'A LO cinnamon bun sounds like a little slice of Saturday morning heaven to me.'

Sallie followed behind as Ben pushed open the door to Pretty Beach Bakery, the little bell tinkling above them and they got in the line of four people waiting for their bread and cakes. Holly looked up and waved.

'Hellooooo to you, how are you both?' She widened her eyes as she looked at Sallie and when Ben turned to move out of someone's way and wasn't looking she nodded her head like crazy and did a little thumbs-up sign.

'I've just been filling in Sallie on the joys of the cinnamon buns.' He lowered his voice, 'Any chance there are some today?' Holly looked around, quickly nodded her head and proceeded to go out the back. She came back with two white paper bags, the aroma of cinnamon and baking hitting them and she quickly passed them over the counter.

'Two coffees for us too please.' One of Holly's girls scooted off to make the coffee and Holly, desperate to know what was going on, addressed Ben.

'Started getting busier now? Not long before it's going to get crazy.'

He nodded and replied, 'Yep, all warming up, the pilots will be here soon and the bookings are flooding in by the day.'

'Ah well, can't be bad. So where are you two off to then?' Sallie smiled at Holly and kept quiet, laughing to herself - Holly really didn't miss a trick.

'I thought I'd take Sallie up to Fairy Bay - do you think she's been here long enough yet to be initiated in the secret waterfall beach?' Ben laughed.

Holly shook her head and tutted, laughing along.

'Oooh, I don't know about that, Fairy Bay, and the waterfall, that's only for the really special ones.'

'Exactly, that's what I thought.' He took the coffees from the counter and popped the little white bags of cinnamon buns under his arm.

'We need to keep this one Holly, she's certainly special.'

***

A brilliant blue sky warmed their shoulders as they walked across to the other side of Pretty Beach, along through a path in the woods until they came to a gate. He opened it and they walked through.

'I didn't even know this was here,' Sallie said as she closed the gate behind her.

'Not many people do, and hopefully it'll stay that way.'

Sallie followed Ben along the narrow path, golden light dappling between the leaves, the sound of the waves lapping against the shoreline in the distance. They walked up and over a hill and down again to some mossy stone steps leading to a small wineglass shaped beach.

'Here we are, Fairy Beach, the waterfall's just over there down over those rocks.' Ben pointed to rocks on the other side of the sand.

'It's beautiful,' Sallie said as she looked around at the secluded bay with only a couple of people set up with sun umbrellas and towels on the sand.

They walked over towards the waterfall, it gushed over the rocks falling into an emerald green pool at the bottom and sat down nearby and finished their coffee and buns. The water trickled down over the sand from the waterfall and the sun warmed their skin - Sallie raised her face up to the sunlight and sighed.

Propped up on his elbow, Ben leant over, Sallie froze, wondering what was going to happen next as he reached over, took her hand and then bent his head to kiss her gently on the lips and ran his hand through her soft honey hair.

She nuzzled into his neck with her eyes closed and his hand ran over the arch of her back. The gentle sound of the waterfall in her ears and Sallie Broadchurch felt as if she might just have landed in heaven.

Chapter 39

Sallie had only been at the fish and chip shop for a few weeks and she was already running it when she was there. Jessica was right, Laura was nice and a hard worker, but she got stressed when it got busy and wasn't very good at thinking on her feet and when you worked in a cafe you needed to think on your feet.

She walked down the back lane, pushed open the gate to the shop to see David sitting out the back with his niece Caitlin, a cup of tea and a large cake on the table. She walked over and said hello. Charming David jumped up and kissed her on both cheeks.

'How're you getting on with it all?' He asked, pulling out a chair for her to sit down.

'Yep, good, nearly there.' Sallie looked through to the take away section of the restaurant, 'Wow, busy in there already.'

Jessica came out of the double doors in a rush, 'Thank goodness you're here Sallie, what the heck did I do before you worked here? It's nuts out there - as soon as the weather warms up even a little bit, the locals come out of the woodwork after their Winter hibernation and the day-trippers start bunking off work on a Friday and getting on the train. We're fully booked tonight including the outdoor tables.'

'I came over early to sit and have a drink before I started, but guess I'll get my apron on.' Sallie said and turned around and looked at the queue.

'Yep, that's why I'm here too, to help out, just having a cup of tea. I'm your back-up tonight Sallie, just tell me what you want me to do,' David said and he winked - he was quite funny with the banter.

She didn't reply to that, he was pleasant and nice and since he'd told her about his wife she had seen that he was quite sweet. A tiny bit up himself, but sweet, and she loved the way he was so close to his nieces. Caitlin had told her that he was always doing DIY around the house and had looked after them a lot when Jessica had first got her new friend and had to work all the time.

It was a long evening. Jessica was definitely right - there were more people around, walk-ins she'd had to turn away and at about seven the queue was out the door. David had been the perfect little waiter; she'd told him what to do and he'd done exactly that, no fussing, and quick and efficient.

Once the last customer had gone and they'd brought the tables and chairs in from outside, Sallie had shut the door to the front, put the bolt across, locked the door and pulled the old wooden shutters shut. She knew if she sat down she wouldn't get up again.

She started to do the clean down and set up for the next night; cleared off the tables, sprayed and wiped them down and turned off all the lights, just leaving the fairy lights on - the music had been turned down so it was low in the background and a calm seemed to have descended on the place.

She looked over at Jessica, who was behind the main counter pulling out all the trays and starting to clean. She looked absolutely exhausted - in fact she looked quite ill. Saying as much to David they went around the back and through the little alley to the back of the counter. She looked up questioningly. It was almost as if she had turned a bit green, her normal beautiful colour and pretty face looked gaunt and her eyes seemed a bit glazed.

'You know what Jess, you get home, we'll finish off all this,' David said looking at her washed-out face.

She tutted at David, 'You don't know how to clean all this up!' He took her by the shoulder and turned her round and pointed her to the back.

'I'm sure I can work out how to clean a counter Jess.' She went to protest and he practically threw her into the back room, picked up her handbag and car keys and pushed her out the door.

'Sallie will need extra for all this staying late she's done...' She trailed off.

'I'll worry about Sallie, she's fine,' said David. He widened his eyes over the top of her head and Sallie added to the conversation.

'I'm fine, gosh I used to do this six days a week and get up again in the morning for the breakfast shift.' Sallie added.

'If you're sure?'

'Go!' They both said in unison.

'Right, you clean down the counter and pans, I'll vacuum and mop the floors and get the lanterns back on the tables and put out the napkins and cutlery in the restaurant, then all we have to do is the serving area.' Sallie said, taking charge.

It didn't actually take that long with each of them doing their bit, and in an hour or so they were all turned off and ready to go. Just as she was grabbing her coat and they were walking to the back door on impulse she suddenly asked him if he fancied coming back for a drink. He looked almost alarmed back at her and she suddenly re-alised that he thought she meant a lot more than a drink.

'I'm so embarrassed I didn't mean anything like that, in fact not anything at all, what was I thinking? I don't want you to get the wrong impression!' She'd looked more alarmed than he did. 'I just meant a bit of a sit down and a decompress. It always takes me a good hour or so after running around working before I can even think about sleep.'

He looked at her, standing there in the navy-blue polo top, hair piled up on top of her head desperate for him to know that she didn't mean anything, and it flitted through his mind that actually he wouldn't mind that.

'You know what, you're on. I've got a day at the club tomorrow but don't have to be there until late and I'm pretty shattered after all that.'

By the time they'd walked over the laneway and into the Boat House yard it was late and Pretty Beach was quiet. The odd couple walked home from the Marina Club and a group of young people were sitting with beers at the end of the wharf. A tiny, slim moon hung in the sky, the light dancing on a calm, dark blue sea. She yanked open the barn doors into the Boat House and David stopped in his tracks.

'This is amazing, how the hell have I not known about this? You didn't explain it like this when we were at the Yacht Club!'

'Seems you're the only one who doesn't know about it,' she laughed. She'd become used to the reaction now but she had to admit, it was looking better and better.

Ben's two lads had worked on it really hard; it was now devoid of any of the old junk and she'd carefully and slowly cleaned up anything nautical and old and put them on display. Piles of old ship ropes had been hung across the walls, old timber ladders were attached from the ceiling and the vintage lights ran through the middle of the whole thing. They'd pulled in a couple of the old clinker boats and leant them up against the right-hand side to hide the entrance to the old toilets. The doors at the end had been spruced up, the yellow paint removed and painted white.

'My God, this is crying out to be a cafe.' David was looking about him in wonder.

'Well that's the plan, but right now I need to get some money behind me.'

'I bet this was some work?' David said and looked up at the ceiling.

'Yup! I've been working on it daily for months without a break now and not getting very far very quickly - if it wasn't for Ben next door's help it would not be looking anywhere near like this.'

His ears pricked up at Ben's name, 'Ben helped sort you out did he?'

'You know him then?'

He brushed it off. 'Only in passing - he came up here about the same time Jessica came back, awful thing with his wife, she literally withered away in front of his eyes.'

'Yes, I heard that. It must have been devastating and just so sad.' She walked over towards the door at the bottom of the stairs, punched in the number, turned the lock, and they climbed up the tiny stairs emerging in the sitting room. She didn't say anything - it did look absolutely stunning. He stood there gazing around at it all.

'Yeah this is a bit of prime real estate right here. What are you doing working in the fish and chip shop? You could knock this down and build a block of high-end apartments and run for the hills!'

She laughed to herself at the way his brain worked, the brain of someone with money, income and options. She certainly had no money or history of it for a loan - she barely had enough to get the boathouse ready and buy food and pay the utilities.

'I have plans David, and I won't ever be selling it, it's listed anyway so it can't be pulled down. This whole strip here including the seaplane shed, and all the way down to the marina and the club is heritage listed. I spoke to the council and I can't even change the old tin roof even if it's falling in, it needs to be kept and repaired with like materials.'

'Well, I guess that's a good thing, we don't really want Pretty Beach built up otherwise it will soon get ruined like Newport Reef.' He walked back over the room and looked out the front window.

'What will you have then? Glass of wine, beer, hot chocolate with a little nip of something?'

He deliberated. 'I know I'm supposed to say beer, but you know what, I think I'll take you up on the hot chocolate.'

She made two mugs of hot chocolate and carried them to the sofa, gave him the drinks to carry out to the balcony, opened up one set of the French doors and took out two chunky knit throws. There was still definitely a nip in the air but it was warm enough with hot drinks and blankets.

They sat there for a couple of hours talking about all sorts of things. He told her about how very boring his job in insurance was but it paid the bills, a little bit more about his ex-wife with the babies and the carpet cleaning man and how Jessica worked really hard to put her children through private school and had fallen head over heels for Camilla.

She told him about her dead-end jobs, (but skipped over the lost babies, the two failed marriages,) all about Nina and how she'd helped her out so much when she was left with no money and no prospects after the second husband had taken the lot.

'Sounds like you've been through quite a bit yourself Sallie - this place will be amazing though. You can't go wrong up here with holiday letting, it's a rare pocket which is nearly year-round, if you nail the whole cosy-by-the beach Winter thing too, I reckon that old boathouse will be occupied most of the time.'

They sat there a bit longer, chatting, putting the world to rights. He was sweet and not at all offensive to the eye.

'Righto, I'll be off then. That was a great evening, can't say I've sat and relaxed like that for a few hours for a long old time. Amazing what the sea and the night air does for you.'

She got up, picked up the throws, folded them up and popped them back on the sofa. He took the mugs in and put them in the butler sink. She saw him to the big barn doors, pulled them across and they walked out into the evening, her bare feet freezing on the pebbles.

Just as she was walking him down to the gate to say goodbye he bent down to kiss her. He felt warm and soft and lovely, and just wonderful... she sunk into his arms and fell into the kiss, but just before it went any further she pulled away. She simply smiled and looked up at him.

'Be seeing you David, thanks for the chat.' He nodded, gave her a tap on the back and she walked back into the Boat House, shut the doors behind her, walked back up the stairs and sighed and thought to herself *'where the heck had that come from?'*

Chapter 40

The vintage sea bell she'd hung outside the barn doors woke Sallie from a deep sleep. The hot chocolates, tipple of Baileys, the 18,000 steps on top of all the work in the week had made her sleep very well.

Pulling on her pyjama bottoms she walked to the back window overlooking the laneway, the glass was still painted on the inside but she could normally see through the cracks to anyone outside. Whoever it was stood too far over on the left and she couldn't see. She didn't know who it was, wasn't expecting anyone, and was going to leave it when they knocked again. She tutted and walked down the tiny stairs, unlocked the barn door and there was David with a huge bouquet of flowers bigger than his head and a bottle of wine.

'I've just come around to say sorry about last night, I can't believe I did that, I really overstepped the mark, I don't know what came over me.'

She didn't know whether to be happy or sad that he was clearly so bothered about it. She liked David, but the kiss had come out of the blue and really it was Ben she was thinking about all the time. She hadn't actually thought much more about what had happened with David and standing there in her bare feet and old pink shirt, she took the flowers.

'Really no need David, you didn't need to bring flowers.'

'I didn't mean it was awful, just you know, you're working for Jessica, I'm a basket case since Rianna left and you've got all this to sort out,' he gestured around them. 'I just wanted to help out and not you know, well, add a complication. It doesn't have to mean anything.'

'Not a problem David, errr, look, I'm not even dressed...'

'Yeah, sorry, I've been up since 6.30am, old habits die hard and all that.' She looked him up and down, he was immaculately turned out, every single hair in place, freshly showered, in shorts, a navy-blue polo shirt and boat shoes. How come everyone here seemed to look like an extra from a television show, while she was like the blow-in who hadn't been briefed properly and in a permanent state of disarray?

'I just had a sneaky look in the window of the boathouse cottage, didn't think you'd mind... my you've got an eye for it alright, you're going to be fighting off the punters on this, trust me. You should be really proud of yourself - it looks absolutely amazing.'

Sallie looked up at him, he genuinely seemed to be impressed with her work and what she'd achieved. She liked that he said that, it felt good. He really was very kind and genuine. She always just got on with stuff, put her head down and worked and here was the head of a leading insurance company (she'd Googled him too, along with Ben Chalmers, he was not poor) telling her she should be proud of herself. In her old life she was lucky if anyone acknowledged her turning up for work, let alone telling her that she'd done well.

They stood chatting for a bit, she didn't want to invite him in, she needed a shower and to get dressed, she felt embarrassed enough as it was. In the corner of her eye while she leant on the door post of the Boat House chatting to David she saw Ben Chalmers get out of his car and walk down the jetty. He looked over and waved and David turned round and saw the way she looked at Ben as if two giant red love hearts were in her eyes.

'What I also wanted to say was I was wondering if you should do some kind of a launch for the boathouse... a lot of the marketing here is word of mouth, I mean I know that digital will be your first port of call but if you can get a few gathered here, then the word will spread. There's no point doing old school marketing these days, no one even reads newspapers nowadays and the Reporter will charge you a fortune for an advert.'

'Yeah, that's a good idea.' Sallie replied nodding and looked up at him.

'I'm not sure if you know it, but there are a couple of Insta-grammers up here, those two fashion women - can't remember their names now, prance about all over the place in big coats and weird boots. They've like a million followers and there's also a couple that moved down here recently, with a little baby with the funny name, oh what is it? Rabbit or something or Apple, no hang on it's Fox - anyway she's all into diet, eating plant based stuff whatever that means and all that old malarkey, but with 1.5 million followers if you could invite them and they post about it, that's the cheapest market-ing you're going to get with a great return.'

She looked at him frowning, the whole thing running through her head.

'What about a name, have you thought about that?'

'Yeah, all sorts in my notebook, Fisherman's Rest, Seaview Cot-tage, Coastal House.' She rattled off a load. He contemplated them and looked over at the old boathouse cottage.

'What about Pretty Beach Boat House? Keeps it nice and simple then and does exactly what it says on the tin.'

'Yes, yes, I like that actually, you're good at this.' She replied en-thusiastically and he raised his eyebrows.

'Not just a pretty face you know Sallie.' *Don't I know that already* she thought - the face alone was worth it, without the brains.

'You know what, you need to put yourself out there and back yourself up. It must be really hard for you, no family or anything and doing this all on your own. I know how hard it is and I've had Jessica and the girls and my mum and dad seeing me through everything.'

'I suppose I should really, thank you, be seeing you then and re-ally you didn't need to bring the flowers.'

She said goodbye, closed the door and thought about what he'd said. He was right. But there was always such a vast difference in what you were supposed to do and what you actually did. *Backing yourself up? Not always quite as easy as it sounded* she thought.

Chapter 41

Sallie opened up her laptop to check her emails, the graphic designer on the other side of the world had said it would take about a week for her to get the logo done. She scrolled through her emails and saw that a message had come in overnight. Excellent. She opened it up.

Hi Sallie, I've worked off the pics you sent me and completed the logo. I got a bit carried away with it to be honest after seeing those photos, I can't believe the real name of it is actually Pretty Beach. I even popped it into maps and had a look around at the place! It's like a dream. I've done the logos, the watercolours of the boathouse and then I've thrown in all the extra stuff I doodled on the side, the waves and seashells, market basket etc. I hope you like it.

Sallie opened the PDF with fingers crossed and opening up each one of the files, she sighed. It was so much better than she had hoped. In beautiful calligraphy, Pretty Beach Boat House was written across a watercolour of the house. Another one read The Boat House Pretty Beach with the same picture and the sea in the background.

Julia from landlocked Texas had included all sorts in the little digital package and still charged her the same. It would be great for Instagram and for the Facebook ads, for her website and for the footer in her emails and website listings.

It all looked very professional and had cost her the princely sum of £57. She'd checked twice that it was that low, had bitten the bullet and gone for it and hadn't expected anything anywhere near as good back.

All she needed to do now was finish the place off and get it photographed. Not long to go and counting.

Chapter 42

Sallie grabbed her jacket from the coat hook in the Boat House and walked over to Holly's to get a loaf of bread and some milk.

'Hey, how are you getting on?' She asked Holly, who was looking tired.

'All good Sallie, how are you?'

'Getting there. I've just received the logo this morning and got the time set up for the photos, I just need to finish it all off now and get the flowers in.'

'Don't forget we're getting you made over for the date!'

'How would I forget that? Also, I'm just popping over to tell you that I'm going to do a lunch at the house, some bubbles etc. and would love it if you, your Mum and Rory could come. I'm going to invite a few locals too.'

'Would one of those locals be David Windsor by any chance?' Holly looked at her expectantly.

'Yes, I'll invite him and Jessica, Camilla and the girls.'

Holly chuckled.

'You mean David who was standing at your door the other morning? Looks like my old mum was right already.' She tried to raise her eyebrows, but they stayed where they were.

'Nooooo, not at all, don't know what you are talking about!'

'Sallie, you cheeky thing. I did see him and he was holding a huge bunch of flowers.'

'What the heck, have you got binoculars trained on me in here?' Holly laughed so hard there was even a glimmer of movement at the side of her eyes.

'Well, well, well, the second most eligible bachelor in Pretty Beach hand-delivered you a bunch of flowers - now that is something else.' Holly chuckled.

'I just stayed late at the shop the other night and it was really busy. The flowers were from Jessica, he was just delivering them.'

'Of course I believe that.' laughed Holly and passed the bread over the counter. Sallie picked up the bread, turned around, looked over her shoulder and smiled.

'You don't miss a trick, do you?'

'I am the Pretty Beach Gazette.' And she laughed her funny little laugh. Nina was calling as Sallie walked back into the Boat House.

'Hi, can't stop, I'm rushing into court, that weird kid who abused little girls at the gymnastics club - all week too. Anyway, just checking we're all good for the dates for the weekend I'm coming down. I need to sort out my diary round it.'

'Yep, all good. In fact, I've decided to do a small gathering, a lunch to get some pictures for the website on that weekend and hopefully get it out there on social media. I thought I'd do it while you were here, knowing how much you love to socialise with a few bubbles.'

'Excellent, it's locked in. Exciting! Any other news?'

'Well I kissed a man six years younger than me on the doorstep the other night, if that comes under news.' She giggled.

'Bloody hell Sallie, nooooooooo, what do you mean the seaplane dude?'

'No, another one!'

'Who, what, how? So much for not meeting anyone up there.' Nina was laughing now too.

'I know it was nothing really, a somewhat mistake.'

'How do you mistakenly kiss someone Sal?'

'Bit of a story actually.' Sallie grinned to herself.

'Well ahhh, I've got to dash, I'll catch up with you when this case is over, if I survive it.'

'Sweet, speak later.'

Sallie got back to the Boat House, made a cup of tea and a fried egg sandwich and looked on her phone at the Instagram account she'd opened - Pretty Beach Boat House had a few followers already. She'd started adding pictures here and there - the pebbles on the beach, the old worn timber of the house, vintage oars she had found about the place, the clinker boats. She'd found all the right hashtags and started a crash course in Instagram and it was all a bit weird, because it was all becoming very real.

What a funny few days... a kiss with a man on the doorstep, an upcoming date with a millionaire, and getting ready to unleash her very own new business to the world.

Chapter 43

Sallie Broadchurch walked across the pebbles to the Boat House after another long day of work and did a double take as she approached - it really did look different now.

Rory had done the first hack at the weeds and then she'd used the strimmer and the mower to make it all a bit more presentable. The whole of the outside had been spruced up and all the junk that had been laying around here and there had been neatly put away, taken to the recycling or the dump.

The old flagstone pathway that couldn't even be seen before had come to light and led the way up to the barn doors. The moss-covered block-paved patio she'd found down the side which led all the way down to the cottage had come up a treat with Ben's jet wash, it still looked old and faded but the patina was fabulous, just the way she liked it.

She went in, washed her hands and face picked up her coat, shut the door behind her and walked out and down the laneway. She couldn't believe the latest reports about the crime in Pretty Beach.

Walking along thinking about it all, she saw David sitting on a bench looking out at the ocean watching the seaplanes coming in and out chatting on his phone. He saw her, indicated he would be finished shortly and for her to join him. She sat down on the bench. He finished the call and turned to her.

'You look exhausted, are you feeling okay?'

'Just really tired. I think I'm bordering on burn out with all of this, I just need to get started on the business and have a few days off.' He touched her on her leg, concerned.

'Why don't I walk you home? You have a shower, I'll pop over and get you some fish and chips and then you can get yourself to bed. I'll lock everything up on my way out.'

'I've just got so much to do, David, I have to upload all the photos to the final lettings website, I'm behind with the social media stuff, I was going to schedule all the Pinterest pics and all that this evening and get more posts done for the Facebook pages. It all adds up and I'm getting quite a bit of interest now. Everything I've seen says you need to post like twice a day.' Her voice was pitching and she had started rambling.

'And then I have to organise everything for the lunch, it's a lot of work to get the table and everything ready for twenty people. I have to start on the menu and start thinking about that. And, it's going to cost so much, what was I thinking?' She chewed on her bottom lip nervously.

'It will all be okay, don't panic, you have a great place there - you've done all the work so far, it's just some catering and a few hours to look after people then they'll all be gone, you will have the photos and you'll be able to start to relax a bit more. What you need is a good night's sleep and a lay in.' David was saying all the right things. Handsome, lovely David Windsor.

'You know what, you're right,' she got up from the bench. Just as they were walking back, a text pinged on her phone.

Ben Chalmers.

Hi, how's it going down there? I'll be back tomorrow afternoon, want to come over and join me for a drink as the sun goes down? BC

She felt bad; she knew that her and David were just friends, but there was the kiss that night and he was so lovely and now a text from Ben and then the lunch with him on the boat. *Was she stringing David along?* She thought.

'Another thing for you to do?' He asked as she looked at her phone.

'Oh no, just Nina seeing how I am.'

She put the phone back in her pocket and would text Ben Chalmers back later when she got into bed. In fact, she might have to leave it until the morning, not wanting to look too eager and all that. Regardless of everything she had told herself, she was definitely playing the game.

She had to admit it to herself, that despite all her self-talk that she was forty, was past romance, was not interested in any kind of relationship at all, she did actually like Ben Chalmers and she did like him quite a lot. And David - yes David was lovely, sweet and kind, and maybe if Ben hadn't come along things would go differently with David... but it was Ben that made something happen to her heart.

Chapter 44

Sallie Broadchurch got out of bed, took her phone off the charging unit, pulled on her oldest and softest pink plaid dressing gown and walked across the bedroom to the corner window. She pulled the heavy curtains back from the middle, and tucked them back from the floor to ceiling window.

It was one of those amazing Pretty Beach days, the sky was totally clear, not a cloud to be seen and warm. She looked over the top of the old willow tree, out across the deck and to the harbour below. Little white boats bobbed up and down and she could just about make out a fishing trawler coming in from the ocean towards the marina.

The room flooded with light as she opened the curtains, they had been a fantastic find on eBay - a woman at Seafolly Bay had been selling up and moving back to the City and had most of her house listed. Sallie had seen the curtains and known they were just what she was looking for - heavy linen drapes with a tiny grey flower on them, lined with blackout fabric and weighted at the bottom. It was like they were made for the place - three pairs of high-end curtains for about two hours' pay.

She walked barefoot over to the other side of the room, it was still chilly enough to need her slippers, pulled open the stripped timber door to the ensuite alcove and walked over towards the clawfoot bathtub. Turning the copper taps fully on the bath, she smiled to herself at the sound of the old plumbing clunking and squealing as it slowly brought the water up from the tank. She was beginning to get used to the place, to the unique noises, the sound of the ocean outside and it was really feeling like home.

Lovely steaming hot water gushed into the bath and she opened the tiny built-in cupboard to the right housing shelves piled with thick, white towels, and little pots and tubs neatly lined up full of bits and pieces to pop into the bath. She chose a tiny pale pink bubble bar and dropped it into the running water... soft bubbles began to form and the room filled up with the scent of jasmine and rose. She shouldn't really be luxuriating in the bath, but there was nothing like a soak to start the day, and after three days of working long hours at the Boat House and then two back-to-back shifts at the fish and chip shop, she thought it would do her good.

She contemplated what lay ahead of her for the day. It was the day she'd agreed for Holly to come over to get her, as she put it, 'made-over' for lunch with Ben. Sallie though, had lost a tiny bit of interest. Ben Chalmers would not be interested in her and her small-town education and even smaller bank balance, so the whole thing was a complete waste of time. The more she'd thought about it, the more she'd realised he was just being kind and a good neighbour.

She soaked in the bath and thought about the lunch. There had been talk from Holly the last few times she had seen her that Ben had only been on one date since his wife had died. She wasn't sure how Holly knew about Ben's dating life, but she did seem to know every-thing that went on in the town, so maybe it was true.

She slowly climbed out of the bath, dried herself and decided that she was going to take the whole day off from physical work. After they'd gone she would do admin, catch up with the washing, clean the apartment and start getting the copy ready for the internet listing.

She was in the mood for soft, what was now called 'lounging' clothes and Holly had instructed her to wear something that could get messed up, which sounded alarming - there wouldn't be much lounging going on, but she decided on soft grey drawstring pants, a grey t-shirt and a very old and very loved faded flannel shirt... it was all she could muster up the enthusiasm to wear.

Holly would probably be in smart jeans, a little cropped jacket with perfectly shiny hair and now she knew how, an unlined face thanks to a precisely placed filler and what was referred to as a 'diluted' quota of botox. Which was certainly what Sallie needed at the moment she thought - cripes she needed half an hour in the morning just for the deep crease to drop out of her cheek.

She took out her phone. Nina had called her twice in the last few days and she hadn't been able to answer, she clicked the contacts and Nina picked up and asked her how everything was going. Sallie told her more about David, the story about his wife, how he'd so much experience and tips for a holiday rental business and that he'd offered to promote her new venture on the Facebook group he ran for visitors to the Pretty Beach area.

'That's fantastic, it's all really coming together Sal.'

'Yes, with lots of help from David on the marketing side of it too.'

'What's he like then?' Nina asked.

'Umm, let's just say you wouldn't chuck him out of bed.'

'Ooh, for you to say that, that means he's gorgeous. I need to get myself to Pretty Beach.'

'He's also heartbroken about a wife who ran off with the carpet cleaner.' Sallie said.

'Goodness, you can't make it up sometimes. I can't believe it, there seems to be so many more available men in Pretty Beach than here.'

'Well, according to Janelle, local expert on all things love, that's exactly right and it's three to one and so far for me that's bang on the money. The three men I've come into contact with are all single. It must be something in the air and water up here.'

Chapter 45

Sallie walked back in after the call with Nina and sat in the bay of the turret in the kitchen of the Boat House. As instructed she'd washed her hair, scrubbed her whole body with handfuls of salt, shaved everything to within an inch of its life and had her soft clothes on ready for Holly's 'people' to get to work.

Thirty minutes later she'd finished her coffee, eaten her croissants and was ready for her makeover. She heard two cars pull onto the drive one after the other, walked over to the window and looked out.

Yikes, she wasn't joking about her people. A slim, pretty woman with long blonde hair got out of Holly's black Porsche, opened the back door, pulled out a huge black and gold holdall and a roll-along, silver suitcase on wheels.

A middle-aged woman with a long, brown bob opened the back door of a small white BMW, took out a gigantic tote bag, threw it over her shoulder, shut the door and walked over to Holly and kissed her hello on the cheek.

A third woman who looked like the joker the way her eyebrows had been lifted halfway up her forehead walked over with a suitcase on wheels, carrying a contraption with a hose and what looked like a pop-up tent. This was getting weirder by the second, why had she agreed to this?

Because at the end of the day, it couldn't be a whole lot worse. She couldn't even remember the last time she had experienced any kind of beauty treatment - she box-dyed her hair, shaved her legs and left everything else to its own devices.

The four women stood chatting, clearly they knew each other well - Sallie went down the stairs to let them in and they all traipsed in with their equipment. The three of them looked around in astonishment at the decor, at the view and a seaplane just coming in to land.

'This is Dr. Leza - botox and filler extraordinaire, Lizzie - tan, eyebrows, nails and eyelashes and this is Kimberly, hairdresser to the stars.' They all laughed, and Holly clapped her hands in glee.

'Nice to meet you Sallie, this place is... my gosh, for once I am lost for words... it's unbelievable!' Dr. Leza put out her hand and shook Sallie's and moved closer to examine her face.

'We're not going to need much here, you've amazing skin! A few tweaks here and there, a little bit of filler in the sides, perk you up a bit on the muzzle, smooth out those forehead lines, yup, no trouble at all.'

Sallie stood back, petrified, this was serious. Dr. Leza sat her down, explained a few things about it all, they decided what she wanted and what she didn't and got to work.

A few hours later, and Sallie had been filled and smoothed. Kimberly had run slices of different caramels and dark blondes through her hair and Lizzie had erected a pop-up tent, sprayed her with an extremely dark brown liquid, painted her nails with a pale pink polish and set them in an ultraviolet light and added a few expertly placed eyelashes to the outer corner of her eyelids.

It had taken hours of dedication and Sallie had wondered at the commitment of women who did this regularly. The three of them had worked simultaneously and Holly had looked on in absolute pleasure, sporadically taking pictures and sending them to Xian.

By the end of it Sallie couldn't wait for them to leave, showed them all out and had already had two of them texting the details of the boathouse accommodation to their friends.

Once it was all over and Sallie was back inside she looked in the mirror; apparently it would all take a few days for it to kick in, but right now her skin was a deep, not very attractive mahogany shade of orange, her eyebrows looked like a couple of slugs had taken refuge on her forehead and small, what appeared to be mosquito bites smattered the whole of her face. She hoped they were right and she would wake up the next morning looking better.

Chapter 46

Sallie Broadchurch woke up on the day of the date with Ben and felt like someone had dragged her under a bus; she hadn't had time to think twice since the makeover - in fact, she'd barely even looked in the mirror. It had been full-on with the boathouse cottage, working at the shop, all the admin for everything which wasn't quite as straight-forward as she'd hoped and getting ready for the lunch to officially get the business onto social media. Plus, there had been the whole day getting made over by Holly's people, which had taken another chunk of her time.

She examined herself closely in the mirror. She had to give it to them, she may have felt exhausted but now the team's work had started to kick in she looked rested. Her face still had the little lines here and there, her top lip was definitely not pouty, but everything was softer and smoother. The scary mahogany colour from the initial spray had faded to a light golden sheen, her hair shone with soft slices of caramel in between the box dye honey and the very expertly placed eyelashes opened up her eyes. It was truly mind-blowing what money and a day of pampering could do.

She was thoroughly shattered inside though, and every part of her now golden body ached, her feet felt like she had been on them for decades and the tops of her shoulders were so tight it was as if someone had opened them up and poured concrete into them. If, and when, she ever made money out of this thing she would be making an appointment for a very long, very deep massage.

She didn't want to look at another linen pillowcase, pot of lavender, or trial any more 'beachy' jazz tunes for the playlist ever again - so today the lunch on the boat with Ben was most welcome.

She walked out onto the driveway and looked over at the jetty to the side of Ben Chalmers Seaplanes, the boat was there all ready to go and so was she. She'd been primped and fluffed to within an inch of her life and her soft blue turned up jeans, oversized white t-shirt and flowing grey cardigan was on point for a day out on a boat worth, oh, about six million.

There'd been much deliberation about what to wear on her feet. Not owning any boat shoes like the rest of Pretty Beach provided her with a dilemma she hadn't thought she would ever find herself in. Would she go laid-back casual and barefoot, plain white with a touch of silver sandals or her white tennis shoes which she'd washed and scrubbed until they had come up gleaming? She decided on the latter, wanting to be able to jump into the boat without slipping.

As she crossed the pebbles Ben appeared from the side door in a replica outfit to hers only with boat shoes, the addition of a very nice watch and instead of the cardigan a navy-blue linen shirt.

She vowed to remain calm, sophisticated and like she regularly attended casual little lunches on boats with men like him. She would replace all errant thoughts of falling into his arms and remember that this was a business-like, neighbourly friendship, whereby he would remain appropriately in the friend department. She would allow herself to enjoy his company and his good nature, even though she liked him very much.

'How are you?' He smiled and walked over towards the low fence, held out his hand to help her step over and placed a large picnic basket down by the door. He eyed her own basket with two bottles of champagne, a rug and sunhat in it.

'Here, let me.' He took the basket off her, 'I'll just pop back and get the cold stuff and we are ready to go.'

Carrying the two baskets and a heavy cooler bag, they fell into step together down the jetty, blue seawater washing underneath, a warm breeze blowing her cardigan around. Ben pulled a hat out of the basket and adjusted it on his head.

'It's a sunburn day, that's for sure. Have you got sunscreen?'

'Yes, Captain Ben, I certainly have.'

They made their way to the boat and as they approached one of the young seaplane pilots Sam poked his head out from underneath. Barefoot and in a Ben Chalmers Seaplanes polo shirt and with the door open to the workings underneath the boat he was clearly the skipper for the day.

'Hi, ready for a ride out on these huge waves, hope you've got your seasick tablets.' He joked - the ocean was a deep blue, not a wave to be seen, and she had never seen it quite as flat.

Stepping onto the boat Sallie was glad she'd decided, after so much deliberation, with both Nina and Holly, to accept the lunch. The thing was built for lovely days out, with a semi-circle of deep comfortable button-back seats at the back, a small table and four chairs built into the timber and a highly polished gleaming deck area designed for lazing around.

'Glass of bubbles?' Ben asked, and Sallie nodded, slipping off her tennis shoes.

'Go and sit up there on the deck, I'll open the champagne and bring it over.'

Sallie stepped carefully up to the deck and sat in a chair in the sun, popping her basket down beside her and putting on her sun hat. It was indeed lovely weather, warm enough to be on the deck of a boat but not too hot it was uncomfortable.

'A glass of bubbles for my lovely new neighbour.' Ben stepped up onto the deck with a tall champagne glass and a bottle of beer, following her lead and sitting down in the chair next to her and putting on his sunglasses.

'It's been a long few weeks, I definitely need a drink. I'll drink to an afternoon out on the water and a lot of Pretty Beach fresh air.' He laughed and took a long swig of his beer appreciatively and clinked the lip of the bottle onto her glass.

Sallie stretched out her legs and crossed them at the ankles, the sun warming through her jeans. Tipping up her glass and luxuriating in the delicate bouquet of the champagne, she was loving the sunshine on her skin.

'Cheers to a new life in Pretty Beach then Sallie Broadchurch, long may you stay. We certainly needed some new faces round here.'

Sallie drained her glass and slowly began to feel the magic softening of her whole body from the alcohol.

'So, what have you been up to then? You've not been around the yard much.'

He started to tell her about his parents. Both of them were suddenly getting health problems when their whole lives they'd been fit as fiddles. He talked about his business and how he'd had to get all sorts of red tape out of the way with lawyers involved for the new tender and how it was the time of year for the annual ball for the charity his mother had set up in memory of his late wife.

'Sorry to hear that, it must be a tough time.' Sallie said sadly.

'Not really any longer,' replied Ben, 'I think it all started to feel better about three years ago, so it took a very long time, seven years of feeling like I was lost. The Foundation my mother set up is just a pain - a load of rich women who lunch in expensive frocks and too much alcohol sitting around talking about their designer bags and how much their husbands earn.'

'A whole other world to mine then.'

'And one you are well to avoid. Enough about me - let's hear some more about you, you know all about my last ten years, the loss of my wife and no doubt the locals have told you I'm a sad, lonely old widower, so what about you?'

The champagne, the sun, the motion of the waves and his what seemed to be genuine interest meant that she started to tell him much more than she would normally tell anyone. She told him about the marriages, the renovating, and then all of a sudden she found herself talking about the stillbirth. As the words came out of her mouth she heard another voice telling her to stop - she was letting on way too much, there was hardly anyone who knew and here she was telling him the whole story. He put his hand on her leg and squeezed it.

'Oh dear, I'm so sorry, grief is an awful thing, isn't it, and there I was going on about myself. I didn't mean to... bring anything up for you.' Sallie pulled herself up and wished fervently she hadn't mentioned it. Not many people understood a loss like it, why would you? It was very private and no one could ever say anything that would make her feel better. All the sympathy, kind words, bottles of fancy French champagne would never be able to change it. It would always be there, right in the middle of her heart.

She poured another glass of champagne and changed the subject rapidly. They both relaxed when the conversation moved on, he popped another bottle of beer and helped himself to the olives on the little table in between them.

'Will you be coming to the unveiling of my empire then?' She giggled, steering the conversation completely in another direction.

'You won't be able to keep me away.'

At that moment, Sam came up onto the deck with more drinks.

'Thought you would be eating out the back, but by the looks of it up here you're very comfortable, what an absolutely fantastic day.' He looked out and gestured to it all, the sky and the sea seemed almost as one it was all so blue.

'I'll come down and get the lunch in a bit, it's much more enjoyable up here, Sallie's had a hard week and needs to rest her weary legs in the sun.'

Sallie could not have agreed more. It was almost like her back and spine had been frozen in the last year with stress, and the champagne, the sun and sea air had made it defrost. She felt significantly relaxed, more than she had for a very long time, perhaps even years.

Ben Chalmers got up with the muscly legs and came back with lunch, pulled out a built-in table from the side of the boat and started to lay the food out in front of them. Slices of apricot, garlic and herb stuffed chicken sat on a bed of green salad, a white bowl holding a colourful Greek salad stood in the middle with a small round loaf of rustic bread. It was simple, non-pretentious food - her favourite.

She very much needed to get some food down her, before she drank too much - so much for the calm and sophisticated neighbourly image she had been trying to project. Had she actually just heard herself stumble over a few words and laugh ridiculously at one of her own jokes?

They tucked into the lunch chatting about all and sundry, it was amazing how well they got on. Polishing off the chicken and bread, Sallie felt instantly better and nowhere near as tipsy when Sam popped back up.

'I'll get you guys back then before the tides change, it's getting on.'

Sallie looked at her watch, she couldn't believe how quickly the time had gone, no wonder she'd felt a bit tipsy and hungry. They'd been talking and drinking for hours, and the lunch had turned into afternoon tea. Sam manoeuvred the boat and before long they'd arrived back at Pretty Beach, he'd tied it all up, sorted everything out and headed off.

Sallie and Ben moved out of the chairs and sat on the boards of the deck below, backs to the edge of the boat watching the sun go all the way down into the water, a chocolate French flan on the floor between them.

She felt better than she had for a long time. Out here on the boat she was away from the stresses of money, from the worry about getting the business going, and the backlash of the last ten years. Out here, it seemed as if none of that existed. It was as if that Sallie Broadchurch, the one who was on her own and always having to keep on keeping on, was someone else. This Sallie Broadchurch out here was sitting on the deck of a boat, legs out in front of her, eating chocolate flan and luxuriating in an afternoon of doing completely and utterly nothing as if she had not a care in the world. This was a different Sallie Broadchurch altogether.

'Funny how life turns out, isn't it? Here I am with a business plan, an apartment by the sea and sitting on a boat with you.'

Ben was looking at her kindly. 'Yep,' he took another sip of his drink, 'You've turned that place around with hardly a glance back, and you've certainly been a hit with the locals.'

'Ha, Ben, not sure about being a hit - more like monumentally messing things up with my big mouth - the episode with Bruce wasn't one of my finer moments.'

'The first time I saw you in the house in the old clothes and cobwebs sticking out of your hair and you turned down the offer of selling the vintage lights as if I was an idiot, I thought to myself, now this is interesting.'

Sallie didn't really know what to think about that, what was he saying? What she did know was she'd thrown all her ideas of not doing anything with Ben Chalmers and remaining sophisticated swiftly out the window.

She took another sip of her champagne and he casually draped his arm around her shoulders as they looked far out to sea. She sat dead still; there was no way she was moving an inch. She rooted herself to the spot and felt like electric charges were racing through her body where his skin touched hers.

She sat there as still as she could, as if moving would break the spell and felt caught in a strange moment of time where she wasn't forty-year-old battle worn Sallie Broadchurch from the wrong side of town, she was just like any other girl sitting next to someone lovely, looking up into kind eyes and waiting to be kissed.

She put her hand on his leg and ignored the voice in the back of her head expressing all sorts of cautions about this going too far, and turned and raised her head to Ben. And Ben Chalmers leant forward gently and kissed Sallie Broadchurch on the lips. They slipped back onto the deck and melted into each other completely. He wrapped his arms around her, kissing her neck, and the whole thing was out of this world better than Sallie had ever felt before or ever could have imagined.

He pressed hard against her and gently stroked the curve of her waist, they slid further down onto the deck and she lost herself in the strong thick muscles of Ben's back underneath her hands. She opened her eyes wondering at it all; the sea, the boat, this beautiful man and the kiss.

It was all just so overwhelming and so filled with... she did not know what. She'd never felt anything like it before and she wondered if she ever would again.

Sallie Broadchurch knew one thing, she would remember this kiss out on the water, the sun going down, the way her hands felt on his back and the way Ben Chalmers smelled in her arms, for a very long time.

Chapter 47

Sallie sat up in bed and looked in the mirror, remnants of black mascara smudged under her eyes, her hair like a haystack. She wiped under her eyes with some cream, scraped her hair on top of her head, took off her pyjamas and threw them in the laundry bin.

She had a big day ahead of her and hair was the last of her worries, but she knew that brand Pretty Beach Boat House today would start with her - how she acted, how well it all went off and how she portrayed herself to the world was all part of her business plan.

She pushed open the stripped timber bathroom door, turned both the hot and cold to full and stood under the shower for as long as she could. She was just getting her jeans and t-shirt on when she heard a car pull onto the gravel down below, she walked over and looked out the window. David was standing at the barn doors downstairs. He'd offered to come along in the morning to give her a hand to set things up. She ran down the stairs, unlocked the door at the bottom, walked over the Boat House floor and opened the barn doors.

'Hi, wow, you're early.'

'I was just at Holly's and thought you might like these before you got going for the day,' he held his hand up and gestured to a bag of chocolate croissants.' He kissed her on the cheek, he smelt lovely, homely and fresh.

'All ready for it then?'

'Yep, I've just had a shower and put some coffee on. I'll come back later on, have another shower and get changed for the lunch. All I have to do today is get the rest of the food sorted and style the outside - all the stuff that can't be done until the last minute.'

He looked over at the boathouse cottage, and up at the sky with the sun shining as the lighthouse glinted in the distance. She'd already dragged out two old trestle tables which according to the scrawled writing underneath had belonged to Pretty Beach Public School c.1944, gathered a bunch of mismatched timber chairs and stacked them up against the side of the house.

'Weather looks great for it.' He followed up behind her with the chocolate croissants. They went up to the apartment, she poured out the coffee and they sat with the croissants and a list on a clipboard with a pencil tied to the side with string.

'Gone traditional?' He pointed at the string and board.

'Yeah, couldn't be bothered to keep getting my phone out, with this it's easy to see and I'll know what's what as we go down. I've prioritised the jobs in order - the flowers go on at the very last minute, all the other stuff goes first.'

They finished their coffee and by quarter past eight had put both the trestle tables up and set them down by the water's edge, checked the tide to make sure it was just far enough to come in and out without anyone getting wet and wiped them both down.

They unfolded all the chairs and tucked in ten each side of the trestle tables. David went to get bags of ice and filled up vintage laundry troughs with it, ready for the champagne. This was definitely not a Prosecco moment - the champagne order had annihilated the budget in one swift movement, but she'd swallowed it.

She'd arranged for all the drinks to be delivered just a couple of hours before the event, alleviating the problem of keeping it cold and had gone over and over with Jeddo that it would definitely arrive and definitely arrive on time. In the end, he'd taken her out the back to the cold room and showed her the order, which had arrived in Pretty Beach the weekend before. All they had to do was drive it down the lane, bring it in, open all the cases and plonk the bottles into the troughs.

Ben, Ollie and Lochie arrived at about 10am. Ben had made a beeline for her, kissed her tenderly on the cheek and put his arm around her waist, calling her beautiful. Every single feeling from the boat came back to her. Just looking at him made her heart swell. She felt the blood rush to her head and quickly scooted off, not wanting to linger on what that meant and made herself busy.

Ollie and Lochie dragged two of the old rowing boats over to the side of the house, stood them up on their ends and fixed them to the side. Two others sat either side of the trestle tables filled with plants and flowers and party lights and white bunting was strung between them.

Ben had flown down his vintage seaplane and parked it just outside the jetty setting the Pretty Beach dreamy lifestyle scene perfectly and an old cruiser bike was propped up against the fence filled with flowers.

Once most things were ticked off the list they all walked back past the Boat House and stood by the laneway looking back down at the whole scene.

Sallie took a deep breath and breathed out, weary and nervous. Standing back looking at it all now though, she couldn't believe how far she'd come When she'd walked up to the place months ago, she'd been scared of snakes in the grass, the roof had looked about ready to cave in, the old boats were piled up like a junkyard and at that point the boathouse cottage down by the seashore couldn't even be seen.

Now it had all been painted a rustic white, the old tin roof and been cleaned up and repaired, a gravel clearing led to its own parking spot, and a stepping stone path ran all the way to the door. A little verandah outside the front porch was set with a French cafe table and chairs and to the left two Adirondack chairs were perfectly placed looking out to sea.

Ollie, lovely funny, talkative, Ollie turned to her, and put his hand up for a high five.

'You, my lovely Sallie, have done an awesome job here.' He spoke as if he was a wise old man.

'Thanks to your help.'

'All we did was the manual work, you had the vision to make this place amazing.' Ben, Lochie and David all looked at Ollie and agreed.

'Mate, I'm going to get some beers, we need to drink to that.' Ben raised up his hand to Ollie.

Just as Ben jogged off next door they heard someone calling out and looked around. Holly wearing wedge flip flops, sleek hair and diamonds sparkling from her ears, throat and wrists and a waft of expensive perfume came walking up the drive laden down on each side with huge brown paper flour sacks, her mum Xian trotting along beside her with four white cake boxes.

'Sallie, your bakery delivery has arrived by moi, Pretty Beach delivery driver extraordinaire.' She thought the whole thing was hilarious, and Xian was chuckling along to herself too. They both stopped in their tracks as they got onto the pebbles and looked down at the old boathouse.

'Oh, my goodness, it looks brilliant!' Holly exclaimed.

Holly dropped both of the sacks down onto the floor and started clapping her hands in excitement. David, Lochie and Ollie looked at the two women as if they were mad and Xian started jumping up and down.

'So good, so good!'

'Glad to see that you like it then,' said Sallie laughing. Lochie picked up the bags and walked them down to the boathouse cottage, Xian following him with the cake boxes.

***

The menu for lunch had been kept as simple as possible, with the addition of lots of champagne - a simple starter of Holly's best sourdough, large bowls of olives and Sallie's special chicken pate. Followed by sides of salmon with French potato salad and a green salad.

Afterwards, were Holly's fruit tarts and a selection of dark chocolates and coffee if anyone got that far. It was very easy and required little work as most of the preparation had already been done. All they needed to do was bring it out on platters and put it on the table. Sallie had worked for ages on a menu that could be prepared in advance, complimented the setting and the weather and was easy enough to serve without any fuss.

Artisan Sourdough with Sallie's Handmade Pate
Pretty Beach Olives
Herb Roasted Rosemary Salmon
French Garlic Potato Salad
Green Vinaigrette Salad
A selection of Fruit Tarts
Dark Handmade Chocolates and Coffee

Ben came back with a case of cold beer, handed them out and they took a breather sitting down on the fence by the sea. Holly, Ben, Lochie, Ollie, David and Xian sat there with the beer, Xian was sitting next to Sallie, she nudged her.

'Ben, I told you to remember, Ben's the one.' Sallie shushed her, they all finished the beers and sat there looking around at it all. It was the last time she would be sitting down until it was all over in a few hours' time.

She walked over and picked up the checklist clipboard from the table. The tables were up and in place, the vintage ladders were strung with dried herbs and huge heads of hydrangea. The old rowing boats were in place and secure, the oars attached above the front door of the boathouse, and the chairs were all tied at the back with linen bows. The champagne had arrived and was chilling further, and Holly's girls had sliced up the bread so it was ready to go.

She worked her way through and ticked all the way down the list. All they had to do now was clean up, get changed, instruct the photographer and wait for the guests to arrive.

Chapter 48

Sallie walked back to the Boat House feeling really proud and even more lucky. She couldn't believe how nice these strange beings of Pretty Beach were, how they had all only known her for a while and were more than willing to help. Apparently, this Pretty Beach 'way' they all talked about was real.

She ran up the stairs with twenty minutes to shower, wash her hair and put on something nice. After much prior browsing through Pinterest she'd decided on a navy-blue linen shirt dress pulled in with a huge tan belt, plaited sandals and a stack of bangles - simple and easy. She wasn't keen on dresses, she spent her life in her uniform of jeans and a shirt, but this was an occasion that called for a dress.

To a playlist titled easy, beach jazz tunes quietly playing from the speaker in the old boathouse, Sallie happily greeted the twenty carefully selected guests for the Pretty Beach Boat House lunch - a local from the newspaper, the family Instagrammers and their little baby, beautiful Nina, Holly and Xian. Then there was Janelle, the two famous women in trendy jeans and Chanel jackets who had millions of followers on social media, and a few other guests from Pretty Beach.

Lochie, Ollie and Lochie's sister Sophie had been paid as waiters and were walking around in white polo shirts and black jeans topping up people's glasses of champagne.

A white ribbon tied to a bottle of champagne had been hung on one of the old rowing boats leaning up against the side of it ready to smash as they officially named the place 'The Boat House Pretty Beach.'

The small gathering of twenty stood on the patio, glasses clinking, a perfect afternoon, the sun sinking in the sky throwing shadows over the whole scene.

Sallie had instructed her photographer and videographer exactly what cuts she wanted and where. Scenes of the house, the boats, the lights strung across the top, the champagne, the Adirondack chairs looking out to sea, the views of the seaplane, and a long line down through the centre of the trestle tables. She'd told them to avoid any of the cliches - no scary overhead shots onto the table of headless people in faded brown clothes, no overly angled shots. She wanted the delicate balance of it all looking lovely but still attainable. She wanted the marketing pitched just right.

As they all stood around chatting, Ben Chalmers, clanked on the side of his glass. Everyone went quiet, and he gave a little story about how he'd had the pleasure of living and working in Pretty Beach for ten years and had slowly watched the old Boat House fade away and now the lovely Sallie had, with a lot of hard work, brought the whole place back to life.

He'd introduced her, and she replied with how lucky she felt to have been included in the community of Pretty Beach and how all the locals had been lovely to her (omitting her verbal abomination of old Bruce) and that she was looking forward to making it very much her home.

'I want to make this place part of Pretty Beach again,' and gesturing round with her hand taking in the house, old shed, the jetty and the floating wreck way out in the water she carried on, 'and hopefully contribute to the Pretty Beach economy.'

Ben handed her the bottle hanging on the white ribbon and she crashed it onto the boat.

'Welcome to The Boat House Pretty Beach.'

Everyone cheered, toasted and naturally started to move over to the tables where Ollie and Sophie had set up huge glass pitchers of iced lemon water, the sourdough bread and the large slabs of Sallie's homemade pate.

The rest of the afternoon flew by in a flurry of food, drinks and laughter. Everything had gone swimmingly well and slowly as the sun went down the first few guests sloped away.

Sallie looked at it all and heaved a huge sigh of relief. She was so very glad it was all over.

Chapter 49

It was two hours since the last of the guests had gone home. Everything had gone to plan; all the guests were tipsy and it had stayed nice and warm all afternoon. The pictures she'd seen already were amazing and the little bits and pieces she'd put up on Instagram had received hundreds of likes. She'd even seen she had some enquiries already.

After the last guest had gone, she'd made one last push to clear up, hating that feeling when you woke up in the morning to a huge mess. Once everything was tidy, she popped the vases of flowers back into the boathouse cottage, folded up the last of the chairs, pulled off the linen tablecloths and turned off the lamps and little fairy lights.

Ben had gone back over to his place to Facetime with his mum who had just come out of hospital, Holly and Xian had walked back home a little worse for wear, the Instagram fashion women had been the last to leave and had already gushed about the place all over their feeds. Lovely David had stayed until near the end clearing up and then rushed off to babysit.

Nel had helped her with the last few bits before she left, kissed Sallie goodbye, had taken off her shoes to walk home along the beach and sent Sallie a text on the way home.

Thank you so much for inviting me, I've had the loveliest afternoon for a long time. The food was delicious. Nel xx

By the end of it all though, Sallie had been on her feet for twelve hours and was exhausted from socialising and making small talk which to her was like pulling out teeth.

She walked back into the Boat House and up the stairs and suddenly realised she was starving; all the chatting and making sure everything went well meant she'd hardly sipped a glass of champagne or touched her salmon. The last thing she could remember properly eating was the croissant from David, and that had been twelve hours earlier.

She walked into the bathroom, let the dress slip to the floor, took off her knickers and bra, rubbed cream cleanser all over her face, tied her hair up, turned on the shower and got in. She scrubbed all the makeup off, black and brown covered the face cloth, pumped her favourite black pepper shower cream and lathered up her whole body. She felt like she could sit down right there on the bottom of the bath and let the water flow over her for hours, but if she did she wouldn't get up again.

She turned the taps off, wrapped herself in a huge white towel, walked into her bedroom and pulled out a pair of her softest oldest pyjamas. There wasn't anything quite like that hair up, bra off and soft pyjama feeling she thought.

Padding over to the kitchen, she opened the fridge, and was just considering what leftovers she could pop in the microwave and pouring herself a glass of champagne when her phone started ringing. Ben Chalmers - he was outside, with a take-away from Pretty Beach Thai restaurant and a bottle of wine.

'My saviour, how did you know? I'm starving!'

She buzzed the app on her phone to open the door and he emerged from the stairs, showered, in soft grey tracksuit pants and a dark blue Ralph Lauren hoody. He told her to go and sit down, pulled the Thai out of the bag, put all the little pots of it straight onto a tray and then onto the coffee table and they sat on the sofa, chatting about the afternoon and how well it had gone.

'You were amazing, and didn't the group just click beautifully? Nel worked that crowd and your friend Nina the barrister, she's a hoot. Where did you find her?'

'Yep they did, she's hilarious, she's been such a good friend to me - I lived upstairs and next door to her, basically in a cupboard and we hit it off from day one.' They chatted more about it all.

'Now I just need to see if I can actually make some money out of all this.' Sallie sighed wistfully.

He held his glass up and clinked hers.

'I know you can, I really don't know how this can fail.'

Sallie downed the wine very quickly and it went straight to her head. She went over to the fridge, poured another one and plonked herself back down on the sofa. Ben was scrolling through his phone looking at The Boat House Pretty Beach on social media.

'You've already got a few questions on here about bookings and where it is, yadda yadda. What will you be doing with all this success and money that's going to be flooding in?'

'Getting a cleaner, a massage every day, taking a few days off and then repeating it all again with the cafe.' She said wryly.

'Who knows, you could be running a hospitality empire - this place is a license to print money. I've never looked back since I've been here, and who would have thought I'd be sitting in the old Boat House looking out on the water, on a white sofa, with a very beautiful new lady in my life.'

Sallie nearly stopped breathing at that. Sitting with her feet tucked up under her, face devoid of makeup and not feeling anywhere near beautiful, she didn't know what to say back so studiously decided to ignore it. What had happened on the boat had not been mentioned - was he saying that this was now a thing? She thought about it for a moment.

'Well you're definitely not wrong there - a few months ago I was stuck in a dead-end job working for a loser, and all along I could've been up here making a go of this place.'

'And now you live next door to me.' He said as he got up and walked over to the sofa, she felt so deliriously tired and happy she could hardly move. He reached over, put his hand on her leg, turned to her and kissed her softly. She kissed him back intensely and he pulled her closer against him.

Ben then picked her up, as she kissed his neck, and she wrapped her arms and legs around him. He carried her through to the bedroom, placed her in the middle of the bed and slowly began to take off the faded pink pyjamas. His hands slid underneath the top, caressing her soft skin, and the beautiful curve of her breasts. She felt his whole body pressing into her and she sunk into him as his movements got more insistent and she lost herself in the wonderful thing that was Ben Chalmers.

Chapter 50

Sallie Broadchurch woke up and for a second had forgotten everything. She'd slept like a log and had momentarily forgotten the afternoon lunch, how it all went, the long day, what she'd had for dinner and how it had all turned out... and then she remembered the end. She remembered the very end bit very well.

Ben Chalmers had picked her up and carried her to bed, and then it all came back to her. It was wonderful and delicious and at the time, she couldn't quite believe it was happening, that he would even glance in her direction, let alone romance her and take her to bed. Whatever she had felt on the boat had become a million times better.

She rolled over, the covers were pulled back and his clothes were gone - he must have left early morning. His blue jumper was left hanging on the chair. She clambered out of bed, picked it up and took a deep breath. It smelled of him, of his aftershave, his body and of last night. She pulled it on over her head and inhaled the scent of Ben Chalmers and pinched her leg as she looked out over Pretty Beach to wonder if this was all real, or whether she was caught up in some stupid middle-aged dream.

She must keep herself in check though, Ben Chalmers was no different to any other man; he liked sex and that was probably all it was to him. Despite the fact that his wife had died and Holly had told him there hadn't been anyone except for one skinny, tanned, model-like creature who drove a convertible Saab, men loved no complications sex. She cringed. Oh no, had she offered herself on a plate to him? Silly little Sallie next door, overwhelmed by the millionaire pilot.

He was hardly proposing marriage - she must keep this real. This was just a little bit of fun since he had finally awakened from the years of grief... a little bit fun he could have with no strings attached.

The thing was, Sallie didn't do casual sex. She'd only ever had sex with her two ex-husbands and only ever had relations of any sort with a few other men, so the no strings thing felt alien. Actually, as she thought about it more, maybe it was a good thing, she certainly didn't want any strings and had been attached twice before and look how that had ended up.

She sat on the end of the bed and thought about how the whole day had gone. Funny Xian nudging her while they'd been sitting there in the morning, and chuckling and telling her that he was the one and to keep hold of him. Maybe there had been something in it after all? She shook her head, what was she thinking? She was turning completely mad in her old age.

And how the night had ended up, she hadn't seen that coming, not at all! But my God she had enjoyed it. It was the first time ever she had felt things like that - it was like a door had opened up to a whole new world. Whatever had happened to Ben Chalmers since his wife had died worked for her.

As she sat there staring out to sea, it reminded her that Nina had told her to call her in the morning - David had dropped her at the station to catch the train home just after they had finished cleaning up.

She clicked on Nina Campbell, and it started to ring.

'Hey! It was great, everything went perfectly, have you seen the pics all over social media already this morning?' Sallie hadn't even looked at Instagram - she'd been thinking more about Ben and them ending up in bed.

'I haven't even looked yet,' Sallie said, a far away, dreamy tone to her voice.

'You sound odd, what've you done?'

'What do you mean what have I done?'

'Sallie, I know you, I can hear it in your voice - what happened last night after I left?'

'How do you know me so well?' She laughed back.

'Well, it can't be David, because he dropped me off at the station to go and babysit, unless he came back later, that is. I know, Seaplane Chalmers!' Nina exclaimed.

'I'm saying nothing Nina, except it was better than my first Honeymoon, actually either Honeymoon, not just the Honeymoon night, the whole thing, in fact... ever!'

'Ahhhhhhhhhhhhhh!'

Ben's name flashed up on the top of Sallie's phone as a text arrived.

Sallie, sorry I had to get up for a plane booking. I don't know what to say, apart from I hope that was ok, see you tomorrow. BC

She didn't know what to reply, was she blase, did she pretend it wasn't good for her? Good for her? It was like an out of body experience! What did she reply? Did she say it was the most fantastic night of her life, ever? Was it okay? It was more than okay!

What did one do when one was literally swept off their feet by a very good looking, multi-millionaire who lived next door, who also just so happened to be a pilot?

Where was the rulebook on this?

Chapter 51

Sallie balanced the Le Creuset Dutch oven full of dahl against her chest and walked across the pebbles all the way down to the water behind the Boat House. She dragged the fire pit in between two Adirondack chairs, rolled up some newspaper and kindling and lit the fire. A beautiful night for a meal outside.

She set the dahl on the table, walked back up to get some glasses and drinks, grabbed a few lanterns and strolled back down barefoot with a bottle of wine and some chocolate.

Ben walked down the seaplane jetty, hopped off the end and ambled over along the beach, looking out over the water. He walked up to her, put his arms around her waist, pulled her to him gently and kissed her sweetly on the lips.

'How lucky are we? Look at this place. I love it when the weather warms up.'

'I was just thinking that. You couldn't make it up really - the water, the lighthouse, the weather...' She went to tentatively say 'us' and then decided to keep that thought to herself.

He sat down in the other Adirondack chair, slipped off his boat shoes and she poured him a glass of wine. They sat there eating the dahl, not saying much, and he tipped her glass with his.

'Here's to beautiful Pretty Beach and more, err, nights like the one after the Boat House lunch, Sallie, that was amazing.' He looked over at her, legs tucked up underneath, enjoying the dahl and looking out over the sea, lost in thought. She blushed and didn't say anything back.

'I nearly forgot! We need to check the Newport Reef Police Facebook page - according to Ollie, they have the scoop on the Marina Club, I can't believe I nearly forgot to tell you. Apparently it was nothing to do with old Pete as some were led to believe, but a nephew of Brucie was in on it all! He'd been up here a few months ago, saw the place was ripe for the taking and tipped off a gang. They were the ones who tied up Bruce and took off with everything.'

Sallie put another marshmallow onto the end of a stick and placed it into the fire, shook her head and let out a long sigh, 'Well, there we go.'

She was so pleased now she had kept it to herself about Pete. So, he wasn't a bad egg after all. Thank goodness it had turned out to be someone else.

'I bet Ollie's Dad will be sad it's all over, it's the most I've ever seen him in the police car in the ten years I've lived here.' Ben smiled and raised his eyebrows.

'Yep, I think that was enough crime for one decade in Pretty Beach.'

Chapter 52

If you had told Sallie Broadchurch a year earlier that she would be standing in a tiny little white church in Pretty Beach watching two of her new friends getting married she would have told you were absolutely bonkers.

But here she was, right up the front of the church, standing beside David looking very dapper in a blue suit, brown brogues and a pretty corsage. Holly on the other side of her in a hat which was nearly as wide as she was tall and Xian in a frothy pale pink cloud dress which was so full she could barely see over the top of it.

The white pitched roof went all the way to the floor of the tiny church tucked up in the hills behind Pretty Beach, bordering Gypsy Bay. Simple carved pews filled the inside, eight arched windows lined the walls and the whole place was decorated by White Cottage Flowers with a profusion of pink country-style blooms. It was doubtful if it could hold 100 people Sallie thought as she looked around.

The two brides were stunning, Jessica's girls standing behind them head to toe in white tulle, their hair curled and piled up on their heads and braided with dreamy white flowers and both carrying small posies.

'They all look so lovely and so happy.' Sallie whispered to David.

'I know, I'm so stoked for all of them, let's hope this is the last of all the people who have given them so much stick over the last few years.' David sighed, lowering his voice so she could only just hear.

Sallie nodded, she wasn't surprised at some of the stories she'd heard. She had to admit, she could see how Jessica's choice of new partner would have been hard for some of Pretty Beach to embrace - ditching her husband and taking up with a woman fifteen years older than her had caused quite the stir in the small community.

Sallie had never seen two people who seemed to genuinely love the bones of one another more than these two though. It made her

sad for the sham that was both her marriages, she had really never felt
the way these two looked at each other about anyone up until now.

The celebrant went through the formalities and she seemed to
drift off into a world of her own as it all went on in front of her. She
thought back to both her weddings. The first one, she had been super young and super stupid, her dress had been a slim, strapless cream
dress with a beautiful mass of fabric at the bottom, a long veil and a
tiny bunch of white flowers. The second affair had been a quickie in a
registry office. She'd bought a pale, oyster pink, slim fitting silky dress
and eight years later he'd kicked her out and she had been scrambling
around in rented accommodation ever since. That all seemed like a
lifetime ago now.

They all filed out of the church to gorgeous music, the brides and
bridesmaids laughing and giggling and as they opened out onto the
grass outside, the guests showered the four of them with dried rose
petals and Jessica threw up her bouquet.

A few photographs were taken on the top of the hill overlooking
Pretty Beach and Sallie sighed at the beauty of it all. She stood next
to David, who was clearly thinking about his wife and his failed marriage and took his hand and gave it a squeeze.

'I think we both need a good drink.' She said to him quietly.

Sallie and David chatted as they trailed down the hill after the
wedding party to the reception in the old timber Scout Hall. Pale
pink flowers adorned the arched front door, ribbons and bunting
were strung throughout and the double doors at the end opened out
to the bay of Pretty Beach.

Ten round tables were dressed in white tablecloths, pink flowers
and chairs with white covers and pink ribbons were tucked in underneath. On a table at the back stood a five-tiered wedding cake tum-
bled with pink flowers and raspberries. Jessica and her new wife and
two daughters sat at a smaller table at the front, all four of them looking as if they were in a dream.

Sallie and David, Holly, Nel, Xian and Rory toasted the happy couple and the drinks started to flow. Rory told them stories about his medical days as a student and had them in stitches with tales of using an orange to practice shots. How the first time he'd done an examination he'd not a clue what he was doing and had been praying and counting to ten in his head until it was all over.

David had them roaring with laughter about some of the idiots he had to suck up to at the insurance company, where their biggest worries were whether or not to buy a new yacht and where they would go next on holiday.

Jessica and Camilla floated around from table to table as the food was served and the champagne flowed and before they knew it the time had come for the happy couple to leave for their honeymoon in Fiji. They toasted the couple, everyone cheered and saw the radiant pair off.

Holly, Xian and Rory hopped in the back of their neighbour's car to go back to the other side of Pretty Beach. Sallie picked up her hat and bag and started to gather all her bits to go home - she'd had a lovely day, one of the best in years. It was so nice to be a guest for once, not to be either serving somebody else or organising someone else's fun.

***

Sallie and David walked along the beach with their shoes in their hands. She was carrying her hat under her arm, nicely tipsy and a bit wobbly on the sand, until eventually David took her elbow and steered her along.

'Lalala.' She hummed to herself.

'I feel like I'm in a magical, wobbly, pink tulle dream David. A lovely new town, some gorgeous friends and for the first time in twenty years I'm not super worried about money.' She chuckled as she told him how much she loved it all.

Just as they were approaching the Boat House and David was thinking he would soon get her home, she stopped at the jetty and decided it was a beautiful night to stargaze.

'Let's lie down and gaze. I used to do this as a little girl, looking up at the stars is free and amazing. You can see all sorts up there. You can see God.' She laughed at her own joke. 'Hahahahahah. Yep God is looking down at you David.'

He tried to stop her laughing and said that he really thought he should get her home. Just as he said that she dropped to the floor, laid flat on her back on the timber of the jetty and looked skywards laughing again and pointing up.

'Look David, look at it all, so pretty, so twinkly, so sparkly up there.' He looked at her flat on her back laughing up at the sky and laid down beside her and looked up.

'I've never done this before, it's amazing!' He said looking up at the stars.

She pointed to all the different patterns and started to explain to him all that she knew about stars. A shooting star went past and they looked at shapes on the moon.

'Sallie Broadchurch, I can't believe I am lying flat on my back, in the dead of night, in the middle of the jetty, looking at stars. You're absolutely nuts.'

They laid there for a long time, chatting more, laughing more, she was enjoying herself so much.

'Come on, it's getting chilly, let's get you home,' he took her hand and pulled her up from the ground. They walked along the rest of the laneway and approached the old Boat House which was lit up with an array of lights, automatically programmed to come on as it got dark.

High-powered uplighters placed at their base lit up the old trees and fairy lights went all the way round the boathouse. From the laneway of Pretty Beach the whole scene sparkled. The image of it all reflected in the water as they approached was dazzling.

They got to the door, David said he would take her all the way up as he didn't trust her stumbling and falling down the stairs. Laughing they clambered up the stairs to the top and she walked over and started to close the blinds.

'I'll get going now then Sallie, now we've finally got you home safely.'

She looked up at him and before she knew it they were kissing, a long passionate kiss. Just as he was about to take her into the bedroom, she pulled away.

'Sorry David, this is not a good idea, we are both tipsy and... well we said this wasn't going to happen again, and well, things have changed.' She was about to mention Ben and then didn't.

'Yeah, yeah, sorry okay, what's changed though?'

'Let's leave it, David.'

He picked up his suit jacket. She followed him to the top of the stairs, heard him go out the barn doors at the front and listened for the notification on her phone to confirm it was locked.

Where had that come from? She was so very angry with herself, she was dating Ben, what was she doing?

Chapter 53

David sipped his coffee while scrolling through the pics of the Boat House Pretty Beach on the website. You had to give it to Sallie - it was gorgeous. He must have been past the place a million times thinking it was lovely but how she'd styled it took it to a whole new level... The pictures were magical and what she'd created was wonderful.

He was really proud of her, he knew how hard she had worked and that the whole thing had come from nothing really. What was more impressive was that she had done it all on a budget - a simple website which looked great, the pictures were unbelievable and she'd created an impressive social media strategy.

He sat there looking through the pictures and thinking about it all - he still hadn't found out though what was wrong with her - she had definitely been edgy the last few times he'd seen her. Even at the wedding and the night of the second kiss, she seemed almost preoccupied. It was all very strange because he had thought that she liked him.

Normally, not that he was being big headed, it wasn't exactly hard for him to get a woman. Since his wife had run off with the carpet cleaner, various women at work had been interested, he'd had a bit of a thing with one of the girls at the Yacht Club in Newport Reef and Nel had offered him a night of pleasure, just as she put it 'for the hell of it'. But Sallie wasn't quite as straight-forward.

He sat there musing the whole thing - what was it about this Sallie Broadchurch anyway? There was something about her that made him interested.

He knew what he would do. It was Sallie's birthday coming up and all of them, Jessica, Camilla, Holly and him had decided they would do her a birthday meal at Jessica's place so Jess didn't have to worry about a babysitter. It would get Sallie away and she could relax and have a good time. He would maybe try to talk to her about it then. Perhaps ask her out for dinner.

He picked up the phone to talk to Jessica about it, if she would like him to cook, to arrange a cake and to get some flowers in. Jessica listened to him discussing it all, and had gone very quiet.

'Oh my God David, you like her, don't you?'

Chapter 54

Time seemed to be flying by; the website was up and running and getting lots of hits and Sallie had taken her first six bookings. The two weeks over Christmas were rented out for an extortionate rate which had taken her by surprise. She'd decided to put it up at a thousand a night, just to see what happened intending to lower the price soon after. Everyone had told her that Pretty Beach sold out for most of the high season, even if you had a Seventies apartment with old shabby sofas and a falling down roof, so she'd decided to give it a go.

She'd put the price on, answered a few enquiries and Instagram comments and gone to bed. The next day she'd had a direct message from a young couple in the US who were coming on a trip of a lifetime. They wanted a high-end, magical, secluded base on the beach but with access by public transport to the City and enough things to do in the evening.

She'd replied all about the details of the beach, some further images of the boathouse and they'd immediately booked. She had a deposit in the bank by the end of the day. The booked income she now had was the same amount as she had been paid in months working her dead-end jobs. She was ecstatic to say the least and couldn't quite believe it.

The other unexpected side was the social media accounts, they had skyrocketed. She'd quickly amassed thousands and thousands of followers and messages and questions from all over the world. The only problem so far was that many people wanted more than a place that slept two and there were lots of enquiries about weddings. Maybe that was the next thing.

***

Sallie had started seeing Ben more and more. After the night when he'd carried her to bed their 'relationship' though she hesitated to call it that, had moved on further.

Was he now considered her boyfriend? Did people even still call it that? They did loads together, and it was as if they were an item. He seemed very casual still though and there was no way she was mentioning it.

Did she want it to go any further at this time? They had nice coffees, walks up to the lighthouse, enjoyed breakfasts, gorgeous meals in Newport Reef, they had been out on his boat and she'd been into the City on one of the planes. She'd even been up to London for lunch and met his family.

It was all topped off with lovely, easy sex, and lots of it too. Really, she had thought to herself, why would she bother with trying to put it in a box and give it a label? She would relax and keep it just as it was.

Chapter 55

Sallie woke up, turned over and looked over at the sun peeking through the windows, a patch of it warming the floor. The floor of her very own apartment, overlooking the sea in Pretty Beach, the place she owned, and would give her quite the nice little income. She curled up under the covers - what a lovely feeling to have.

If only she had taken up the offer of the place earlier. With the internet changing the way people worked and one high-speed train, a back-end town like Pretty Beach had turned into the amazing place it was to live and work in today.

And the new friendships, potential new income and then dare she say it, the new romance in her life... unbelievable. She had certainly not been looking for a man when she had arrived, in fact she had taken the decision that she would be alone for the rest of her life and look how that was turning out.

She got up and walked across the wide plank floorboards to the kitchen, put the kettle on, threw a few teabags into the pot, made a cup of tea, warmed up a slice of brioche, put the whole lot on a tray and went and got back into bed. She sat there propped up against the pillows with the tea scrolling through her phone, a lovely day off ahead of her and after a few days of lashing down rain, now a change in the weather.

If you ignored falling into bed with him at any opportunity, waxed and primped to the nines, with gorgeous new underwear and tipsy from the best champagne, she had really tried to play it cool with Ben Chalmers. She'd let him do all the romancing, all the asking, all the texting and all the initiating. She wasn't going to get caught out again liking someone too much, ever. But he hadn't put a foot wrong. Charming, witty and appeared to genuinely like her and they just seemed to click even though they came from completely different backgrounds and completely different ends of the spectrum.

Since the kiss on the boat and the night after the lunch, he'd popped over to the Boat House often, she had been over to his place for a candlelit dinner, they'd gone out for breakfast, walked on the beach, had sex under the stars - it was casual and easy and she liked him very much.

She sat in bed thinking about it. Yes, he had done all of the running, and now it was her turn - she now felt comfortable enough to initiate something herself. She would surprise Ben Chalmers with a late brunch picnic. She would wander over to his place and take him on a walk all the way to the lighthouse to sit up there and watch the cruise liners go past on their way out to sea.

She opened up the curtains, pushed open the half glass door to the ensuite, ran herself a bath, washed, dressed, braided a French plait through the front of her hair and tied the whole lot on top of her head. Popped on a quick layer of bb cream, mascara, slick of eyeliner and some blusher. Done. She was, for once, quite happy with what looked back at her in the mirror.

It was quite staggering what had happened to her since the makeover with Holly's ladies - the box dye honey was still there but it had been lifted with slices of different colours, the little wrinkles around her eyes had miraculously softened courtesy of a special botox and filler mix which had been stamped all over her face and the two little dents between her eyes which had begun to give her the permanently cross look had disappeared. She could no longer frown, but who the hell cared about that?

She went downstairs, opened the barn doors and collected the loaf of sourdough from the doorstep and took it back up to the kitchen. Sliced the top off and filled it with layers of salad, salami, roasted red peppers, mozzarella and spinach for an Italian picnic loaf, which wasn't actually that fancy (but looked it). She cleared all the bits off the chopping board, carefully wrapped the loaf in grease-proof paper and secured it together with some butcher's string. Then made up pink elderflower cordial in a vintage glass bottle, took a bottle of wine out of the fridge and put everything in a wicker picnic basket, together with a tartan rug, two wine glasses and a little tub of strawberries.

A crisp oversized white t-shirt, cut off faded jeans and a pair of white tennis shoes, sun hat and sunscreen finished it all off nicely. She'd even been using some moisturiser with tan in it so her skin was plump and glowing.

She was quite pleased with herself; she never did anything impromptu like this. Her confidence in herself and self-esteem over the last few years had barely let her do anything, let alone take a surprise picnic around to a multi-millionaire. The audacity that she now thought enough of herself to turn up announced.

She sprayed her skin with another layer of sunscreen, popped on her hat, put the basket over her arm, shut and locked the Boat House doors behind her and walked down the little pebbly path.

Walking out onto the road and along to the left Pretty Beach was already quite busy, there was a queue at Holly's place and she could see Jessica in the shop getting ready for the day. She waved to Jessica in the distance and a couple of seconds later felt her phone buzzing in the basket.

'Where are you off to looking all done up with a basket over your arm?'

'Off for a picnic.' Sallie smiled and shook her head laughing.

'Picnic for one?'

'Ahhh, well that would be telling!'

'I knew it, hope you have fun, don't do anything I wouldn't do!'

Sallie Broadchurch was even humming. It was a beautiful, windy day in Pretty Beach after all the rain and for the first time in her life, dare she even think it, she was feeling good about herself. Yes, her clothes were budget but she felt secure and hey ho, it was all paid for, all by herself and she wasn't relying on anyone else.

She turned the corner into Ben's place. Two of the planes were on the side bobbing around in the water, his car was parked in the garage with the door up and the little carport to the right had a small black sports car parked in it. Probably one of the pilots. She knew that he had two coming up for the Summer season and that one of them was driving all the way to Pretty Beach. She thought he'd said they were arriving next weekend but she must have got that bit wrong.

The back of Ben Chalmers Seaplanes had been renovated a few years after his wife's death. It was in total contrast to everything Sallie had done at hers. He'd had to keep the outside the same because of the heritage status and keep the colours in keeping, but everything else had been upgraded and modernised. The triple garage had an electric door and stairs taking you up to an open plan area with a huge kitchen with a six-metre-long marble centre island running along the whole of the back of the property. Four sets of black bi-fold doors looked out over the ocean, down towards the workshop and out over the landing strip for the planes.

She'd never been up the back stairs before, she normally got into the house via jumping over the fence at the front and through the workshop but she knew it was shut for the day. She walked up the stairs, smiled to herself, she could smell coffee brewing and hear the radio playing over the sound system. She got to the top of the stairs and turned right; there was Ben shirtless just in shorts, back to her making a coffee at his Italian coffee machine.

She walked in, as bold as brass, he hadn't seen her yet, quietly tiptoed across the tiled floor and made a noise just in time for her to pop the basket down on the counter and him to turn around. She beamed at him.

'Good morning, what are you up to? Fancy a walk up to the lighthouse with a picnic?' Was she imagining it, or did some of the colour drain from his face? He looked a bit unsettled.

He didn't come over to kiss her, which was strange - he normally did the whole two kiss I'm posh thing and since that night after the lunch it had moved on from that and now normally involved a longer kiss too.

'Umm yeah, morning Sallie.' He replied looking awkward.

She suddenly realised that she could hear the shower going... and saw that there were two coffee cups on the side not far from where she had put the basket down.

'Oh sorry, I didn't realise you had one of the pilots here already.' He didn't say anything back.

'No worries we can do it another day, it's only a sandwich and a bottle of wine.' Sallie said trying to sound as if she wasn't bothered.

He nodded, 'OK great, yep look sorry, why don't I pop over later on this afternoon?'

'I won't be here later I'm helping out at Jessica's again as Laura decided she couldn't handle the stress of it any longer.' She rolled her eyes and picked up the basket, turned around and started to walk away.

'Look, I'll leave you to it.' She turned around, he was behind the counter in front of the bank of glass bi-fold doors overlooking the sea. Just as she was crossing she heard the shower stop, the bathroom door open and a voice.

'I can't wait for that coffee, how long are you going to take to get that machine going, as long as it took last night?'

A female voice. A glossy female voice with a very well-bred accent, followed by a skinny, dark haired woman in a towel, who came strolling into the room. Sallie stood there in her tennis shoes and stupid market basket over her arm.

The woman took in the situation, smirked, and paraded like some sort of model from the front of Vogue.

'Hi.' She almost sneered and then the recognition went through her face.

'Yes, right, you must be the one from next door? Yes, makes sense now, yes he told me you were a bit... different.' The skinny woman's eyes swept down to the floor and back again as she looked Sallie up and down, took in the clothes and the basket and the rolled-up picnic blanket.

'Going for a picnic, how lovely...oh and I just love that little, errr, braid in your hair.'

Sallie looked from the woman to Ben, turned and walked away. The blood had run from her face and back up again, her skin prickled with she didn't know what - adrenaline, anger, embarrassment? She felt horrified, stupid, like some idiotic, middle-aged, overgrown teenager in the throes of love.

She got to the stairs, ran down them as fast as she could, taking them two by two and nearly tripping at the bottom kicked his stupid gleaming black car as she went past, bashed her hand against the wing mirror and raced out onto the driveway.

'Asshole, absolute asshole. Idiot, what a complete idiot I am. Why did I do this? Knew it was too good to be true.' She whispered to herself under her breath.

'Sal, Sal, wait, it's not like that, hang on!' Ben called out to her frantically.

She turned around. Ben Chalmers was standing there in nothing but his shorts, muscly legs and now she also realised he had wet hair straight from the shower. Wow, not only had she walked in looking like some stupid little teenager with a crush and a picnic basket over her arm, it now dawned on her that they'd been having sex in the shower.

'It's not like what? Take you a long time to get going does it Ben? I can't believe I trusted you!' She turned around and stalked off.

'Wait!'

'I won't be waiting for you or for any other man for that matter. You can take your seaplanes, your stupid rich friends, your big watch, your ridiculous car and big frigging head and go and ram them sideways up your arse.'

Sallie raced down Ben's drive, jumped over the fence, stalked past the boathouse with hot tears running down her face. That made it even worse - she didn't want to cry over some stupid man.

Chapter 56

Punching the number in the keypad, she opened the door, slammed it behind her and got her phone out of her bag. She tried phoning Nina, but knew it would be highly unlikely that she would pick up at this time, opened the inner door to the apartment and raced up the stairs. She threw the basket on the coffee table, pulled out the wine, ripped off the lid and poured the wine in a glass, all the way to the top.

All sorts of thoughts were racing through her head. A panicked feeling engulfed her, and she lugged down the wine to numb the pain. She tipped the wine glass back and drained it like it was water, poured another one, kicked off her shoes and leant back into the sofa. There was no way she was crying over this prick. This multi-millionaire prick who had obviously thought she was a neighbour with benefits.

How could she have been so stupid? What an absolute fool she had been, swept away by the Pretty Beach air, the film star looks and the fact that he was witty and charming and seemed to fancy the pants off her too.

He obviously hadn't factored in that she would pop over unexpectedly. You had to give it to him and the front of it - they hadn't even tried to hide the car! The rich bitch even had a convertible frigging Saab on his drive.

What were the odds of her turning up with a picnic, with a stupid braid in her hair and walking straight into another woman coming out of his shower wrapped only in a towel?

She didn't know how she had controlled herself, at least she hadn't hurled abuse at the woman or worse thrown the wine or the picnic basket at her, or both.

Why hadn't she seen this coming? Everyone in Pretty Beach had been just as surprised as she was about Ben Chalmers and her. Holly had told her that she'd only ever seen him with one dark haired, model looking woman - this was obviously her!

She'd been so wrapped up in him, maybe she had missed all the signs, maybe he had been seeing this woman too and he thought that Sallie wasn't interested in anything more. Should she have made it more obvious that she was mad about him?

To be fair, she had told him she didn't want a relationship, but that was months ago, before he'd carried her into the bedroom and stayed the night. Before he'd invited her for lovely breakfasts, taken her to dinner and kissed her under the stars. Before he had taken her home and she had spent more than a few blissful nights in his bedroom in his arms.

All the crap about being heartbroken about his wife, blah blah blah, and how sad he had been. Not sad enough to mess around with two women at once though.

She pulled the throw from the back of the sofa, wrapped it round her, hobbled over to the doors, opened them up to the sea, poured herself another glass of wine and sat nursing it in front of her. She sat there going through in her head any of the signs that she had missed that she'd completely barked up the wrong tree when Nina called back.

'Hi, you okay?' As soon as she said that Sallie promptly burst into tears.

'No, I'm not.' She started to sob. Everything over the last year hit her - the awful man she had been working for before, the move up to Pretty Beach, the stress of getting the Boat House up and running, the making of new friends, the crime when she had first arrived.

'I've only just walked in on Ben with another woman in a towel coming out of his shower.'

'What? Are you sure? The lowlife!'

The wine was starting to hit her now too, Nina could hear the alcohol in her voice.

'Right Sallie, you need to get a grip on this or you will be two bottles down and in a right old state. This is not a good combination, you'll get more and more morose and sad and it will not be good.'

'I don't care.' Sallie blubbed into the phone, tears pouring down her face. 'How could I have been so stupid?'

'You will care. Take that wine now and go and put it back in the fridge, or pour it down the sink and go and make yourself a nice cup of tea. I'm driving, I'll be home in twenty minutes. I'll have a quick shower and I'll WhatsApp you. Start running the bath too, you can get in there later and soak it all away.'

Sallie stopped sobbing, she knew Nina was talking sense. She picked up the empty bottle of wine, walked into the kitchen, put the bottle in the bin, put the kettle on and stood back leaning against the counter. As she looked out the window she saw Ben walking across past the boathouse and heading in her direction. She walked over to the table in the turret, leant over, undid the catch and stuck her head out.

'Sallie, I need to talk to you.' He shouted up to her urgently from the drive.

'Get lost, back to your seaplanes and that skinny bitch with the big nose.' Ben shook his head and turned around, she slammed the window so hard she thought the glass might shatter, pulled down the blind, made herself the tea and spooned in two heaped sugars.

She went in and ran the bath, sat on the loo with the cup of tea and WhatsApp started ringing with Nina. She went through the whole story, standing there with the picnic, being made a fool of by some rich woman with a convertible black Saab in nothing but a towel and a big smirk on her face.

'I can't understand it Sallie, I think you should wait, there may be an explanation for all of this, he genuinely seemed to like you and I thought this was going well...'

'Too late, I just shouted out the window for him to get lost. What is there to wait for? How can he explain this?'

Nina sighed. Sallie finished up the call, got in the bath and let Ben Chalmers, the vision of the woman in the towel, and all the alcohol she'd downed in less than an hour slowly soak away.

Chapter 57

Sallie spoke to Nina the next morning.

'So, what are you going to do?' Nina was getting ready for work putting her makeup on. Sallie was in the kitchen drinking her morning tea before heading over to the boathouse to get it ready for its first guests.

'I don't know. I've gone and had sexual relations with my neighbour and then walked in on him with another woman and now I have to see him every day. Thank God I took your advice last night and stopped drinking... it could have ended awfully.'

'Have you had any texts or anything?'

'No, but I did see him go down to the plane quite early. I think the river lunches have started so they are going to be very busy picking up people from now on, which means I'm going to be seeing him walking down the jetty all the time.' Sallie sighed, took a sip of her tea and rested her chin on her hand.

'I'm surprised you haven't said anything.' Nina looked into the phone as she fluffed her cheeks with blusher.

'I can't be bothered. What is there to say? I will just end up looking even more stupid. At the end of the day it wasn't really official between us.'

'True, true. Would be great to get back at him somehow though, wouldn't it? Like rent a hot handsome man to come over and have dinner with you in the garden in his full view.'

'Too much effort, time and money for that! Anyway, so what do I do, keep ignoring him, what if he texts?'

'For now, you act not bothered, as if he's inconsequential to you. Have you told anyone else? Like Holly or anyone?'

'No not anyone. I've not been out. Ahhhh, what's worse the whole of Pretty Beach will know. Silly little Sallie thought the handsome man next door might actually like her.' Sallie propped the phone up on the dressing table and started to make her bed.

'So much for Xian's matchmaking.' She laughed wryly, 'I don't know why I'm so upset - I repeatedly told myself not to let this happen and not to get involved with anyone.'

'It would be great to get some revenge but maybe best to just leave this for now, just keep away from him. Okay, I've got to go, I'll check in with a text later - remember, no irrational acts.'

Sallie went and had a shower, got dressed, and did her hair. She could quite easily have hibernated in bed all day under the duvet with a carton of ice-cream and her favourite movies but she'd promised Jessica to cover at the fish and chip shop while she was away on honeymoon in Fiji.

She made herself a coffee, grabbed the chip shop apron, opened up the door and walked unseen down the side path behind the trees. She didn't want to see anyone, and especially not Ben Chalmers - he was the last person she wanted to lay her eyes on.

Pretty Beach was busy, she'd never seen so many people around, ambling along enjoying the sunshine, coffees in their hands, little children skipping. It was going to be busy this lunchtime by the looks of all of this.

She avoided going past Ben's and turned right down the little lane, quickly past Holly's place and in the back gate of the fish and chip shop. David's big Mercedes was in the parking spot and she remembered that she was in charge today and he was helping out. She'd forgotten that.

'Hey.' He got up and kissed her on the cheek, the smell of him reminded her of the kiss outside the doors.

'How are you?' he looked at her, 'you look awful, what's happened?'

'Oh no nothing, I'm fine.' She wiped the edges of her eyes.

'Have you been crying?'

'Oh no, no, no, just got a fit of sneezes this morning, really weird, hope I'm not allergic to anything up here in the warmer weather.'

He clearly didn't believe her for a second. There was no way now though that she was going to tell him about Ben. It wasn't as if she had lied to him about her and Ben, he knew that she was seeing him now and then, but she had neglected to tell him that the night of the lunch party it had developed further from a coffee and a few dinners. Not that she owed anything to David, it was only a couple of kisses, but she had definitely avoided the truth and it was all just a bit awkward.

She made herself busy getting everything prepped for the lunchtime onslaught and by eleven the customers had already started. It was manically busy, with lines of people out the door; it was clear that the season they had all been telling her about for months had arrived.

She didn't get time to go to the toilet, to catch her breath and certainly didn't have time to think about Ben Chalmers. The next time she came up for air was closing time when she walked down to the end of the shop, brought in the chairs from outside, closed and bolted the door, turned the open sign over to close and pulled the blinds a third of the way down to shade the place from the afternoon sun. David made them both a cup of tea and they sat down in the garden out the back, warming up from the sun in contrast to the hours in the air-conditioned shop. She put her head back and let the sun bask on her face. He could tell she was fed up and tried to cheer her up.

'How about we go out over to Newport Reef tomorrow night? I've got a yacht club meeting in the afternoon, I've booked a water taxi there and back. I've had a crazy few weeks with the merger at work and I've been run ragged trying to do the rota here for the last ten days.'

She was sure he was not wrong about being busy at work. What lovely, humble David had forgotten to mention when they became friends was that his boring old job in insurance was actually CEO of one of the world's biggest insurance companies. He was more interested though in the carpet cleaner who had run off with his wife rather than bragging about his work.

'I don't know David, not sure I'm up for a night out actually, but thanks.'

***

Sallie walked back down her drive to see a white card stuck on the door of the Boat House. The logo on the heavy white paper was embossed with White Cottage Flowers. A little note was attached to the top of it noting that they had left her flowers over in the shade at the back of the out-house area. She had no doubt who the flowers were from, unless she had some secret admirer, or maybe Nina had sent them to cheer her up, she very much doubted that - it wasn't Nina's style. She carefully opened the envelope and pulled out a thick white card with beautiful calligraphic lettering.

Sallie, please just let me talk to you and explain.

She walked behind the Boat House and down to the log stack, a massive bunch of flowers which probably cost more than she'd just been paid for her shift, possibly the whole week's work had been perfectly placed in the cool shade. Pink and white peonies were wrapped in white paper the whole thing enveloped in tissue and tied with a thick, white grosgrain bow.

She grimaced, *even the flowers are high end and not in my world* she thought. This wasn't your bunch of lilies from the supermarket, no wonder that woman had looked down her nose at her like she was some small-town idiot. She felt the anger rise in her again. How could she have been so stupid to think that a man in his league, a man who sent flowers that cost more than her pay packet, would look twice in her direction?

She picked up the flowers, started to walk over to the fence where she was going to deftly throw them over so that they landed in his car port and preferably on his car. But as she looked at them, they were so beautiful and someone had arranged them with so much skill and care that she couldn't bring herself to do it.

She walked back and let herself in, took out two huge old antique enamel jugs, peeled off the wrappings, folded them up and carefully placed them in one of the kitchen cupboards to recycle. She filled up the jugs with water, placed the flowers inside and put them on the coffee table.

Nothing like a bunch of peonies to shove it in your face that the millionaire next door you trusted had turned out to be a knob.

Chapter 58

Sallie stared at the text on her phone from Ben. She'd been completely ignoring any kind of attempts from him to call her, she'd not acknowledged the flowers and she had deliberately kept away from his side of the Boat House so that there was absolutely no chance of bumping into him.

She had ignored texts from him for three days and let three calls ring out. In the old days she would have been playing stupid games, but she wasn't in the slightest bit interested in all that. She'd learnt that if a man treated you badly, or let you down too much, there were no two ways about it, he just wasn't that into you.

She tried to convince herself that she didn't care about Ben Chalmers - there were more important things to worry about. Plus, she had a group of new friends now who were nice to her... and the other night with David, well maybe David was what she wanted.

As she sat down on the sofa in the boathouse cottage whilst getting it ready for the next guests, her phone started ringing again, on impulse, she answered it.

'Ben, what do you want?' She almost barked it out.

'I miss you Sallie, and I really need to talk to you to explain about Pippa.'

Of course she had to be called Pippa, no doubt next in line to the throne or related to the nobility of Europe like his wife had been. That took the wind right out of her sails.

'Ben, I haven't really got much to say to you, how you can explain that I don't know? Look, I'm really busy, I have to arrange everything for guests and I'm helping out at Jessica's while she's away... let's just leave it. It was just soon enough along for it still to be a little dalliance. We can both leave it at that, I'm happy with that. I shouldn't have thought for one minute that you would be interested in me. Seriously, my fault to expect more to be honest.'

She still hadn't let him speak.

'You know what Sallie, if that's the way you want to leave it that's fine, you won't let me explain so I won't. Let me tell you though, it wasn't a little dalliance to me.'

Chapter 59

David Windsor carried on aimlessly scrolling through pictures on Facebook - his ex-wife with the carpet cleaner, his ex-wife pregnant and holding a toddler, his ex-wife beaming into the camera her new man's hands shaped together as a heart over his ex-wife's tummy.

He clicked the search bar and typed in Sallie Broadchurch. What a different Facebook page this was. None of the crappy inspirational quotes and stupid memes. No pictures of what she'd had for dinner. No showing off about the Boat House. Crikey, this woman even had her Facebook page just right - a few pictures of her, looking beautiful, smiling in selfies with Nina and silly snaps of them out on the town. He scrolled through further, more pictures of her - at Christmas, at a restaurant in Freshlea, laughing on the train in a pair of sunglasses.

He poured another neat whisky into the heavy glass and pressed the right arrow on the images to the more recent ones. Lots of happy snaps of him and her at Jessica's wedding, her huge blue eyes looking into the camera, her throwing her head back in laughter, her throwing confetti at the two brides. It had been a wonderful day and he'd loved having her standing at his side, it was the first time since his ex-wife he'd felt even a glimmer of hope that he might ever feel human again. There was a modest but definite stirring and it had given him promise.

He lugged back the whisky, drained the glass and refilled it. He'd made a right mess up of it all with Sallie, and just carried on as if nothing had happened. He'd played the game all wrong.

Ben Chalmers had beaten him to it and let's face it, he wasn't going to be able to compete with the seaplanes, the overall charm of the man and even though he hated to admit it, the fact that from what he knew Ben was all around quite a decent guy who had been through crap of his own.

Why hadn't he chased her more? Why hadn't he asked her out to dinner? Why hadn't he made a play for her? She'd been standing there all tiny, barefoot on the pebbles looking up at him and kissed him and fireworks had gone off in his head. Dammit he hadn't even so much as glanced at anyone since Rianna and then boom, this out of nowhere!

What was he thinking going back the next morning saying to forget it, when he loved every single second of it? It was the first time since Rianna he'd felt anything, who ignored that?

He had wanted to wrap her up, take her home and never let her go. He should have wined her and dined her and given Ben Chalmers a run for his money... and telling her it didn't mean anything? What an absolute idiot.

Chapter 60

Sallie knocked on the door of Jessica's gorgeous beach house, the smell of garlic and cooking hitting her nostrils even before she'd got to the door. Jessica, in a beautiful white cotton maxi dress, came to the door and ushered her in.

'Hello, hello, birthday girl.' She kissed her on both cheeks.

'Come in, Holly, Nel and Xian are on their way. Rory's coming too, hope that's okay with you?'

'Of course, it's your house.'

'Yeah but it's your birthday celebration...' she beckoned Sallie to the kitchen.

'Nina will be here shortly, she's getting a taxi from the station.' Sallie said happily.

'The more the merrier, as long as it's not Ben Chalmers eh?' She raised her eyebrows to Sallie. Sallie hadn't told anyone what had really happened with Ben; the only person she had told the full story to, including the flowers and phone call was Nina. She'd just told Jessica and the others that she'd seen him for a few dates and then he had decided to call it off when he thought it was getting serious and then changed his mind back again but she'd said no.

Jessica wasn't stupid though, none of them were, she could tell that Sallie was upset and even the mere mention of his name made her go quiet.

'You feeling alright about it all now, then?'

Sallie brushed it off and replied, 'Just neighbours, it's as simple as that, I don't even want to talk about it, yes he's said sorry and everything but, well, you know, I just don't want to get into it again, not worth the pain.'

Sallie handed her a bottle of champagne, a bunch of flowers and a plate of shortbread she'd baked.

'Are you sure that's the right thing to do though? He had a tough ride with his wife, maybe you should give him a chance - maybe he just got scared all of a sudden.'

Jessica didn't want to encourage anything with Sallie and Ben, but she had seen them together, and it worked like magic. The way he looked at her was something you didn't see often. She'd also seen her brother and the way he had perked up since Sallie had been around. She would much rather that Sallie started seeing David, but she was trying to be a good friend and they could all see the sparks going off between Sallie and Ben.

'Yeah absolutely, I should never have got into it anyway, why would he like me in the first place? I knew it was too good to be true.' Sallie said, turning her attention to unwrapping the shortbread.

'Ahhh, I don't think he's all bad to be honest. I've never seen him with a woman, ever and I have never heard a bad word spoken about him from anyone in Pretty Beach in the ten years he's been here. The only thing I know is he's helpful and friendly and very handsome and he has brought a lot of economy into the area with his business. So I'm not going to slag him off but yeah they're all bastards.' They laughed together and walked into the back of the house, the doors opening out onto the garden, David sitting under the cabana with a beer chatting to Alex, Jessica's neighbour.

They both jumped up and kissed Sallie on the cheek, David put his arm in the small of her back and directed her to the seat next to him. Holly, Xian, Nel and Nina arrived and they all sat around chatting and then got up to the table to eat.

Sallie looked around the table as she took a sip of her white wine - a lovely roast chicken, green salad, garlic rice and salsa, just right for a casual birthday.

She took it all in and felt really lucky to have these few people around her, it was amazing how quickly they'd become her friends.

Jessica, Camilla, Nel, Rory, Xian, Holly, David and the only friend from her old life who had really bothered to keep in touch, Nina.

They finished the meal, polished off a few bottles of wine and then Jessica came out with a lovely double layered, homemade chocolate cake covered in candles.

'Happy Birthday to lovely Sallie.' They raised a toast, she felt a tear in her eye, she'd never had anyone bring her out a birthday cake covered in candles before and they toasted her with bubbles.

'Sallie, it's all downhill from now!' Jessica laughed. Camilla and Holly looked at each other over Jessica's head knowingly - if only she knew they thought.

Holly pulled out a beautiful turquoise gift bag topped with a large white bow, Sallie opened the bag and box to reveal a fine gold bracelet, adorned every so often with a tiny flat gold heart.

'I love it, how did you all know?' Sallie said, putting the bracelet onto her wrist.

'Caitlin saw you looking at it on your phone in a break at the shop and we decided to go for it. You are definitely not a cheap date!' Holly laughed and David stood up, holding his glass aloft.

'I propose a toast to Sallie Broadchurch, the best new addition to Pretty Beach since the revolutionary high-speed train.'

They all clinked their glasses and for once in her life Sallie felt content and surrounded by love.

'To Sallie Broadchurch.'

The rest of the afternoon flew by with lovely drinks, cake and chatting and a few hours later David walked Sallie and Nina back home to the Boat House, walking along arm in arm. Everything was good, the meal had been amazing and the night was clear, warm and still. She'd even tried to put everything that had happened with Ben at the back of her mind and put it down to bad luck.

'Thanks so much for everything this evening,' Sallie said, 'it's been lovely.'

'You're worth it.'

'I am, hahaha, it's been a great night, just the right amount of everything, food, friends and not too much wine. How about we stop in at the Marina Club for one for the road?'

Nina widened her eyes at David. They weren't drunk but well on the way, laughing and being silly all the way home to the Boat House.

'Think we've all had enough for the night Sallie.'

'Booooorrrrrrinnnnnnng,' Sallie giggled.

They got all the way to the Boat House driveway and as they approached the barn doors sitting there in front of them was a large bouquet and a large white box. David picked up the box, Nina picked up the flowers and they went upstairs, David put the box on the coffee table while Nina got them all a glass of water and they sat down with the box in between them.

Sallie slowly peeled the thick white gift paper off, finding a very small deep red box inside. She opened the lid to find a keyring engraved with:

The Boat House Pretty Beach
established 2020

It was a heavy gold from Cartier, Sallie had certainly never had a gift from anywhere like it. David was standing back quietly. Sallie opened the card, read it, said nothing and put the card back on the table. She felt tears stinging the back of her eyes and jumped up all of a sudden before they could see and headed off to the bathroom.

Dear Sallie, Happy Birthday, you still haven't let me explain and I miss you and the amazing nights you stayed at my place. I miss all that's between us. Please call me, I want to be with you again. Love Ben x

David read the card while she was in the loo, put it back on the table, looked sadly at Nina and was just heading off to go when Sallie came back.

'Where are you going? I was going to get you a nightcap.'

'Yeah, I'll be off Sallie, I think you've got other stuff to sort out.' He gestured to the card.

'Oh, don't be like that, it was nothing, I told you that!'

'You didn't tell me it was as serious as spending nights over - anyway, it's none of my business, but I thought we were more than that, more honest. I've had a few too many drinks to talk about it now. I'll talk to you soon.' He walked off down the stairs. Nina followed him down, locked up and sighed when she got back up.

'That was awkward, I didn't realise you hadn't told him what happened between you and Ben.'

'I didn't see the need to, but now it just looks like I was lying and stringing him along when Ben didn't want me. It just wasn't like that at all.'

'Hmm, a bit of a mess.'

'Well, it's a lesson learned. I knew I should've kept myself to myself. David is lovely and we get on so well, but you know Ben Chalmers, well he did something very good to me Nina.'

'Oh Sal, you don't need to tell me that my friend. I know.'

Chapter 61

Sallie had just finished stripping the beds in the boathouse cottage after another set of guests had stayed. Before they had even left they'd added glowing reviews on the website and hashtagged #theboathouseprettybeach with beautiful pictures of the views out to the ocean, the clinker boats lined up outside and the pretty lights in the evening. They'd put a story on Insta of their walk up to the lighthouse, the fish and chips at Jessica's, stargazing, the bath overlooking the ocean and an evening by the firepit with marshmallows. It was all working out much better than she had hoped.

She walked out of the boathouse with an armful of sheets and saw Holly coming out of the bakers and over the laneway tottering on a pair of wedge sandals, a blue Chanel jacket and a pair of silky pants, looking as if she was off to somewhere nice. It wasn't Tuesday so she wasn't off to the casino. Sallie waved cheerily and Holly waved from the other side of the road and then pointed to a bag she was holding. Holly always made sure to deliver Sallie extra little bits, it was normally a good excuse for them to sit and have a coffee and catch up.

Guests had a delivery of croissants, fresh orange juice and a loaf of sourdough every morning and Holly would normally leave a package on the doorstep of the Boat House for Sallie too. Sallie indicated that she would meet her at the end of the drive, Holly crossed the road and Sallie watched her tottering towards her beaming.

'I have cakes for you, lovely rock cakes, new recipe, only for locals though.' She thought this was funny. The in jokes were all around town and Pretty Beach Locals Only Rock Cakes was one of them, along with the LO special batter in Jessica's fish and chip shop, the LO candle in Watermelon Home the homewares shop, LO curry at Ashiana Curry House and the LO pale ale beer in the Marina Club.

As Holly was crossing the road Ben Chalmers came driving along the lane, indicated to turn left and Sallie's heart banged in her chest, cripes she even liked the look of him driving along in his car. He wound down his window.

'Good Morning to my best neighbours!' He called out jokingly.

You had to give it to him, he had obviously taken all this on the chin and instead of him scooping her off and taking her to bed, he was now going to casually wave to her in the mornings, leaving her pining, love struck and sad. Something happened to her heart just seeing him driving past and whenever she set eyes on him, it was like her whole body got warmer. She banished the thoughts, *what am I a teenager with a crush? Pathetic.*

He pulled onto his drive and Sallie turned her gaze back to Holly trotting along the laneway, watched her hop over the stream, she came up to Sallie breathless and kissed Sallie on the cheek.

Holly was breathing heavily and the colour had gone from her face. She gave Sallie the little bag with the rock cakes and just as Sallie was about to look inside, Holly touched her forehead.

'Oh dear, it's quite hot, I think I need to sit down.' Sallie was alarmed and took the white paper bag and Holly's massive Gucci tote bag and took her by the arm.

'We'll go and sit inside out of the sun and I'll make you a cup of tea.'

They started to walk towards the house and suddenly Holly went wobbly.

'I think I'm going to faint!'

The next thing Sallie knew, Holly was lying on the floor and Ben Chalmers, who'd been on the phone finishing up a business call had sprinted across from his yard via the muscly legs, leapt the fence and came running over to them. Holly was lying on the gravel and pebbles. Her breathing was laboured and sweat was pouring off her forehead.

'We need to call an ambulance,' Sallie said as she clutched Holly's arm.

'You're joking, the traffic on the road in is backed up for the weekend, I've just been sitting there for nearly forty minutes, it's bad enough on a normal day for the ambulance to get here quickly...'

Holly lay motionless and they both knew the quickest way to Newport Reef and the hospital was on the water. Ben was already phoning Louisa from Pretty Beach Water Taxis.

'Yeah flat out on the floor... no I think it will be ages, there's a long queue in already and not much better on the other side. I know it's best not to move her but she's not looking in a good way.'

There was a pause while Ben waited for the answer and Sallie stroked Holly's hand.

'OK, yeah, cheers.' He turned to Sallie, 'She'll be here in two minutes.'

Precisely ninety seconds later Louisa pulled up on the old jetty down the side of the Boat House and they gently lifted Holly into the water taxi and laid her down on the side.

Ben jumped in and untied the ropes and Sallie pulled out an umbrella from underneath and held it over Holly to keep off the sun. She'd come round a bit now, had raised her head up and taken a sip of water.

Ben Chalmers phoned ahead to Newport Reef where the paramedics were waiting on the public wharf. They skimmed over the water, Louisa had done this trip a million times and negotiated every wave with ease.

They could see Newport Reef wharf in the distance, the ambulance was already there and it wouldn't be long before she was in their capable hands. Holly had fallen back onto the seats, her hands were limp and her head was railing around.

'We should call her Mum and Rory, oh no I remember, he's in LA, what a nightmare.' Sallie said as the boat approached the wharf.

'Maybe we should wait until they've got her in the ambulance and in the hospital, and then Louisa can go back and collect her Mum.'

They pulled up at the wharf. The paramedics climbed on board, put a mask on Holly, strapped her to a stretcher and put her into the back of an ambulance. Sallie turned to Ben and Louisa.

'Thanks, I'll see you later.'

'You're looking pale yourself Sallie,' Louisa indicated Sallie's face.

'Yeah you know what, I'll come up there with you,' Ben was looking down at his phone. 'There are a couple of Ubers nearby - but by the time they get here we might as well walk, it's only five minutes by which time she'll be in and we can find out what's going on and call Xian.'

They left it that Louisa would go back to Pretty Beach, on call for Xian, and they started walking up the hill. Neither of them said anything, Ben touched the back of her shoulder and gave her a squeeze.

'Bit of a fright for you on a Friday morning eh, someone passing out in your garden?'

'I just hope she's okay, the blood literally drained out of her face and she fell to the floor!'

'I know, I saw it happen.'

They arrived at Newport Reef Emergency Department not a lot more than ten minutes later, three ambulances lined up outside the main double doors but there was no sign of Holly or the paramedics who'd brought her in. The doors automatically opened and they approached a large circular reception desk where a very tall, very blonde woman with a face in a permanently wide smile approached them.

'Welcome to Newport Reef Hospital, my name is Veronica, how can I help you today?'

'Holly Nguyen from Pretty Beach has just been brought in via ambulance, she collapsed down by the old jetties, we brought her up by water taxi and she was collected at the public wharf, we're just coming to see how she is and we need to inform her family etc.' Ben had taken charge of the situation. Sallie stood there silently.

Veronica, tapped onto her iPad and walked around to the other side of the desk.

'She's being assessed at the moment. This is the main lobby and there is another waiting room down to the end there, through the corridor and out onto the west side of the building. Just follow the signs.'

Sallie and Ben walked along the corridor, Sallie looked down at herself, still in her cleaning jeans, a grey t-shirt and three-day old hair tied up with a pink velvet scrunchie and trainers. Ben got them both a coffee and started calling through to Pretty Beach, he tried a few numbers to get hold of Xian. It went through Sallie's mind that she really was still not a local, whereas he knew everyone.

'Yeah Ben here, yeah, ok mate, thanks mate - I'll try Jessica.'

'It seems Xian is at home and neither of the girls in the bakery have her mobile number,' he said dialling another number.

'Yeah, Ben Chalmers.'

She heard a man's voice on the other end of the phone.

'Not sure if you've heard yet but Holly's been taken ill and we need to let Xian know.'

She heard the other man talking back but couldn't make out what he was saying.

'OK, thanks David, too easy, thanks mate.' Ben closed the phone and looked at Sallie.

'David from the fish and chip shop is going to go up there, no one can get hold of her, apparently the girls next door had already been in to see if he could give them a lift up to get her. He's going to go up and get Xian, take her down to Louisa and she will bring her in, I'll go down and get her and we'll see how we go from there.'

Sallie sat back, leant her head back against the waiting room chair and sighed. Two hours later, Sallie and Xian were sitting in the waiting room, Ben had gone back to Pretty Beach for work, instructing them to call him as soon as they knew anything and he would come and collect them. A nurse came out, ushered them through the double doors to the inner area and gave them another seat where a young doctor came up to them.

'Well, she's looking a lot better than when you last saw her, so that's a positive, it was a complication of the diabetes. We think she might have made an error with the insulin.'

Sallie kept quiet, she didn't even know Holly was a diabetic and Xian nodded gravely.

'She's been very busy.'

'We've got on top of it, she's settled and just about to go up to the ward, she should be ok. If you go back out and up the lifts you can meet her up there.' They went up in the lifts, Sallie texted both David and Ben the same text that she was ok and going to the ward.

They arrived at the ward and in a small side room Holly lay on the bed with cannulas in both arms, a blue hospital gown, monitors attached to her, her head back on the pillows and looking up to the ceiling. She smiled weakly as Xian and Sallie came in, and Xian gingerly gave her a hug.

'I'll be fine, so sorry to do that to you.'

'Don't be silly, I was so worried about you.'

'I've had a few of these before, haven't I Mum?' Xian nodded her head and fussed around with the sheets on the bed and the water jug.

'You can't get rid of me yet Sallie, I'm not going to kick the tin yet!'

Sallie laughed, 'It's kick the bucket Holly!'

They all chuckled and Sallie heaved a huge sigh of relief.

***

It had been a very long day. Sallie Broadchurch walked up the stairs to the apartment and had started stripping her clothes before she'd even reached the top, she needed a long hot shower to get rid of the awful smell of the hospital, she couldn't abide the places - they always reminded her of the stillbirth and the sadness of that whole time.

Holly had stabilized and had been let home and was safely tucked up in bed and Sallie had got home feeling grubby, starving and in need of decompressing.

She'd hated seeing Holly there in the bed, but all the rallying around of her family and friends had made Sallie realise that if anything happened to her she had no one really who was interested; no mum or dad or siblings, not even a twenty-year friendship - she'd lost touch with all of them when she had been married to her first husband. The closest she had to anything was Nina.

She stood in the shower, shampooed and conditioned her hair twice, got out, dried off and wrapped herself in her dressing gown. Then she padded into the kitchen, pulled open the blinds, opened the fridge and took out some wine and cut up an onion and some bacon and put it into the oven. This was a moment for comfort food. She turned on the water for some pasta and sat down at the kitchen table looking over towards Ben's place.

He had been a lifesaver. A lifesaver with lovely legs, that smell she wanted to bottle and just generally being resourceful and pragmatic in a crisis - getting it all done with no fuss, much confidence and little words. Just how she liked it.

Chapter 62

Holly seemed in much better form in the morning and had texted her to say thank you for the day before.

You seem brighter?

I've had these before, it's a horrible complication of diabetes, I'm all good, still here.

I didn't know you were a diabetic.

Never even crossed my mind to tell you, I've been fine for years & then bang this happened, good job I was wearing my identification. I was trying to point it out to you on the boat.

Yes, I realise that now.

I'll pop up later and see how you are.

Sallie put the phone down, she needed to get the boathouse ready. With a whole day gone yesterday she had to clean it, get the new linen on the beds, collect the flowers and put the evening dinner in the fridge.

She walked out into the sunshine, waved to Ollie who was working on one of the seaplanes and looked at the sky over the water. The sun glinted off the sea - it was definitely warm enough to go for a swim. She would power through work quickly and go for a sit on the beach and swim in the afternoon hoping the therapeutic powers of the sea would do her good.

She walked past the boathouse cottage all the way down to the shore, slipped off her flip flops and let the water run in and out over her feet, it was cool but lovely. She put her hands over her eyes to cover them from the sun and looked past the jetties and down to the beach on the other side. It was busier than she had ever seen it - sun umbrellas dotted here and there, children played at the water's edge and the picnic tables which had been unused since she had arrived were set up with families.

Sallie spent the rest of the morning getting the boat house ready for the next lot of guests, cleaned the bathroom going over every inch of it, folded the thick white luxury towels into neat piles and placed them on the vintage chair next to the bathtub. She replaced the French milled soaps, placed a vase of flowers on the side, vacuumed the ceilings for stray spider webs and stacked new toilet rolls in a large old fishing basket beside the sink.

She pulled out everything from the kitchen cupboards, cleaned and restocked them, emptied the fridge and put their chosen dinner in - homemade dahl and rice in a special heat-sealed bag and labelled with the Pretty Beach Boat House logo. Ran and emptied the dishwasher and left the tea pot and special blend of Assam tea and a French cafetiere ready on the side with the Boat House Pretty Beach blend of artisan coffee. She went outside and picked little bunches of fresh herbs, and strung them from a line of string in the kitchen and put a bottle of champagne in the fridge. The sourdough, croissants and orange juice would all be delivered the next morning in Boat House Pretty Beach cake boxes, the orange juice in a glass ceramic topped bottle.

Sallie changed all the throw cushions on the sofa, pulled up the sisal rug and changed it for another one, placed a huge jug of flowers in the centre of the coffee table and popped a new copy of Beach Style magazine in the middle.

Outside on the verandah, she swept all of the old bricks until there wasn't a stray fallen leaf to be seen, placed a huge vintage vase full of bay and olive in the middle of the table, refilled the fire pit with fresh kindling and wood and replaced the grey and white striped throws with clean ones.

Everything was ready, the guests had their unique code, they had downloaded the comprehensive guide to Pretty Beach and all the local information. They had the orders in for their food delivery and a trip with Ben Chalmers Seaplanes for a ride to Ocean Point for lunch all ready to go.

She walked back over to the Boat House, got changed into her bikini, slipped her faded blue shirt dress over the top, popped a cardigan in her basket, slipped her feet into her tan sandals, grabbed a sunhat from the vintage hooks in the hallway and popped on her sunglasses.

Sallie pulled her pale blue bike out from under the apple tree down the side of the Boat House, put the lock and her cardigan in the basket and pedalled out of the Boat House and down the laneway towards the other side of Pretty Beach and the bay. After the last few days and then getting all that completed, she was ready for a couple of hours on the beach with her Kindle and a new book.

A couple of hours on the beach later and a swim and relax in the sunshine had done the trick - amazing how it made her feel better. The locals were right that the ocean water had worked its magic on her.

She rode along the laneway to Holly's house; the Porsche was sitting on the drive alongside Rory's car, who had been overseas in LA on a medical conference. She knocked on the door, and lovely, handsome Rory opened it with a smile. He took in her dress, bikini and hair still damp from the beach.

'Been for a dip, how was the water?' He asked, gesturing for her to come in.

'Still chilly, but warming up at last.' He ushered her in telling her that Holly and Xian were in the main room.

'Thanks so much for sorting everything out, I had no idea it was all going on, luckily I was on the plane on the way home. She's fine now, not had an episode like that for years, thank goodness for you and Ben.'

Sallie and Ben. Sallie and Ben sitting on the back porch. Sallie smiled up at Rory.

'Yes, Ben was pretty fabulous actually, and, well, it could have been really awkward considering, you know, the circumstances.'

'I heard all about the situation from Mum,' Rory replied. 'You know what, none of my business, but I'm really surprised about Ben, always thought he was a good egg.'

'Well, it seems everyone thought that, doesn't make me feel any better though, you never judge a book by its cover right Rory?' She looked at Rory with the lovely skin and the huge, kind, brown eyes.

'Cup of tea, glass of wine or one of my grandma's special drinks?' He laughed, and looked at Sallie as if to say she should definitely not try one of those. He came back with a cup of tea for all of them and left Holly, Sallie and Xian to it.

'What about Ben, what are you going to do about it?' Holly was questioning Sallie.

'I'm not doing anything about it, I told you I want to keep it strictly neighbourly from now on.'

'Strictly neighbours, are you joking Sallie, there's an electric spark between the two of you!'

Xian looked up from the iPad and joined in, 'Sallie, I think you've made a mistake, I think you need to give him another chance.'

Chapter 63

Sallie woke to the sound of Nina, who was down from the City for the weekend, putting on the coffee and the sea crashing on the beach outside and a text from Ben.

Still haven't explained and it was not the right time at the hospital the other day, please let me talk to you today. I will meet you out on the jetty with a coffee at 11am? BC

She didn't answer, she wanted to run it through with Nina first. She could, she supposed, go and speak to him - she had to be his neighbour and it would maybe clear the air. She showed Nina the text.

'Look, he's made a lot of effort here, I'm not defending him, but he's sent you two huge bouquets of flowers, had a keyring engraved with a sincere not smarmy message, phoned you multiple times and left messages. I say go and see what he has to say for himself.'

It was ten, she texted him back and said yes, she would meet him there. She had an hour to think about it and get ready.

***

'Pippa and I are just friends, my parents have been friends with hers for a very long time, we went to the same University too. Yep I did sleep with her then and a few times since, but that was before Tana and she's always been a pain. Her family are so close to mine, so I sort of have to keep in with her.'

Sallie stood, hands shoved in her pockets, looked up at him and said nothing.

'It's like meeting you opened up a door that had been shut for a long time. I suddenly felt alive again, but Pippa is the last person I want. I want to carry on with what we had Sallie, with you - I'm not saying it will go anywhere. I can't offer you any guarantees. I've

240

been through a lot of grief and wasn't expecting this to happen but we were getting along really well and I thought it would be just nice to amble along and see where it goes.'

Sallie didn't know what to think, she just looked at Ben's legs and up at his eyes with that same warm, I'm home feeling deep in her heart. Did this man with the very nice life and so many options really want to carry on with their little romance? Was he really interested in her?

He looked at her questioningly.

'What do you think?'

She sighed a big, long, sad sigh.

'Well, I think you have a point, but I can't trust you Ben, and I can't trust anyone to tell the truth and I let myself fall into it all. I never should have got involved, we should have kept it as neighbours, I totally regret the whole thing.'

'That's harsh. You totally regret it? We've had so many laughs and nice times. Very nice times.'

'Yep I know, but Ben, I just can't do it, I need it to be a success up here and I don't ever want to go back to that old life again, not being able to fend for myself and if we carry on again then I won't be able to stay if it all goes wrong. It will all get horrible and ruin it all for the both of us.'

He took her hand.

'Well, Sallie Broadchurch, I suppose I can see your point but I don't want it and I'm telling you now that the moment you say jump I will say how high.'

***

Sallie walked back down along the jetty, hands still in her pockets, head down, not looking up at Pretty Beach and the lighthouse in the distance as she usually did. Was this all in her head, this crazy feeling she had?

The thing was, there was something about Ben Chalmers. Something happened to her when she was with him; it was like she wanted him to open up his coat, pull her into it and never let her go. She had never had that feeling before, so why was she now telling him no?

As she walked back to the Boat House to Nina she knew she had done the right thing... she wasn't willing to gamble on this because Sallie Broadchurch did indeed like Ben Chalmers a lot, in fact she loved the bones of the man. But she had done the right thing. For her, for her business and for her new life in Pretty Beach. If she felt like that, so deeply and it all went wrong, she would be the one to have to pick up the pieces, not him.

She walked back into the apartment, Nina was sitting in the window seat of the turret propped up with lots of cushions, sipping a cup of peppermint tea. Sallie made herself one and walked over.

'So?'

'He reckoned they are just friends, there's nothing in it, and she's an old family friend.'

'Right.' Nina looked back at her glumly.

'I think I believe him. I don't know, but I think he was telling the truth.' She trailed off sadly, looking out the window. 'It's much better to just leave it as it is though. I'm not in his league and never will be, and there will always be people like Pippa around and the memory of his perfect wife. It's just not worth going into it and then down the road it's not working out and I am the one who comes out worse from it all.' Sallie said sadly 'The thing is, I like him, I think I love him and I don't know what to do.'

'Maybe you need to give it a chance, maybe you should listen to your heart.'

'The sad thing is Nina, is he said he can't give any guarantees, and well, I don't want to settle for no guarantees...'

Chapter 64

Ben Chalmers dropped his towel on the floor and looked in the mirror. What the actual hell was happening to him? He was skulking about like a lovelorn adolescent over the woman next door, who not that many months ago he'd never even set eyes on.

He didn't even want or need anyone in his life. He had been more than happy as he was. Trundling along with the business, helping out his brothers, finally accepting everything with Tana and looking forward to a life with no drama, no sadness and no complications.

And then she'd arrived and whipped the rug out from under him. He'd wined her and dined her and stars had shot across the sky when they'd kissed. He'd felt things he hadn't even felt before with Tana and enjoyed the most amazing few months with her and then, not only had he gone and messed it up completely, he'd followed it up with a load of waffle about keeping it casual.

After telling her that she only had to say the word he'd bottled it and backed it up with the fact that he couldn't give her any assurances.

Like some idiot, he'd looked down at her, her gazing up at him with the huge blue eyes and the messy hair, and told her there were no guarantees and he'd seen a look go across her face.

You didn't tell Sallie Broadchurch there were no guarantees.

Chapter 65

Sallie Broadchurch clicked close on the spreadsheet, she wasn't one for numbers but this simple document had shown her that she'd made more money in the last three months with The Boat House Pretty Beach than she had in the last year.

She sat chin on her hand staring out to sea. This time last year her life was completely different - she'd had no money, no prospects and a life going nowhere fast. She looked behind her at the apartment. Now she had a lovely home in a lovely little town, a circle of friends who genuinely seemed to look out for her and a business that had started well and was already expanding.

Boat House Weddings at Pretty Beach was in the planning phase, with a tentative booking in place for Christmas awaiting approval from the council, and every single penny of extra money she had over her living costs was going into it. There'd been so many enquiries for intimate, boutique weddings at the magical spot she had created she'd decided to shift the cafe idea to the back burner and play to the market which was clearly asking her to provide a wedding venue in her signature style.

She let out a huge sigh. There was something missing though and she knew what it was and so did everyone around her and an off the cuff comment from Xian after a few of her special drinks had made Sallie sit up and take notice.

Xian had told her that she'd had the chance with a man she had fallen head over heels in love with but she'd taken the safe option, the one that had given her no drama, and she had spent the next fifty years regretting it.

'Sallie, it will be hard for him, he lost his wife. He'll be worrying as much as you about getting into something again.'

'I asked though, and he said he couldn't commit.'

'Of course he did, he wasn't going to stand there and say he could certainly do this or that after what he's been through.' Xian was gently shaking her head. She tapped the back of Sallie's hand softly.

'Do you really think so Xian, do you really think he would like someone like me? I mean he's done nothing about it since.'

'All I know is you don't want to stand by as the next-door neighbour and watch him do it all with someone else, while you spend the rest of your life, like me, wishing you'd had the strength to give it a go.'

Sallie felt tears welling up in the back of her eyes - she knew Xian was right. She knew that Holly and Xian had seen this whole thing play out in front of them like a screenplay and now this was the part where the wise old woman imparted what to do next. She'd never had a mum there for her, and it almost felt like for the first time someone was actually interested in helping her to make a decision. Maybe she should take the advice.

'Have you actually told him Sallie, told him what you feel like inside?'

'No, he told me the way he felt, but well, I was too nervous to say it back.'

Xian took a sip of her special drink and didn't say anything for a minute. They sat there in silence, Xian lost in her thoughts.

'It's quite simple, there's nothing to lose - don't be like me, don't spend the rest of your life wondering what may have been.'

Chapter 66

Shadows danced on the pebbles, the glow from the lighthouse shimmered on the water and the fairy lights in the trees twinkled when Sallie walked out of the Boat House. Butterflies raced in her stomach as she walked over towards Ben Chalmers Seaplanes. Xian, sitting outside the bakers tipped her hand to her head and gave her a little salute.

What was she going to say - how did you tell someone they made something happen in your heart? He opened the door, surprised to see her standing there, before he could speak she blurted out.

'I've missed you, Ben.' She almost whispered.

He stepped out of the door, took her hand and they walked silently down to the end of the jetty.

'I've missed you too Sallie.' They sat down on the edge of the jetty, looking out over the sea.

'The thing is, I know you can't give guarantees, but I... well, before this I didn't even know there was a feeling like this, and... well, if it doesn't work out then at least I can say I gave it a shot.'

Ben Chalmers turned to her, took her in his arms and kissed her gently, full of longing and love. They looked out across the water and Sallie placed her hand on his leg.

The lighthouse beam swept across the bay, their shadows falling on the water. He didn't take his gaze off the water.

'I love you Sallie Broadchurch, that's my guarantee.'

She sat there at the end of the jetty, her legs dangling over the edge, gazing at the lighthouse in the distance. She'd decided to give Ben Chalmers a chance, she turned and looked up at him.

'I love you too.'

The Boat House Pretty Beach 2

Have you loved immersing yourself into Sallie's world and all the go-ings-on at Pretty Beach?

Well, you'll adore Summer Weddings at Pretty Beach - the deliciously cosy little sequel to The Boat House Pretty Beach.

In Summer Weddings we delve back into the wonderful seaside town, find out what happens to Sallie, the fabulous expansion of Pretty Beach Boat House Enterprises and immerse ourselves further into the sweet little town by the sea.

We find out that for someone who wasn't looking for romance, she certainly finds it and we explore more with Sallie on life, love and friendships. Throw in an utterly gorgeous setting, a plethora of heart-warming characters and a dash of intrigue to curl up on the sofa with and dream.
Perfect for those who love funny romantic books.

***

Be part of Polly's World!

If you've loved reading along...
You might want to be part of the Babbettes and the Polly Babbington Reader Club - little bits and bobs from Pretty Beach, excerpts from up-coming books, pretty things and covers and the like that I'm working on... we'd love to have you over there. Xxo
Just go to Polly Babbington Reader Club group on Facebook and re-quest to join.
Send me an email at pollybabbington@gmail.com if you're interested or even easier send me a message - Instagram & Facebook @pollybab-bingtonwrites

Thank you so much.
pollybabbington@gmail.com
If you've enjoyed Sallie, Ben and all the lovelies at Pretty Beach please leave a review xxx.

Author's Notes

Thank you so much for reading all about the wonderful world of Pretty Beach.

I actually adore immersing myself in the Boat House and Sallie's life. Oh to live right on the beach with a pilot next door. ;)

Pretty Beach was inspired by a beautiful coastal town where the water really is that blue and the little unique pocket with its very own microclimate really does have more sunshine-y days than the rest of the country.

I moved to this little town about fifteen years ago and it captivated me from day one... the slower pace, the happy faces and the benefits of the wonderful fresh sea air.

Sallie and the boathouse actually came to me while I was deep in the dark recesses of editing another book - this one involving three women, including Chloe who lives in a huge old white house on the top of a hill in a seaside town. This book is a crime novel with a few nasty characters and my mind kept wandering to a character like Sallie and the old falling down shed I walked past every day on my walks by the sea. The Boat House at Pretty Beach was the result.

Right now, I am well stuck into this series and am looking in the eye of at least six for this little lot. If Sallie can survive them all, hopefully more.

I wrote the second book, Summer Weddings at Pretty Beach hibernating in the Summer House down at the end of the garden surrounded by thick white snow and tucked up under a blanket with a little pot belly fire next to me and many a flask of tea.

Book three it was a bit warmer and I shuffled between the cosy little cafe at the end of my road (complete with resident white puppy and a plethora of homemade cakes) to the Summer House with the doors open, and surrounded by David Austin roses whereby writing breaks consisted of a blue and white striped hammock under an old oak tree.

Right now, typing these author notes I am sitting at an old timber table at the back of the house, surrounded by little terracotta pots of lavender and herbs... there may be a weeny raspberry gin by my side, a sweet little cat on my lap. There were chocolate croissants earlier and lots of coffee.

If you get a chance, do come and say hello on social media - I have new accounts for Pretty Beach and certainly could do with, like Sallie, some new friends.

Love

Polly

PollyBabbington.com

Summer Weddings at Pretty Beach

When dreams really do come true...
*Get ready to fall in love with Pretty Beach all over again, where the
sweeping, sparkly blue beach town surrounded by water, overlooked by
a quaint old lighthouse and filled with wonderful characters welcomes
us into its fold once again.*

*We catch up with Sallie Broadchurch who followed her heart to a new
life, new friends and an old house by the sea. She didn't think it could
get much better... until she met Ben Chalmers, the dashing pilot who
just so happened to live next door and her life took on an unexpected
turn she hadn't seen coming.*

*We follow the next part of her journey as she settles into her new world
with a beautiful old orangery, the bonniest baby in Pretty Beach, a so-
ciety wedding and it seems as if her dream life really has come true.*

*But not everything is as simple as it seems and when Sallie starts re-
ceiving unwanted messages she realises not quite everyone is as happy as
she is and Pretty Beach begins to take on a whole new look.*

*'Addictive, absorbing and does the trick to get you lost in a whole, new
delightful world.'*

Winter at Pretty Beach

The delightfully romantic story of Pretty Beach continues as the sweet, little coastal town is covered in a blanket of snow. Sallie Broadchurch is undoubtedly living the dream with her own wedding business, a gorgeous old boat house and a vintage orangery she's bought all ready to host events. Then, when luck comes her way she finds herself creating a winter wonderland at the Orangery on the beach.

But not everything is quite as dreamy as she thought...and real life throws up a few problems.

If you love romance in the snow, an utterly gorgeous setting, a plethora of heart-warming characters and a dash of intrigue to curl up on the sofa with and dream you may just have found the book for you.

Winter at Pretty Beach is the perfect read this Christmas for those who love romantic snowfall, cosy fires and funny, romantic books.

Immerse yourself back into the next part of this cosy little town by the sea, guaranteed to brighten your day and leave you pondering a new life on the coast.

***

Will Sallie and Ben get what they really want for Christmas or will fate deal a blow that will overturn all their plans?

Books for Babbettes

The Boat House

The Boat House Pretty Beach
Summer Weddings at Pretty Beach
Winter at Pretty Beach

A Pretty Beach Christmas
A Pretty Beach Dream
A Pretty Beach Wish

Secret Evenings in Pretty Beach

Printed in Great Britain
by Amazon

30485064R00145